INNOCENT DEATH
A Steve Donaldson Thriller

By Craig Simpson

INCHBROOM

IndieAuthors
World

Dedication

FOR DAD

Who always believed in me.

Also Available from Craig Simpson

Jigsaw

Acknowledgements

Thanks to my lovely wife Marion for her love and patience, understanding and helpful research which made the writing of this book possible

Thanks to Kim & Sinclair Macleod at IAW for their assistance in the publication

Chapter 1

The blue eyed blonde with an attractive figure sat across from Steve. 'As I said Mr Donaldson, on a need to know basis.'

Steve sighed! He didn't need this. The death and loss of Maria was still fresh in his mind, and right now he did not want a repeat of the Rosenberg case.

Claire Monroe uncrossed her legs, stood, and extended her hand to seal their contract but Steve just sat there, making no movement and no commitment. Claire hesitated for a moment, then withdrew her gesture. She turned to leave in full anticipation that her private detective would make an effort to stop her. It was not to be.

She opened his office door, the lining of her skirt rustling against her body and departed, the clicking of her heels echoing down the dimly lit corridor. Steve watched from his window as she crossed the street.

The quick movement from the dark coloured car at the kerb was unexpected, its speed and direction finding its target as it ploughed into her, then continued on its way.

A crowd gathered around the dead body of Claire Monroe as Steve closed his window blind, his mind in turmoil.

He knew instinctively Claire's death was no accident.

Chapter 2

Back in his apartment Steve poured himself his second Jack Daniels. He left the bottle uncorked as he felt his need for the liquor would not be done with for this evening.

Claire Monroe's death was recorded as a hit and run, but Steve suspected otherwise.

'On a need to know basis,' he said out loud, repeating Claire's last words to him before leaving his office and being killed.

Whatever she knew had died with her, but whoever killed her wouldn't know that. She was obviously followed and that someone knew she had visited himself. Claire wanted to employ him and yet was reluctant to impart all the information she had and only drip-feed him as and when necessary. She didn't appear frightened, or even nervous but she obviously, for whatever reason, was holding something back.

Steve pondered over various questions that ran through his mind.

What did she know?

Who was involved?

Why had she not gone to the police?

What was her background?

Why had she felt the need to employ him?

So what was it that she couldn't divulge completely, and what could be so important that she was eliminated?

Steve mulled these questions over and over in his mind. He didn't know the answers and at this stage could walk away, but the fact remained that whoever killed Claire Monroe would believe she had imparted her knowledge to him. She was dead. Was he next? He certainly was implicated.

His telephone burst into life. Steve stared at the instrument but didn't answer. Instead, he switched off his lights and moved quickly to the window. The telephone stopped ringing abruptly. He searched the street below, his observant eyes recording any movement. He saw no one. He switched his lights back on and within seconds his telephone began to ring. Hesitantly, he picked up the receiver. The line was live but nobody spoke.

'Hello! Who's calling?' Steve said. 'Come on, I know you're there.'

Silence reigned, then the line went dead.

Chapter 3

Steve sat in his armchair, his mind on Claire Monroe and the obscure telephone call he'd received. He took another gulp of Jack Daniels and savoured the liquor as his mind turned over recent events. He now wished he'd listened before dismissing her out of hand, but he was still too raw after losing Maria in the Rosenberg case and had stopped taking assignments for a while. He had only known Maria briefly, but the chemistry and electricity between them was instant, just as it had been with his first wife Gill.

Steve thought about Gill. How they met; him in hospital fighting for his life. She a nurse, his saviour. They loved each other and had a good marriage until his career in Special Forces and his missions overseas took their toll. Missions he could never talk about. Missions that changed him. He then joined the New York Police as a detective, but the long hours of the job were just as bad, causing friction between them. Their marriage ended and Gill moved away.

Steve never thought he'd find that love again. That was until Maria.

Maria had protected him when he was framed for crimes he did not commit. She believed in him. Now she was dead, gunned down in a mad frenzy by a stupid, rich, scorned woman by mistake. A woman who had hired him "ON A NEED TO KNOW BASIS."

Once again, Steve allowed his mind to reflect on Claire Monroe. She was dead. The question was, why?

'A dark coloured Sedan,' or, 'it all happened so fast,' were the familiar statements from innocent bystanders who witnessed the incident. He had expected an attack on himself, especially after the telephone call, but nothing had occurred.

Was he still under surveillance? If so, by whom?

Did these persons think Claire had imparted information to him? If so, what had Claire Monroe known, and more importantly, about who?

There was no further investigation by the police, just a newspaper headline.

'WOMAN DIES IN HIT AND RUN.'

Claire Monroe suffered fatal injuries when a speeding vehicle collided with her as she crossed the street on Flatbush Avenue. Brooklyn police are appealing for anybody who may have witnessed the incident to come forward.

Contact 911, or your local police department. All information will be treated in the strictest confidence.

Chapter 4

Claire Monroe was raised in Austin, Texas. Her parents were hardworking Americans who encouraged their daughter in all aspects of life. Claire worked hard at school and soon drew the attention of her tutors who persuaded her to extend her education and go to college. They told her she was too intelligent just to leave school and find a job, so Claire attended college and enrolled on a secretarial course which she believed would lead to a better career in the outside world. She was attractive and her sense of humour made her popular with her fellow students.

It was at a dance where she met Gerald Northorpe who, like others, changed the course of Claire's life. Society was changing; more improvements, more inventions, and a new Space Programme had begun with NASA. Gerald Northorpe had suggested Claire apply to the Spartan College of Aeronautics and Technology in Tulsa, Oklahoma and after much consideration, Claire set her sights to learn about navigation and embrace the new world of flight. Claire surpassed herself and after a course of five years graduated with full diplomas which allowed her to secure a job at Andrews Air Force Base in Maryland.

Another five years had passed and she found herself in a relationship with pilot Dan McKinley. Dan was older than Claire by ten years but their mutual respect and ambition for anything that could fly developed a close friendship between them. They were seen everywhere together and soon were regarded as a couple. The only time they were apart was when Mac was either away on training, or indeed on a mission.

It was a lovely day at Andrews Air Base and an air show was taking place. There were many spectators, all in awe of the aeroplanes that stood before them and imagining when each aircraft was originally commissioned and used in the World Wars and Korea.

There were all types of fighters, fighter bombers and of course heavy bombers with the crowds inspecting them, all snapping photographs and watching as airmen took them to the skies, displaying their pilot abilities together with the performance of what those planes could achieve.

Dog fights between Grumman P/12 and Hellcats, Cobras and Hawks took place, the crowds cheering with enthusiasm at each manoeuvre.

Andrews Air Base was also famous for the training of the pilots in the well-known B25 Mitchell Bombers and there were displays and fly-passes to enthral the crowd.

Charlie Donovan was ready. His slot in his B25 was all scheduled for take-off, but his co-pilot had failed to appear, and although Charlie was as keen as mustard to fly the organisers would not permit him to proceed. Arguments broke out as Charlie pleaded as all he wanted was to take his bird skyward.

Claire was standing in the enclosure and overheard Charlie pleading to be allowed up on his own. Henry Ryman, the organiser, spoke indignantly.

'You can't go up there on your own, Charlie. You know the rules. Besides, it's more than my job's worth to authorise such behaviour.'

'Listen, Henry, you've known me a long time, cut the programme, or whatever, but let me get me and my crate up there,' Charlie said, pointing to the skies in his leather and sheepskin flying jacket.

'And what if something should happen and you're on your own? What if ...?' Henry said.

Charlie interrupted him. 'Well, at least I won't have a black eye.' Henry looked puzzled.

'A black eye, who's gonna have a black eye, Charlie?'

'You are, Henry, if you don't let me up there!' Charlie shouted, now raising his fists. 'I have to be a part of the show. Come on ... please ...'

Claire stood and listened quietly and momentarily watched the display performing overhead. 'Excuse me,' she said, stepping forward. 'My name is Claire Monroe. I'm an experienced pilot and navigator at the base here. I don't mind going up with Charlie Donovan as long as you okay it with the rest of the judges, or whoever.'

Henry Ryman turned and appraised Claire. 'How many flying hours have you had, Miss ...?'

'Monroe,' Claire answered. 'The name is Monroe. Listen, my boyfriend will vouch for me. Dan McKinley. We've both got enough flying hours and experience for this little sortie.'

'And where is this Dan McKinley?' Henry Ryman questioned.

Claire's eyes took to the skies above. 'That's him currently up there, doing that loop de loop.'

Both Henry and Claire stared above into the bright sunshine, watching Mac now flying his fighter aeroplane upside down, bringing applause and cheers from the crowd of spectators.

'How many flying hours?' Henry Ryman repeated, only to find that he was addressing fresh air. Both Charlie Donovan and Claire were already running towards the aircraft, their chutes being put on as they climbed aboard.

Henry Ryman shouted and waved his arms but it was too late, the engines fired and the propellers turned as the aircraft then slowly taxied to take-off position.

'You can really fly and navigate?' Charlie asked.

Claire smiled, her eyes lighting up. 'You bet, Charlie. Now, let's show them what you and this ole girl can do.'

Charlie Donovan braced the machine for take-off, its engines roaring, its frame vibrating like a bee as he slowly pushed the controls forward and allowed his aeroplane to release its power and make its journey down the concrete runway before taking to the sky.

'You really are the complete package,' Charlie said. 'You fly, you navigate, good lookin' in all the right places,' he said as Claire caught his wandering eyes. 'Yeah! Your Mac sure is a lucky guy,' he said, as he stared into Claire's gorgeous blue eyes. Their display went well and cheering spectators encouraged them.

Their flight over, Charlie returned his aeroplane to its parking bay and climbed down. He thanked Claire for her part in enabling him to participate.

'I hope you two enjoyed that,' a voice from behind bellowed.

It was Henry Ryman.

'Charlie Donovan, you've flown your last flight if I have anything to do with it and as for you Miss Monroe, your superiors are waiting to see you. I think you'll be disciplined also and I wouldn't be surprised if the same fate awaited you. Most irresponsible, both of you,' he said, displaying his dissatisfaction.

General Bob Harris just happened to be listening. He'd understood what had occurred and had heard enough of Henry Ryman's babblings. 'Miss Monroe,' he said. 'It *is* Miss Monroe?' he repeated. 'Let me introduce myself – General Harris. Quite a performance you put on up there. Understand you work on the base here.'

Claire turned and admired the man before her. He was handsome in a rugged kind of way, obviously over-weight, but no bullshitter. 'Thank you, General, but Charlie here did all the flying.'

'You got any other qualifications?' General Harris asked, liking the package in front of him.

Claire smiled. 'I have my pilot's licence, can navigate and I trained and graduated from Spartan Aeronautics in Tulsa, plus I have a secretarial qualification.'

'Secretarial qualifications, eh! Graduated in Tulsa; quite a résumé if I may say so.'

'Thank you, General,' Claire said, her eyes smiling sheepishly.

'You got grit, Monroe, I like that.'

'Thank you, General, I like to think I get things done,' Claire replied.

'Oh!' General Harris exclaimed as he thought of his own mental attitude. 'Well, what will you do if they ground you?' General Harris said as he glanced at Henry Ryman and Charlie Donovan.

'Well ... I'd be upset, 'cause I love my job, but I don't think, or expect that to happen after all the money Uncle

Sam has spent training me.' Claire stopped, then added, 'and I'm sure I've a lot more to give which shouldn't be kiboshed just because of a little sortie at an air show. Besides, the public loved the display and it was good to take the old crate to the skies one more time.'

General Bob Harris liked her immediately. He picked his moment. 'How d'ya like to come and work for me? Be my personal PA. I need someone who can organise, be diplomatic, has initiative, can take action and most important can think and look out for me. Is that you, Miss Monroe?'

General Bob Harris's question and offer took Claire by surprise. She fell silent, then answered.

'I could give it a go, see how ...'

'Stop! No!' General Harris said, shaking his head negatively. 'You're no use to me if your attitude is just to give it a go,' he sneered. 'I can get "give it a go" people ten a penny.' General Bob Harris turned to leave.

'Sir, General Sir, sorry, I mean, I want the job ... I would very much like to work under you,' she said, more confidently now.

General Harris turned and faced Claire, reappraising her. God, she was attractive. He liked the cut of the young woman before him. She had grit. 'Okay! Start Monday morning, I'll clear it with your superior.'

Again General Harris turned to leave when Claire spoke again.

'And where shall I report to, General? Where is your office?'

Harris smiled. 'The Pentagon, of course – Virginia. Oh! And Claire? Be punctual. I don't do excuses.'

Chapter 5

Charlie Donovan and Henry Ryman just stood there, in awe of what had just occurred when Mac arrived.

'Hey babe, they tell me you were up there,' he said, averting his eyes to the sky, then back to Claire. Mac was smiling, his dark brown eyes and dimpled cheeks making his rugged, manly face appear friendly.

Claire's words flew out in an overwhelming rush like autumn leaves blown along the sidewalk. 'Mac, guess what, I've just landed a new job with General Harris at the Pentagon. I start Monday. Isn't that great?' she said, smiling enthusiastically as she wrapped her arms around his neck.

Mac's body tensed, his voice lost for words. After a few moments, when they broke free from each other, Mac spoke. 'You takin' it?' he said, searching Claire's face.

'Mac, it's the opportunity of a lifetime, my career. I mean, we'll still be able to see each other, okay it won't be as often, but we'll still have weekends,' Claire said, believing her words were the truth.

Mac lowered his head; his words were slow and softly spoken. 'Claire, I'm not going to persuade you either way. I want you to stay here at Andrews. Tell this General that you've changed your mind.' Mac now held her shoulders with outstretched arms. He spoke gently. 'Claire, as I said, I want you to stay. Don't do this, but if the job or your career is that important to you, make the friggin' goddamn career move. But I know how that will end for us. In short, Claire, if you do we're through. You and I are over.'

'Mac, what are you saying?' Claire said, now standing back and free of his arms.

'How clear do you want me to be?' Mac said. 'It's me Claire, or the fuckin' Pentagon, so which is it to be?'

Mac was angry now, his gentle tone had changed. Then softening once more he whispered. 'I want you to stay, Claire. Stay here, don't go to Virginia. Please …'

Claire was so hurt by Mac's lack of understanding. She'd already accepted the job; she had never thought that there would be a problem between them. 'Well, you listen to me, mister hotshot pilot, I've decided it's my life, not yours, and if you're so hell bent in obstructing me to further my career, well you know what you can do.'

'Claire, think about this,' Mac said, attempting to change the row now between them.

Claire just stared into his dark, brown eyes. 'I already have, Mac. Goodbye!' With that, she hurried away, not wanting him to see her tears.

Chapter 6

The rest of Claire's weekend was spent in turmoil, and she decided it was impossible to attempt the move in one go. After all, General Harris had promised he would clear everything with her superiors and have accommodation arranged for her arrival. With that in mind, Claire relaxed a little. She was still upset with her break-up from Mac, but he should have been pleased for her. Instead, he had behaved like a spoiled teenager. Claire contemplated their situation and decided that maybe some time apart may actually be good for them both. She therefore continued packing, giving Mac no more thought.

Mac paced his room. He didn't want Claire to leave. He knew she was headstrong and swore at himself for being so stupid, and acting so selfish and immature. He wanted to call her but his stupid pride stood in his way, and he let the opportunity go without taking any action.

Claire waited, hoping Mac would have calmed down, and telephoned her to apologise and the two of them could save their relationship, but his call never came and Claire went to her bed that night, again with tears in her eyes. 'Goodbye, mister hotshot,' she said to herself, as she cried some more, then thought of the General and the Pentagon.

Chapter 7

Monday morning arrived, and Claire reported to the Chief of Staff at the Pentagon. She felt over-whelmed with the bustle of employees all moving quickly to various departments, all with very little time to converse.

The officer sat in front of her took her particulars and eyed her up and down as he checked her identity. 'Cleaver can sure pick them,' he said, smiling, as he processed her new official pass.

Claire hesitated. 'Who's Cleaver?' she said, unaware of General Bob Harris's nickname.

'You are with Cleaver Harris?' the officer said, as he stared upwards into Claire's gorgeous blue eyes.

Claire still looked puzzled. 'I'm supposed to report to General Bob Harris,' she replied.

'Yeah! That's correct. Cleaver. That's what we all call him, everyone does, well, nearly. You'll no doubt find out why in your own good time. Now follow me. I'll take you and introduce you to some other colleagues. Normally I would just give you directions to the third floor, but since its Cleaver, I'll make an exception in your case.'

Claire was introduced and remembered everyone's name. She stood in an outer office on her own. It was 8:30am when General Bob Cleaver Harris appeared.

'Good morning, Claire, coffee, black, no sugar, and a blueberry muffin. That's my usual every morning. Once you've organised that, bring your pad and I'll run through today's agenda.'

Claire smiled nervously as she observed her new boss. General Bob Harris seemed taller. He was 6ft 1", broad-shouldered with a very close-cut hair style, clean-shaven and sharp dark brown eyes, which missed nothing. They were not like Mac's eyes, not as soft or as gentle.

His body language and large frame exuded presence and Claire reckoned that there would be no messing with this man. He was used to having his own way, and, more importantly, used to achieving. Claire set off to organise his breakfast and before re-entering his large offices checked herself out. Hair still in place, make-up and lipstick still on; she felt good in her white crisp cotton shirt, black pencil skirt and jacket, and so grabbed her pad and, best foot forward, stood waiting as her General read over some papers. He glanced up and motioned her to sit opposite, then continued reading for a few moments. General Bob Harris looked up, sat back and stared at his new recruit.

'So, Claire, no problems with your superiors at Andrews?' he said, then continuing before she could reply. 'I need someone, Claire. Someone here working very close with me day and night, twenty-four-seven, if need be. Someone …' Harris paused, '… someone with utmost discretion, diplomacy, but with enough initiative to think on their feet. You've already proved you're not of the timid variety and your service record to date is exemplary,' he said, tapping the file in front of him.

Claire smiled with her eyes, although she remained pensive, not wanting to jump in or be too familiar on her first morning.

'Now, each day, my agenda is put on my desk, but I expect you to have summarised it for me. Given the most important details, the background of the people I am meeting that day. Now I expect a settling in period Claire, and please ask any questions you like, I don't expect you to be up and running, knowing everybody and their functions immediately, but you've got one month to learn who's who so to speak, and then I expect you to be truly my eyes and ears, no matter what you hear or see, you tell me. I'll judge what has to be done. Now, today, I have this agenda. Please cancel this, this, and this, there won't be any amendments or rearranged meetings. I don't give reasons for my decisions Claire, but whatever I say goes, is that understood? I will, however, once we get to know each other, be privy to your opinion – should I ask for it of course. Anything you hear in this office from myself, or at any meeting with anybody, remains within these four walls. Under-stand?'

Claire nodded, then, clearing her throat, answered 'Yes, General, Sir.'

General Bob Harris smiled. 'And you can drop the yes General Sir stuff. I'm known as Cleaver. You may call me that. It's my nickname. They gave me it because no matter what, I always got the job done, no matter who or what is in my way. In short, Claire, I always win – always.' Cleaver's voice fell silent. Again, Claire nodded.

'Thank you, General, I ...'

'Claire, call me Cleaver. We'll be working very close together, assuming my judgement of you is correct, so I don't need all this General bullshit. I ... we'll keep that for the numbskulls out there.' Cleaver raised his arm, obviously indicating to persons' outwith his close allies.

Claire smiled. 'Do you require more coffee, Gen .... Cleaver?'

Cleaver Harris let out a loud laugh. 'Maybe this morning I do. Yes, Claire, that would be most appreciated. Now, go take this afternoon to get acquainted with the other staff; let them know your position as my PA. Then get yourself sorted and we'll start seriously tomorrow.'

Again, Claire smiled, then departed to attend to the three amendments Bob Cleaver Harris had made and organise his coffee.

Cleaver Harris watched his new PA vacate his office. He hoped she would work out, as he had future plans for both of them.

She was so goddamn attractive, he thought as he drummed his fingers on his desk.

Chapter 8

Claire's trial month passed quickly, and although she had organised proper accommodation, she found that she very rarely domiciled there. She was always working and very often she would just camp down in one of the guest suites within the Pentagon as she was always on call. Cleaver Harris never seemed to sleep; day or night he would contact her and she had to appear ready and immaculate at all times. The work was endless and tiring but she was learning and her quick mind and initiative was slowly impressing other members of staff and, of course, Cleaver.

It was coming up to her first year's anniversary when she had joined the staff, and Cleaver invited her to join him in the Caymans. He was taking a well-earned rest over the weekend. 'Do some fishing, meetings with the Governor; that would be the boring shit, Claire, but it'd do you good; meet some influential people too. Take some time out, you've earned it. I'll be fishing on Sunday, so you won't have this old fart to contend with. What do you say?'

Claire stood before her boss. It was a fabulous invitation and she could certainly use the break.

'Thank you, Cleaver, your offer is very much appreciated, but I've not been home for a year and I ...'

'This is your home, Claire. Well, it is now,' Cleaver interrupted, his eyes searching her face.

'Well,' Claire hesitated. I did leave rather unexpectedly and I have a few loose ends to tidy up.'

Cleaver fell silent for a moment. 'Oh, I see. It's not Austin, Texas that beckons you, is it? It's your hotshot pilot ... Mac somebody at Andrews.'

Claire blushed. 'Cleaver, our relationship ended badly, I would welcome your understanding in this matter. It's over for Mac and me. It wouldn't have worked but we went back years. I owe him some explanation.'

'Explanation my ass, tell him you've moved on, because you have, haven't you?' Cleaver waited for Claire's response.

'It's not that easy, Cleaver, I want to put the matter to bed. Face-to-face. Tell him on a one-to-one. You surely can understand that?'

Cleaver's mind had only heard the phrase put the matter to bed. He shook his head negatively. 'And if I order you to accompany me this weekend, what would your answer be?'

Claire felt her legs go shaky but gathered herself. Then quietly she answered. 'There would be no doubt Cleaver. An order is an order. I would accompany you to the Cayman Islands'

Cleaver smiled inwardly. He'd made his point. He paused, then spoke in a monotone voice. 'Go, Claire. You take this weekend, go to your flyer. Settle your differences. Finish it. I'll manage this weekend without you.' Cleaver now bent his head forward, reading some papers.

'Cleaver, you surely understand?'

Cleaver never raised his head, he just uttered 'I said go, Claire. Get this monkey off your back.'

Cleaver now sat up and faced his PA. 'You're the best personal assistant I've ever had, Claire. Thank you for that. Take the long weekend, sort it out, but be here first thing Tuesday. You're dismissed,' Cleaver added abruptly.

Claire went to the Ladies, her handkerchief drying her tears. She looked at herself in the mirror and started sorting the black mascara lines that had ran down her cheeks before redoing her face make-up and making every attempt to hide her red eyes.

In her mind Cleaver did not understand and certainly was not being fair, but in any event she would make arrangements to return to Andrews and meet up with Mac. Their conversation on the telephone was muddled and hesitant but somewhere deep down she felt pleased that she would see Mac again.

They had arranged to meet at one of their old haunts where they would be guaranteed privacy and away from friends. Mac waited patiently in a seat in the corner of the bar where he could keep a lookout on the main entrance. He was already on his second beer and did not recognise the young woman as she entered. He watched as she spoke quietly to the barman who pointed in his direction, and it was only then he realised it was Claire. He stood up and greeted her.

'Hell, look at you,' he said, admiring her from head to toe. 'You're different,' he said, forcing a smile.

Claire smiled awkwardly. 'I've changed my hair, but I'm still the same.'

Mac ordered her a club soda and now paid more attention to the girl he'd missed and her blonde hair. It used to be long and tied back in a ponytail when she was flying, otherwise it was curled and left down, but now it was cut short, very neat, tapered and squared at the neck. Claire looked very professional.

'You suit it,' he said, still appraising her.

'Thank you,' Claire answered, beginning to feel more comfortable. 'You're looking good too,' she said, as she admired his warm, soft, friendly eyes.

Conversation was hesitant between them. Everybody had expected them to marry, but each had a strong personality and each determined in their own careers had seen them part company.

'So, how's life with you, Mac? Still got your wings, they've not grounded you yet?' Claire said, attempting to lighten the atmosphere between them. Mac had a reputation for breaking the rules and protocol and discipline was not his strongest point. He was, of course, a first class top-notch pilot.

Mac smiled. 'Oh yeah, still appeasing those desk jockey head cases,' he said, allowing a smile to escape. Must be doin' somethin' right, they haven't grounded me yet. How about you, Claire?' Mac said. 'How is life in DC? Do you miss Andrews?' Mac left his question hanging in the air. Inwardly he was hoping that his former sweetheart would respond all gushing and explain how she missed him and her life at the base.

Claire paused. 'Kept very busy. There's not enough hours in the day. Working for Cleaver is not for the faint-hearted.'

'Oh, very intimate are we Claire? 'Cleaver'?' he said sarcastically, in a tone which implied something else.

'Listen Mac, if you're going to condemn me or him, I may as well leave right now,' Claire said, now rising from her chair.

Mac sat back and appraised her. 'Oh Claire, sit down … please. People are looking,' he said as he directed his eyes to other customers.

Mac saw the change in her. Her hair was one thing, but her attire was so classic; knee length skirt, polished high heels, shirt and jacket and a single strand of pearls around her neck. Not the casual Claire he remembered or loved at all.

'You've changed, Claire,' he said, slowly glancing between her and his beer glass.

'Really?' she replied.

'Yeah! Washington has changed you. I mean, look at you. Where's the Claire I knew? The fun-loving woman who couldn't be controlled and now one year, one lousy year with General fuckin' Cleaver Harris, and all of a sudden you're this prim and sophisticated bitch …' Mac paused. '… Yeah. As I said Claire … you've changed.'

Claire stood there. She listened to Mac sprouting forth his opinions, well after all, he was always good at that, but maybe Mac was right, maybe she had changed. One thing was for sure, she now knew and realised that life back with Mac at Andrews Air Base was not for her. She had moved on.

Mac sat now, expecting Claire to retaliate, defend her position; plead with him that there was no change between them, but it was not to be.

Claire simply stood quietly for a few moments, and stared into Mac's rugged, tanned face and captivating eyes.

'You know what Mac?' she eventually said. 'You are absolutely correct.' With that statement made, she leant across the table and gently kissed him. 'Goodbye, Mac,' she said for the second time in her life, but this time she knew would be the last.

Claire departed leaving Mac rooted to his chair as he watched the woman he loved leave. He watched as he waved, expecting his gesture to be returned, but Claire just started her car and was gone.

SIX MONTHS LATER

Chapter 9

It happened unexpectedly. One afternoon, Steve had purchased a newspaper and was about to cross the street when he heard the screech of tyres biting the tarmac and the noise of quick acceleration. A car's engine revved at high speed and sped towards him.

His quick reactions, fitness and physical strength avoided the inevitable as he vaulted over the hood of a parked car, the offending vehicle glancing its fender as it hurtled past and vanished into the distance.

A crowd gathered, making sure he was unhurt, but once again no one could give a description of the vehicle, or its driver. Steve was shaken but unhurt and examined the damaged fender of the stationary car that saved him. There were dark green scuff marks where it had been hit; obviously the paintwork from the other vehicle. Steve scrutinised them closely, whatever make the vehicle was would probably have to be repaired to avoid detection. He would commence his enquiries of all bodyshop repair garages, beginning with the smaller ones.

'Hey, bud, I need a statement! What's your name and address? What happened?'

Steve turned towards the beat officer. The last thing he needed right now was to get involved with the police. The crowd of bystanders were pooling and now jostled the officer.

'Okay! Get back!' he shouted, waving his arms, his whistle now blowing, signifying for the crowd to disperse.

The officer turned back towards his witness, but Steve had gone. Panicking, the officer searched the street, the adjacent sidewalk and the crowd of pedestrians, but could not see his man. He pursed his lips and shook his head. This would not look good on his report of the incident. The officer turned his attention back towards the damaged stationary vehicle, its owner now present, aghast and yelling.

'What the fuck's happened here? Officer, officer, where's that son-of-a-bitch that's wrecked my car?'

'Okay, okay, calm down. There's no one hurt and not much damage sustained.'

'Oh! And who's gonna pay to repair this, eh?'

Officer Bradley did not observe the dark green Sedan moving slowly on the other side of the street, its driver and front seated passenger's sharp eyes scanning the sidewalk. It looked as if they had slowed to glance at the traffic incident, but in reality they were searching for their target.

Donaldson watched from a distance, then tensed as he caught the stare from the driver's eye who, when realised he'd been spotted, accelerated his vehicle and sped off.

Steve stood motionless, now realising even though six months had lapsed without any incident he was obviously a loose end that required to be tidied up. What had Claire Monroe known, and more importantly, about who? He cursed himself and once again tortured his mind, wishing he had taken her case.

Next morning, Steve spent his time checking small repair shops but no green Sedan had been booked in for repair. He pondered and reflected on the incident. Even the fact that another car had been damaged would have prompted action to hide the offence, and yet his enquiries drew a blank.

He was walking towards a park when the thought and word came to his mind, and Steve uttered the word 'destroyed' out loud. Have the car crushed, why not? No questions, no evidence, no records if an unscrupulous trader were used. It sounded a bit extreme, but Steve allowed the thought to permeate his mind.

If he could still locate the dark green Sedan, it may just be the tip of the iceberg.

It was late afternoon when he meandered into the breakers yard.

Chapter 10

Rusty's junkyard with its corrugated tin fenced walls and barbed wire top appeared to be just another typical breakers yard with bold warning signs positioned at regular intervals, of:

DANGER

KEEP OUT

HEAVY MACHINES OPERATING

Steve approached with caution. He heard the clanging of a conveyor belt machine and its functions on the metal bodies that passed along, crushing and thumping as it worked through its day. He heard the sound of the crane, its noisy engine and gears changing as its driver operated the machine from his small cabin, his headphone protectors making him oblivious to anything or anyone outside. Old automobiles were lifted by the crane's claws which gripped them as they were individually selected, and swung through the air before being placed on the conveyor belt which would crush and destroy the metal carcass before it was flattened and compacted into a cube, making it ready for sale and reuse.

Steve waved his arms at the crane driver, who seemed to ignore him as he continued to operate his crane, keeping faithfully to his work schedule.

Steve's shouting 'STOP!' didn't seem to work either, the driver's ear protectors cancelling any outside noise as he swung the arm of the crane towards him.

Steve now waved frantically as the claw grip of the crane came towards him, then at the last moment its engine cut, jolting the cabin as the claws swung in its cradle in the air before coming to a standstill.

Steve still frantically waved his arms as the crane driver removed his ear protectors and commenced his descent from the cabin. His red curly hair and heavy growth lived-in face and broad frame told Steve he did not seem the type of character to be pushed around.

Rusty wore a red baseball cap with his favourite team logo. His red and black-checked shirt hung outside his dark blue denim jeans with a white sweat-stained t-shirt underneath. He pulled his heavy, well-worn leather gloves off as he approached Steve.

'Anything wrong, bud? What d'ya want? Can't you read? Nobody's allowed back here.'

Steve appraised the man before him before replying. 'I'm interested in this dark green Ford Sedan behind me here. You were about to put it through the crusher.' Steve's statement hung in the air. A blank expression stared back at him in silence.

'It's not like any of the other rust buckets you got in the yard,' Steve added, as he ran his hand over the scraped paintwork of the Ford's dark green damaged fender.

'What's it to you? It's not your friggin' car!' came the reply.

Steve stared into the man's blue eyes. 'How do you know; you got the paperwork for it?' Again, Steve's statement stung the air.

The crane driver's eyes narrowed as he spat on the ground. 'Maybe I do,' he replied dryly.

Steve knew any information he would derive would have to be fought for and so considered the man's comment. 'Could I take a look at the paperwork? Please? Steve added, as if any pleasantries were going to cut any slack with the bonehead before him.

'What concern is it of yours? You a cop or somethin'? Show me some identification, bud,' Rusty said, as he now stiffened and stretched his body upwards in readiness to take action.

'No, I ain't no cop,' Steve replied, then ran his fingers along the body of the car beside him. 'My car was stolen last week, one just like this. Same colour, same model; believe it was used in a hit and run, but that's just what the police think. There's no proof and they haven't found the offending vehicle yet, just as they haven't located my car.'

Steve smiled, his eyes scrutinising the crane driver's face, seeking any reaction to his comments.

'You think it's your car, bud? You got the registration documentation?'

'Yeah!' Steve replied. But not for this plate. It's obviously been changed,' Steve said, staring at the new screws that shone from the registration number.

Rusty shrugged his shoulders. 'Ain't my concern, bud. I just crush them.' Rusty paused. 'So you think this is your car, eh?'

Steve nodded. 'Yeah, I think so.'

'It's a common model,' Rusty added, not making any movement or offering any help.

'These marks here,' Steve said, 'I made these myself last week, hit a goddamn wall while parking. It was due to go in for repair until it was stolen and now here it is.'

Rusty could tell Steve was not going to be fobbed off; he also looked fit and had a determined nature, and anyway if it was this dude's car then he would have to play along; well, in the meantime anyway.

'Okay, bud. I keep my paperwork in the Portakabin. You prove it's yours, and we'll take it from there.'

Steve followed Rusty into his office. It was as he expected, primitive, dirty, with old, chipped furniture and a smeared Playboy calendar on the wall that had not been changed for months; the well-endowed model leaving nothing to the imagination.

There was a dark green metal filing cabinet in the corner, its top covered with telephone books; its face disfigured with constant use over the years. The heavy wooden desk with its black, torn inlay at one corner, and scuffed with age housed two telephones; one black and one red, accompanied by three vodka bottles; two empty and the third half full.

'You wanna drink?' Rusty said, as he poured a three fingered measure into a dirty stained mug and offered it at arm's length to Steve.

Steve shook his head, negatively. The small Portaka-bin was confined, its wire grills fixed over the smeared, foggy windows, and dull fluorescent lights with only one tube illuminated told Steve that visitors were not welcome.

'So, let's see your documentation,' Rusty said, as he gulped a large swig of vodka from the dirty mug.

Steve hesitated as he reached slowly into his pocket inside his coat. 'You first, Rusty. I mean, let me see your authorisation to have the vehicle crushed.'

Rusty sniggered. 'That ain't your car out there, is it?' he taunted.

'Maybe it is, maybe not,' replied Steve. 'But I'd sure like to know who authorised such a good car to be crushed just because it's got a few marks on its fender. Maybe you could enlighten me and then let me look it over before you do your job. I'll make it worth your while,' Steve added.

Rusty stopped drinking his vodka and put down his mug. 'You'll make it worth my while,' he said, repeating Steve's words.

'What's your interest in that heap out there? It's certainly not your car, unless of course you do have the paperwork.' Rusty let his comment ring as he took another sip of vodka, his eyes now glinting at Steve, feeling he was back in control of the situation.

Steve took a bundle of dollar bills from his wallet and started counting them out on top of the desk. '$10, $20, $30, $40. I'd like to know who brought the car in,' he said dryly as he continued to place more dollars on the old desk. '$50, $60, $70.'

Steve stopped at $70, but still held a bunch in his left hand. Rusty eyed the remainder of dollars in Steve's hand.

'I think you can do better than that,' he said. 'That is, unless you have the necessary paperwork to …'

Steve's actions were quick. He grabbed his man and pulled him close across the desk. 'Now you listen my friend,' Steve said, as he held Rusty by the throat, smelling his stale breath tainted with tobacco and liquor. 'I want to know who brought that car in … understand? Now, you gonna tell me. It's up to you whether we do it the easy way, or …' Steve paused '… the hard way, now, which would you prefer? If it's the hard way, that'll suit me just fine, 'cause that car was used to kill my little sister and I'm mighty upset right now.' Steve had just made that up for effect, hoping it would serve his purpose to gain more information on Claire Monroe, as any information that would lead to her killers would ease his conscience.

Rusty, now aware of Steve's motive, answered. 'Okay, okay, but let me go, I'll see what I got.'

Steve momentarily released his grip but had repositioned himself beside Rusty, still holding him and warning him not to try anything. Rusty attempted to move.

'Ah need to get into the cabinet,' he said, eyes pointing towards the filing drawers beside the desk.

'Okay, but you try anything and it'll be the last thing you do.' Steve now held the man's left arm in a vice grip, ready to break it if any attempt was made to get free.

'Ah need both hands,' Rusty said, obviously in pain as Steve jerked more force on his body and arm.

'Just get the information, shithead, or so help me I'll finish you now and find it myself – understand?' and with that, inflicted another round of pain, now pressing pressure points in his neck.

Rusty nodded his head, his eyes bulging and then flickering, but signifying that he understood and his situation was not negotiable.

Steve released enough pressure to allow movement, and after some difficulty a file was retrieved from the cabinet. The name on its tab was Riker. Another sheet inside the main folder was headed "Automobile", followed by its description:

Type   Ford
Model   Sedan
Colour   Dark green
Year   ~~1958~~

The year date had been obliterated but there was an authorised scrolled signature. Steve squinted at the name, but couldn't decipher it.

'Whose signature is that?'

Rusty just stared back at Steve, a terrified expression on his face, indicating that no further information was forthcoming.

'You can keep $20,' Steve said as he re-pocketed his remaining $50 from the desk. 'I'm going to look at the car, okay? No objections, I presume?' Steve said, giving another jerk of the man's arm. Rusty stared back at him, unable to speak or move.

Steve, now inspecting the inside of the Sedan, glanced through its windscreen. The junk man was on the telephone. It was time to go.

Chapter 11

Steve would have liked to know who Rusty telephoned, but he had to keep himself loose meantime, after all, he now had the name Riker. Momentarily, Steve thought of his fellow marine buddy George Hunter, whom he used to rely upon for information. George was employed in the records department of Social Security and could trace nearly anybody. He had been a good friend and the information he supplied was mostly correct, as George was a very methodical character who left nothing to chance. But George was dead; murdered by Luther on the Rosenberg case. That case had cost Steve dearly, as once again he reflected on his personal losses. He had not found a substitute for George; to be truthful he hadn't actually tried as his mind had been in meltdown after losing Maria. He missed George, with his quirky ways and old-fashioned habits, but Steve realised to move on he would require to recruit somebody he could trust to replace his friend. Everyone in his business needed informants to enable investigations, and police departments to solve their crimes.

It would be a long slog, but surely there couldn't be many Rikers listed. His main concern was the fact that after an attempt on his life, the vehicle involved was to be scrapped rather than repaired. It seemed an excessive action to take, after all he had not been killed, or even hurt badly, so there would have been no follow-up by the New York City Police, as their workload was so immense. Therefore, the question still remained – why? It was obvious, as far as Steve was concerned he was the only link to Claire Monroe's death. He would need to revisit the breakers yard. He wanted a closer look at that file in Rusty's Portakabin, but right now he headed for one of his favourite bars on 45th street. He needed a drink. He also needed time to think.

Steve was on his second Jack Daniels when the two men wearing overcoats and wide-brimmed hats entered. They acknowledged Steve, but made no advance towards him. Steve casually observed the two men but didn't make any connection with himself until one of them approached the counter and shouted 'Hey, Riker, it's a beer for you, yeah?'

At the mention of the name Riker, the man being addressed had Steve's full attention. Riker was a heavy-set man, double chin, and puffed-up cheekbones, with narrow eyes. His broad chest and large stomach caused the multi-coloured tie he wore to bend, and as he sauntered towards an adjacent table, Steve could see the outline of the butt of a handgun concealed beneath his coat.

Rusty's file had the name Riker on its tab. This was too much of a coincidence to find the two men in the same bar as himself. Steve now turned his attention to the other man. Where Riker was heavy-set, his partner was slim, his facial features sharp, especially his nose. His thin lips gave off an Italian appearance. His black hair was swept straight back with no parting and when he carried the drinks over to his partner, Steve observed that his little finger of his left hand was shorter than normal; in fact, most of it was missing.

Riker sipped his beer and stared at Steve. It was obvious he was watching him.

'What's your problem?' Steve shouted, acknowledging the stare.

'Hey! No problem, bud. Just having a quiet drink.'

'You're watching me,' Steve replied, then quickly strode towards the two men. Steve reckoned if there was going to be trouble then he stood a much better chance standing up.

'Ah, don't want no trouble, pal,' Riker said, now also standing and eyeballing Steve.

'Oh! No!' Steve said, his voice changing the tone, as he delivered his accusation. 'You attempted to run me down, and don't deny it. I found the car and the file with your name on it … Riker … isn't it?'

Riker smirked, then turned to his partner. 'Hey Frank, this joker's accusing me of trying to kill him, what dy'a say, Frank?'

'Well. He's way off the mark,' Frank replied. 'Cause everyone knows if you'd been out to kill this motherfucker then he'd be dead by now.'

Steve smiled. 'So, you guys have never been to Rusty's junkyard I suppose?'

'Who? Rusty, Rusty's … yard … what?'

'As I said Riker, your name is on a file, you've obviously had previous dealings with Rusty, and his yard doesn't just deal with old rust buckets if the dark green Ford Sedan you left there to be crushed is anything to go by. You know Riker, the one with the damaged fender, after you attempted a hit and run on me, just as you accomplished with Claire Monroe.'

Frank now moved beside Steve; his gun was pressed against Steve's ribs.

'I think we should all go somewhere more private.'

He had provoked them, deliberately. Besides, Steve felt confident he could handle the two of them, but he needed to be outside. He would play along meantime, and hopefully find out more about Claire Monroe.

The three men vacated the bar, Riker leading the way, Steve in the middle, and Frank bringing up the rear, his handgun still firmly pressed against Steve's back.

'Don't try anything, Donaldson. I won't hesitate to use this,' Frank grunted between his teeth as he reminded Steve how close he was, prodding the weapon deeper against Steve's body.

Riker turned to face Steve. Steve, now with confirmation that Frank had addressed him by his surname, spoke. 'So, you know my name, Riker. You and your buffoon friend here.'

Frank immediately stepped closer, his weapon now ready to fire.

Riker stared at Steve, then glanced at his partner. He raised his right hand. 'Okay, let's go for a ride,' he said, as his eyes darted at other pedestrians and watching for anybody else who should show any interest.

All three walked for a few minutes towards 10th Avenue, then Riker stopped and unlocked his parked car.

'Get in!' he shouted at Steve, as he opened the rear door of the automobile. Steve hesitated. He knew he stood a much better chance of survival outwith the confines of the vehicle.

'Ah said, get in,' Riker repeated, his voice now carrying a venomous snarl. Steve once again felt the sharp prod of Frank's handgun and realised he'd have to comply.

Riker, now seated beside Steve, produced his own revolver, keeping it aimed squarely at Steve's chest. Frank started the car and pulled out into the flow of traffic, causing horns to blast. 'Where to?' he shouted, as he half turned his head while keeping alert of other motorists.

'Let's return to Rusty's,' Riker replied. 'See what our friend here really knows. Besides, I want to know how Rusty allowed him to know my name, and whatever else he told this schmuck. '

'What 'd'ya say, Donaldson? What exactly did Rusty tell you … eh?!'

Steve remained silent.

'Not talking … well … we'll see,' Riker said, then gave out a ghoulish laugh. 'I'm gonna take great pleasure in making you talk, you son-of-a-bitch,' as he pushed his face into Steve's, his gun menacingly digging into Steve's chest.

Steve didn't respond, or even flinch, but his mind was racing.

They approached Rusty's Junk Cars, which appeared different at night; the high piles of rusty old metal bangers stacked on top of each other, creating an eerie outline against the moonlit sky. A single lamp glow could be seen from the Portakabin, and the figure of Rusty talking on the telephone, a bottle of vodka in his other hand topping up his mug.

The sound of their car approaching distracted Rusty and he abruptly ended his call and downed his liquor before appearing at the door.

'That you, Riker?' he shouted, as he recognised the familiar figure approaching him. Rusty was about to continue talking, but stopped dead mid-sentence when he saw Steve bringing up the rear with Frank.

'I believe you've already met our Mr Donaldson here,' Riker said, thumbing his fist in Steve's direction.

'I …. I … never seen him before,' Rusty replied, his voice quivering.

'Oh! That's odd,' Riker replied, "cause he seems to remember you, Rusty. Said you and he had an interesting chat regarding my affairs here. I see that car is still parked out there, still not done.'

'Tomorrow, Mr Riker, I would have done it today, but …'

'But nothing,' Riker interrupted. 'You were too busy filling Donaldson's head with information. What 'd'ya tell him?'

'Nothing! I swear … ah don't know how he got your name … Mr Riker, you know me, wouldn't tell anybody anything.'

Rusty was about to continue with more excuses, but once again Riker interrupted.

'Shut up, you schmuck, just don't say nothin' more …' Riker turned towards Steve. 'Okay, bud, sit down. Now, tell me who you're working for, and what's their interest?'

Steve formed a smile.

'Hey! Don't get smart with us,' Frank said, waving his gun under Steve's nose.

Steve shrank back in his chair; he didn't like the gun so close to his face, but nurtured up his reply. 'First, I ain't workin' for anybody. I'm a private eye.'

Steve volunteered this information openly as he suspected Riker and Frank knew that only too well.

'No case, meantime,' Steve continued, 'but you know how it is when somebody deliberately attempts to kill you; make it look like an accident. Well, it's my experience to find out more and obviously why anybody would want me dead. The car led me here. I had already searched repair shops, which begs the question, gentlemen: why destroy a perfectly good automobile just because it's got a damaged fender. A small repair and it'd be good as new. So, Riker, what's the story? Then Steve turned to face Rusty.

'And what's in all this for you, Rusty, apart from being paid to destroy a car?'

'You askin' too many questions for your own good,' Rusty replied, wiping his mouth with the back of his hand. 'Ain't that right, Riker?'

'Okay, okay!' Riker responded, his facial expression blank. 'So you think me and Frank here tried to kill you?'

Steve nodded. 'Looks that way to me,' he answered.

'What makes you think you're so important? What makes you think it wasn't an accident?' Riker sneered. He tilted his head at his partner Frank while Rusty poured himself another straight vodka.

Steve held his stare and watched the three men in front of him. ''Cause of what I do know.'

Riker laughed. 'And what do you know, Mr Private Detective?'

'Well, I know you have some kinda racket goin' on with Rusty here, and I know certain autos are being scrapped. Maybe you guys are stealin' them, robbing the parts to order, then scrapping them, so there's no trace. Everybody's a winner.' Steve hoped his naïve explanation would satisfy Riker and his associates.

Riker laughed again, his tobacco stained teeth showing more clearly this time. 'Well,' Riker replied, still laughing as Frank and Rusty joined in. 'I ..., we ... can all see how you're such a good private eye. Does the job pay well?' Riker said, continuing to laugh.

Steve just sat there. They were all laughing at his expense and it wouldn't be long before they let their guard down. He would need to escape before they tumbled his bluff.

'How many autos you stolen this month, Frank?' Riker asked, his mouth still full of laughter.

'And how many you crushed, Rusty?'

All three repeated laughing out loud, staring at each other and momentarily forgetting about their prisoner.

Steve took his chance; he sprang up off his chair, karate-chopped Riker in the throat, which made his gun drop. Steve hit Frank in the solar plexus and he slumped to his knees. Rusty was in shock and certainly no fighter. He had fallen on top of his old desk and Steve pushed him off the other side. He grabbed the gun on the floor and ran outside. He managed to hotwire their car before they came round to what had just occurred and sped off as gunshots from Frank's weapon pierced the air. He had one of their guns, maybe Stuart Chandler could give him more information on its identity.

Steve didn't go home that night. Instead, he ditched the car and made his way to find a cheap hotel for the night.

'Hey honey, want some company?' the short-skirted hooker mused, bending forward to show off her wares.

'Thanks, but not tonight,' Steve replied.

'Give you a special deal, honey,' the voice called, but Steve just kept walking.

He spent the night in a shithole of an establishment, the noise from adjacent rooms making him realise he would have been better going home and taking the chance that Riker and his mates wouldn't visit.

He made up his mind that he would call Lieutenant Stuart Chandler tomorrow, and although he had very little information, anything at this stage that would further his enquiries could only be helpful.

Chapter 12

Riker didn't like loose ends. He took his vengeance out on Rusty.

'If you'd crushed that auto when you were told, none of this would have happened.'

'Hey, Riker, ah just do my job. You think it's so easy, you get up in that crane and do your own dirty work.'

Riker, taken aback by Rusty's outburst, grabbed him by the collar. 'Now, you listen to me, you little shit motherfucker. Don't tell me what my job is, or what I should be doin'. You failed big time, Rusty, and if this guy Donaldson returns or makes any more waves, I'm warning you, those cars out there won't be the only things that are crushed. Do you understand?'

Rusty knew Riker's temper and started to shake uncontrollably.

'Do you understand, motherfucker?'

'Yeah! Yeah Riker, I do. I'll make sure the Ford is done first and any details destroyed.'

'You'd better pray, Rusty, that Donaldson does not get in my way again – understand?'

Rusty nodded; Frank just smiled.

Riker and Frank Gennero vacated the Portakabin. They borrowed another vehicle from Rusty and instinctively knew they had to find Donaldson. They checked his apartment first, but when there was no reply, proceeded to his office, but again drew a blank.

This was not good, their contact would not be pleased.

55

Chapter 13

Steve made his way to the precinct in Manhattan South. He wanted to involve his old adversity, Lieutenant Stuart Chandler. They had a mutual respect for each other and instinct told Steve that whatever Claire Monroe knew must involve some prominent people and therefore he would require the assistance of the Authorities.

Stuart Chandler, being a stickler for detail, was what this case required, and so in trepidation he approached the steps of the precinct that not long ago he had held his ex-wife, Gill, at knifepoint to escape Chandler and custody.

Steve drew a deep breath and entered. 'Hi guys,' he said, smiling as he approached the reception desk.

'Well, look what the cat's dragged in,' Sergeant Murphy cried out as he saw Steve approach. Other officers looked up and there were several mutterings from some of them who knew Steve when he was on the Force.

'Well, what can us humble beings do for His Lordship and what brings you downtown on this lovely day?' Murphy said, appraising Steve, who, with his previous night's escapade and lack of sleep looked like an unmade bed.

'Hi Murph,' Steve said, extending his hand. It was not reciprocated and Steve felt uneasy. 'Is Chandler in?' he asked, now realising how he must have looked, unshaven and dishevelled, and wished now he'd taken time to have gone home, washed and changed.

'Chandler? Well, ah don't rightly know,' Murphy replied. 'Maybe you tell me what it's about, and I'll see that he gets your message.'

Steve just stood there, then spoke quietly. 'Why you being so difficult, Murph? Is Chandler in? It's a simple question, even for you, so I'll ask again. Is Lieutenant Stuart Chandler available, Sergeant Murphy? I'd like to see him.'

Murphy was standing his ground and was still being uncooperative when Detective Sergeant Johnston entered the lobby.

'Steve Donaldson,' Johnston said, extending his hand. Steve hesitated for a moment, then shook Johnston's hand, pleased that someone still showed him some courtesy.

'Is the man in?' Steve asked, now totally ignoring Sergeant Murphy.

'Am still here,' Murphy's voice bellowed, but Steve not only ignored the officer but turned his back on him and spoke into Johnston's ear.

'I want to see Chandler. I'm working on a case, well, a hunch, to be more precise, and I think the Department can help fill in a few gaps so to speak, and probably find what info I have interesting.'

'Anymore to add? Give me a clue before I disturb him,' Johnston said. 'You know what he's like,' he added.

Steve smiled, 'Yeah Johnston, I remember, but I need to see him myself.'

Detective Johnston glanced over at Sergeant Murphy; the extended pause making Steve feel uneasy once more.

'You do remember, Detective that Chandler invited me back anytime, especially if I had something of interest to discuss.'

'Our workload is way over the limit, Steve,' Johnston said, hoping Steve would divulge more, before he interrupted his superior. 'Maybe tell me what it's about?'

'I have to discuss this myself. Now, can I see him?'

'Okay, I'll see if he will spare you five,'Johnston said, and disappeared, making his way to Chandler's office.

Steve took a seat in the lobby and stared at Sergeant Murphy square in the eye, but kept his mouth shut as other officers crowded beside Sergeant Murphy.

Johnston reappeared. 'Steve, the Lieutenant will see you now.'

Steve nodded, then gave a sarcastic smile in Sergeant Murphy's direction, pleased that he'd won.

Stuart Chandler stood up and extended his hand when Steve entered. He had not forgotten the Rosenberg affair, as it was down to Steve that the riddle was solved, but also, and more importantly, the fact that Michele Salvadori died and many of his soldiers in organised crime were arrested and who were now serving long prison sentences. It was a feather in Stuart Chandler's cap and Steve Donaldson had played a key role in bringing all that about.

'So, what happened to you?' Chandler asked, scrutinising Steve's untidiness.

'Oh! Had a rough night, that's all. You know how it is.'

Chandler paused. 'So, what can I do for you? You didn't confide in Johnston, but I do owe you, well, owe you enough to listen, anyway.'

'Thanks,' Steve answered. Any chance of a coffee?'

'A coffee! What do you think we are, Steve, a hotel?' Chandler exclaimed, then lifted his handset. 'Johnston, bring two coffees in here.'

Steve smiled. 'Thank you,' he said.

'Don't thank me yet, you ain't tasted what they serve for coffee in here.'

'I do, you know, Lieutenant. Remember I used to work here.'

Chandler sat down behind his desk. He had a mountain of things to do, but he was wise enough to realise the detective before him would not normally have requested police assistance and therefore was very interested to hear what Steve may tell him.

Pleasantries over, both men sipping their coffees, Steve opened the conversation.

'Do you remember, Lieutenant, about six months ago, a young woman by the name of Claire Monroe was killed? It was reported as a "hit and run" in the newspaper, and by the authorities who dealt with it in the normal way. There were no witnesses that came forward, no trace of the vehicle and after the usual procedure the case was closed with no further action. Claire Monroe just became another statistic; just another unsolved accident.'

Chandler shrugged his shoulders. He replied vaguely. 'Hit and runs rarely find their way to this desk,' he said, pointing at the higher priority case files that lay before him.

'You see, that's just it,' Steve said. 'I believe Claire Monroe was murdered. She was taken out for another reason. She knew something. Something important. Something that I think involved some very important people and because of what she knew they killed her. An organised hit, but one that would leave no trace and therefore would not draw too much attention and not be investigated further. A simple hit and run accident.

'What information do you have that collaborates all this, Steve?' Chandler asked, still unsure if this was his bag.

Steve hesitated. 'I don't really have too much information at this time. I was hoping that's where you and the Department would come in … I mean …'

'Stop! Hold it right there, Steve,' Chandler interrupted, his arm raised. 'We don't have the time, money, or manpower to go investigating a hit and run from six months ago, unless of course you have solid evidence; names, dates, the whole caboodle, so I don't think I, or the Department, can help. Have you any idea what's on my plate, Steve? You don't have to answer to the DA or my superiors. I …., I don't have the luxury of taking on one case at a time. So I'm sorry Steve, I'm passing on this one.'

Steve rose to go. He knew it would be pointless to press the Lieutenant. He had hoped that Stuart Chandler, with his stickler for detail attitude, would have at least made further enquiries and maybe have let him see the police report of the incident.

'Let me leave you with this, Lieutenant. Claire Monroe came to me six months ago; an attractive young woman, professional career in the city. She had information on somebody in a prominent position. She wanted me to take the case "on a need to know basis". Feed me titbits as we went along. Like you, I told her I wasn't interested.' Steve paused.

'Claire Monroe left my office. Five minutes later she was dead on the sidewalk. I watched it all from my office window. I didn't come forward, as I expected that whoever took Claire out would also come after me, but guess what, nothing. I checked everything, waited patiently; cautiously for the hit, but nothing happened. As I said, that was six months ago, but four days ago I was the victim of a hit and run. The vehicle that attempted to run me over damaged its fender. I traced that vehicle but not to a repair shop, but guess where? A crusher's yard. Two or three scratches on a 1958 Ford and it was to be crushed, along with the other rust buckets. The owner of the yard is as reputable and professional as my ass and then of course I was abducted last night at gunpoint by the two jokers who had attempted the hit and run on me, and probably the two schmucks who took out Claire Monroe. I managed to escape, stayed in a small, cheap hotel last night, hence my appearance, but I know there's a connection with whatever Claire Monroe was hiring me to investigate. I know I'll be stopped before I find it, unless of course I can enlist your help, 'cause I don't really want to end up in one of your files.'

Detective Chandler listened. He respected Steve Donaldson, but knew on what he'd just heard his hands were still tied and he could not authorise the manpower to the case without more evidence. Chandler therefore once again shrugged his shoulders.

'I'm sorry, Steve, that still doesn't change my decision. If, however, you do find anything more concrete, something that I can work with, come back and we'll take it from there. In the meantime Steve, I suggest you be vigilant and keep your head down.'

Steve realised it was pointless to try and persuade Chandler for assistance and therefore had no option but to leave.

'Before I go, Lieutenant, I'll give you a name.'

Chandler remained unmoved.

'Riker,' Steve said. 'Works in the Department of Justice. He's got the standard weapon issue. Has a partner, Frank. Don't have another name.'

With that, Steve departed. The air outside felt good. He needed to rest, so headed home to his apartment.

Lieutenant Chandler drummed his fingers on his desk. He picked up his handset. 'Johnston, find out what you can about somebody named Riker. Works in the Justice Department. Oh, and Johnston? Don't use the normal channels, do it yourself. Tell nobody. Just report back to me – okay?'

Chapter 14

Steve made his way home. He was pleased he'd spoken to Lieutenant Chandler, even although he and the Claire Monroe case had been dismissed, but the fact remained he had at least brought another dimension of the incident to Chandler's attention, and maybe, just maybe, with his attitude, Chandler may just make further enquiries. Steve could only hope, but for now he needed to wash and rest.

He entered his apartment block. He was in his corridor when Gerry the maintenance man approached.

'Did your two friends get you?' he said.

'What? Who?' Steve replied.

'Two guys, said they were friends of yours. Flashed their badges, said you were expecting them.'

Steve stared at Gerry. 'Oh, yeah, eh, that's right, Gerry. Did they leave you a contact number?'

'No sir, said they'd be happy to wait. I let them into your apartment with my pass key. I did right, didn't I Steve?'

'Thanks Gerry – you did right. Do you know if they're still there?' Steve said.

'As far as I know. Never saw them leave.'

'Can you describe them, Gerry?'

'Yeah, sure can. One was heavy-set, chubby face; the other sharp-featured, Italian-looking,' replied Gerry, now staring at Steve.

'Thanks, that's who I'm expecting. By the way, Gerry, you're pretty good at observation.'

'Well, thanks, I have to be. Can't just go letting anybody in, ya know.'

With that, he walked off, unaware of what he'd done.

Steve waited until Gerry was out of sight. So Riker and Frank were inside, waiting for him. He had to think out his next move.

He returned to the street and the phone booth on the corner, and dialled.

'Lieutenant Chandler, please, it's personal.'

A few moments passed, then the line was connected.

'Chandler here, who's this?'

'It's me, Lieutenant.'

Chandler didn't respond, so Steve started talking.

'The two dudes I told you about, Riker and his pal Frank, well they're in my apartment right now, waiting for me, and I don't think it's a social visit. My maintenance guy let them in by mistake; passed themselves off as police. If you want to help me close the Claire Monroe case, I suggest you pick them up.'

'Donaldson!' Chandler snapped. 'There is no Claire Monroe case.'

'Well, there should be,' Steve replied. 'Something stinks here Lieutenant, and I ...'

Steve's never got to finish his sentence. Stuart Chandler had hung up.

Chapter 15

Blaspheming, Stuart Chandler shouted for Johnston.

'Get a car to Donaldson's apartment. There are two guys there, Riker's one of them; bring them in. I'll question them myself.'

'Well, that'll save some time,' Johnston replied. 'I really wasn't looking forward to investigating someone from the Justice Department.'

Chandler cut Johnston short. 'Just bring them in, Sergeant. Don't give any reasons why, just that I need to see them.'

'Okay, Lieutenant,' Johnston replied, not sure what reasons he could have given anyway. It was obviously to do with Steve Donaldson.

Riker and Frank Gennero were about to leave Steve's apartment. They had waited long enough, but Donaldson was a no-show, or so they thought, when Detective Sergeant Johnston approached with two patrolmen.

Johnston held his identification shield high for both men to see. 'I need you both to accompany me downtown. My Lieutenant wants to see you.'

'Your Lieutenant?' Riker said. 'And who's that?'

'Lieutenant Stuart Chandler, Manhattan South.'

Riker stared at Frank. 'What's this about?' he asked.

Johnston thought impulsively. 'Well, Steve Donaldson is down there, you know him, you've just been in his apartment. Chandler's questioning him, but he said you guys could vouch for him. Told us you guys were here.'

Riker considered the detective's statement. 'Steve Donaldson's downtown with your Lieutenant, and he knew we were here and he's requested we come with you and vouch for him?' Riker repeated.

Frank Gennero now spoke. 'Maybe we should go. Find out what's going on; after all, if Steve needs our help then help him we shall.'

Riker glanced at his partner, then smiling, said 'you may just have a point there, Frank. Okay, Detective, we'll follow you in our own car.'

Johnston nodded.

Steve watched them all depart. So Chandler had taken action. Maybe he would find out more about Claire Monroe after all. Steve wished he could be there, but right now he really needed to rest and then freshen up and try to assemble the jigsaw in his mind.

Chapter 16

Riker and Frank Gennero entered Chandler's office, who promptly requested full identification. Chandler read their shields, thinking that Steve Donaldson's assumptions were correct.

'So, you wanted to see us, Lieutenant. Understand you have Steve Donaldson here. You want us to vouch for him, or something?' Riker paused, then added, 'so, what's he been up to now?'

Lieutenant Chandler eyed the two men in front of him, hesitated, then, ignoring Riker's question, asked 'so, where does Claire Monroe fit into all of this?'

Chandler let his question hang in the air, while his experienced eyes absorbed every expression and movement of the men before him.

'Claire! Claire who?' Riker eventually responded. 'Never heard of a Claire … Monroe!'

Chandler interrupted. 'Claire Monroe, Claire Monroe,' Riker repeated, his brows furrowed as if attempting to recall the name and the person. 'You ever heard of a Claire Monroe, Frank' Riker asked his partner.

'Monroe … Claire Monroe …' Frank answered, shaking his head. 'Can't say I have.'

'What's all this about, Lieutenant? Thought we were here to collect Donaldson,' he said, attempting to change the subject.

'Donaldson?' Chandler responded. 'Oh! He left here some time ago. I don't know where he'll be right now,' he said, as he checked the time on his leather-strapped wristwatch.

Riker mopped his brow with his handkerchief. The overhead fan was whirring, but it was only moving the hot air of the office around and Riker's overweight body was struggling in the confines of the small, warm office.

'Thought Donaldson was here, Lieutenant? We were told you required us to vouch for him, or something, so what's this really about?'

Chandler once again observed the two men. Instinct told him dubious characters, if ever he saw them.

'So, what do you know about Claire Monroe's hit and run of six months ago?'

'Lieutenant, we've told you, nothin'! Nothin' at all. Don't even know a Claire Monroe, so what the fuck's goin' on here?'

Chandler was not phased by Riker's outburst.

'What do you know of the attempt to kill Steve Donaldson; make it look like a hit and run?' Chandler pressed.

'An attempt on Donaldson's life, Lieutenant? Don't know what you mean,' Riker replied.

'So you weren't driving a 1958 dark green Ford Sedan a few days ago?' Chandler asked.

Riker replied too quickly for Chandler's liking. 'Dark green Sedan! You must have the wrong information, Lieutenant, and as far as Steve Donaldson is concerned we, that is, Frank and I, haven't seen him for a few months.'

'So, why were you in his apartment then, waiting for him?' Chandler asked, a stark expression on his face. He was fishing, but didn't know what for, and was trusting his instincts.

'Oh! You know ...' Riker started.

'No! I don't know, Riker. Please explain.'

There was a moment's silence, then Riker spoke. 'Listen, my superiors are working very confidentially with Donaldson. Me and Frank are the go-betweens and were instructed to visit him.'

'For what purpose, Riker?' Chandler pressed.

Riker hesitated before replying. 'That's not your concern, Lieutenant. This matter does not concern you and it's certainly out of your jurisdiction.'

'I'll decide, Riker, what I think concerns me, or my department,' Chandler replied, raising his voice.

Riker mopped his brow again, then rubbed the back of his neck around his shirt collar. He was perspiring heavily now.

Riker composed himself, then stood up, his partner Frank Gennero mirroring his movements.

'Listen, Lieutenant. The matter with Steve Donaldson is *not* your ... understand ... *not* your jurisdiction, or your affair. Now, don't make me call my superiors 'cause they'll rain down on this department like hells fury and you sure as hell don't want that.'

Lieutenant Chandler stood back and stared into Riker's eyes. 'Hey, only following up a hit and run on Claire Monroe. We know Donaldson is somehow involved, so what's the beef? You guys want me to back off, then give me some information so that I can do just that and keep my Captain happy, okay?'

'Lieutenant Chandler, we're not tellin' you nothing,' except to say this does not concern you, so stay out of this, it's not your business …. understand?'

Riker had moved closer to Chandler, eyeballing him. Chandler felt the pressure of intimidation, but experience told him to stay calm. Riker and Frank Gennero then moved to the office door to vacate the premises, when Chandler spoke.

'So, Riker, I'll, or *we'll*, forget about the attempt on Donaldson; he's a big boy and can look after himself, but we'll need to follow up why a perfectly good car was to be crushed along with other rust buckets. That, Riker, requires investigation.'

'What'd you say?' Riker now strode back towards Chandler.

'We'll need to speak to Rusty, who we believe owns the breaker's yard and who was being paid to destroy a perfectly good vehicle which may have been used in a crime. That, Riker, is our jurisdiction and we'll be using all our means at our disposal to find answers to that one.'

Riker stared a threatening stare into Lieutenant Chandler's face.

'I'd be very careful, Lieutenant, just what you investigate right now. You might just find that you've bitten off more than you can chew.'

Riker now stepped really close to Chandler and whispered in his ear. 'Drop it! Understand? It's not a warning, Lieutenant. It's an order … got it?'

Riker and Frank vacated the precinct. Lieutenant Chandler sat at this desk. He lifted his handset.

'Johnston … get me that son of a bitch Donaldson and get him in here now!' he yelled.

Chandler, upset, banged his handset down in its cradle.

Chapter 17

Steve had washed, showered, changed and now felt human again. He knew he needed to rest, but his curiosity was aroused and he wondered how Lieutenant Chandler's interrogation was going with Riker and his sidekick Frank.

Maybe in the meantime he could find out more himself and so he decided to revisit Rusty's junkyard; he was sure he'd find a link to Claire Monroe in Riker's file.

He took his time, his mind retracing recent events and his first meeting with Claire Monroe six months previously, and even allowed himself time to have a coffee and a doughnut in a nearby café. He thought again of Riker. Lieutenant Stuart Chandler would not be intimidated and hopefully he would delve more closely into the hit and run on Claire Monroe.

A few hours had lapsed when Steve found himself outside Rusty's yard. He was not alone, however. The emergency vehicles of fire tenders, ambulances and police patrols were all in attendance as the black, acrid smoke blackened the skyline, followed by an occasional bang from exploding fuel stored on site. The smell of burning rubber filled the air, causing the emergency teams to choke. Steve pushed his way through the crowd.

'What happened here, officer?' he said, as he approached the patrolman standing guard of the taped-off area.

'Nothin' for you to worry about, bud, just stay that side of the line – okay?'

Steve nodded and stood motionless as his gaze wandered over the officer's shoulder and into Rusty's yard.

'Bit of a mess,' he casually commented.

'Ah told you, stay back, now please leave.'

Steve thought it better to move on; after all, he didn't want to attract any unnecessary attention. He found himself another position and let his eyes rotate around the other spectators that had now gathered. He recognised a small figure with a soft hat tilted backwards, his press identification slung around his neck, his notebook and pen at the ready. Jimmy Malone of The Times was talking to a fireman attending the scene.

Steve moved towards the two men, but was distracted by medics shouting 'coming through' as the crowd parted to allow them access to their ambulance. Steve recognised the badly burnt body on the stretcher and stopped the medics momentarily.

Steve looked into the black, frightened eyes of Rusty, who blinked very slowly, as he stared into Steve's eyes. Rusty's mouth opened, but no sound came. Steve bent closer, his ear at Rusty's mouth. A faint whisper and a name filled Steve's ears. He was expecting Riker's name, but that was not the name Rusty spoke before he died.

Jimmy Malone had secured enough information to run a small article in his newspaper, but Malone had experience and the cunning sense of a wolf and knew there was more to the tragic death of a scrapyard owner than met the eye. He too witnessed Steve bending over old Rusty, gleaming information before he died. Malone therefore searched for Steve but he had obviously departed. His investigation and interview would have to wait.

Chapter 18

Johnston had been unable to locate Steve, and Lieutenant Chandler was not happy. The call came in about the fire, but only received Chandler's attention when Rusty's junkyard was mentioned as the location and the owner Rusty had died in the blaze, which to all accounts appeared like a tragic accident.

Lieutenant Chandler now realised Steve Donaldson had stumbled onto something, and given the threat by Riker earlier Chandler was in no mood to roll over and play dead. His intelligence had been questioned. His department and him intimidated, Lieutenant Stuart Chandler was not about to roll over on this one.

He opened his door and signalled to Johnston to come to his office.

'Six months ago, a hit and run, a woman was killed; goes by the name of Claire Monroe. No suspicious facts, just an accident, apparently. I want the report and the file on my desk by tomorrow morning, oh, and Johnston, find out all you can on her background. I want a full picture and history of this Claire Monroe, understand?'

'You got it, Lieutenant,' Johnston replied.

Chandler nodded. 'Any news on Donaldson?'

'Not yet, Lieutenant. He's not at his office or apartment; we're watching both places. He's bound to turn up sooner or later.'

'Johnston, find Donaldson, I want him in here today, not tomorrow, today, got it?'

'Anything else, Lieutenant?'

'Yeah, I want you to keep tabs on that Riker and his partner Frank Gennero. I still need you to find out about them, but as I said earlier, make these enquiries by yourself and no matter what you find, only report direct to me, and only me.' Chandler's tone of voice made the situation clear.

'Yes, Sir, will do.'

Johnston had answered affirmatively, but inwardly didn't like all this cloak and dagger stuff within the department.

Chapter 19

Riker and Frank Gennero mused over the interview Lieutenant Chandler had put them through.

'Somethin' ain't right, Frank,' Riker said. 'That Lieutenant knew more than he was letting on.'

'You think Donaldson got to him?' Frank replied, his eyes narrowing questioningly.

Riker paused for thought. 'Probably, after all, the son of a bitch was on the force, wasn't he, bound to have connections.'

Both men sat in their car; silence now reigned between them. Riker was first to speak.

'How much can Donaldson know? I mean, it's at least six months since Claire Monroe died, and there was no follow-up; at least not implicating us, and as for Rusty, well, he only met him this week and I don't think he'll be speaking to anyone ever again. So, the question really is, how much does Donaldson actually know?'

Riker wiped his brow and neck with his handkerchief. 'Maybe we should do nothing, just let things slide meantime; I mean, if no more evidence or action is taken the New York City Police will drop the case. That Lieutenant Chandler won't keep a case open just on the word of a PI, even if he was on the force before. He couldn't justify the cost, time, or anything. That means we do nothin'. Let Donaldson go, well meantime, but *"you know who"* will still want to know what Claire Monroe told him and if we can't find that out then Donaldson will remain a loose end. And you know what happens to loose ends, Frank?' Riker smiled.

'Yeah, they get tidied up,' Frank replied.

Riker nodded at his partner. 'All in good time, Frank. All in good time.'

Riker and Frank Gennero sat reflecting on the events of the last few days.

They hadn't wanted to kill Rusty, but hey, he had become a liability and therefore of no further use. They sipped their beers, contemplating contact with their boss. They felt that the incidents were moving too fast and required instructions of their next action.

It had always been agreed that they were never to make direct contact, unless of course a dire emergency arose. Riker and Frank considered their immediate position as such, resulting in Riker dialling the private direct number.

Its tone rang out. A voice answered on the third ring.

'Randall, is that you?' Riker whispered into the mouthpiece. There was no confirmation from the receiver. 'Listen, its Riker; me and Frank think we should meet. There's been developments in the Claire Monroe case.' Riker paused. 'Randall, you still there?' Silence reigned. 'Randall,' Riker repeated. He was about to hang up, when the voice spoke.

'Where are you?'

'Is that you, Randall?'

Again, there was no confirmation, but the recipient of the call repeated his question. 'Where are you, Riker, and is Frank with you?'

'Yeah, Frank's here.'

'Where are you?' Randall asked.

Riker looked across the street from the phone booth.

'We're on 49th and Eleventh Avenue. There's a bar, Gillies, across the street. Do you want the number of the booth we're in?'

Silence reigned again.

'Randall, we have important information. We need to talk.'

'Go to Gillies. I'll have someone contact you.'

Riker began speaking, but the line was dead. Looking at the handset, aghast, he replaced it on its cradle.

'Did you speak to Randall?' Frank asked.

'Yeah, but the son of a bitch hung up. Told me we were to meet at Gillies across the street. Said someone would contact us.'

Both men ran over to Gillies, jumping between the blaring horns of the heavy traffic. The bar was dimly lit inside; the red draylon velvet booths with dark tables and small lamps giving discreet light but privacy to their customers and hostesses. The glitter ball above the stage area rotated as the girls performed, rehearsing their set for that evening, while other long legged ladies propped themselves on their high stools at the bar, smoking and eyeing their latest arrivals.

Two hostesses wandered over to Riker and Frank. 'Want some company, big boy?' the red haired hostess said to Riker, as she placed the palms of her hands on his lapels.

Riker smiled. 'Maybe later, honey. We're meeting someone, so fuck off.'

'Don't you like me?' she replied.

Riker didn't engage in any further conversation, he just removed the girls' hands and headed for a booth with a wave of his head for his partner Frank to follow.

Another scantily clad hostess appeared.

'Two beers,' Riker said. 'We're waiting on someone, don't want to be disturbed … understand?'

The blonde waitress nodded, smiled and returned to the bar to place their order.

Riker and Frank were sipping their beers quietly and whispering to each other when the barman approached. 'Any of you guys called Riker?' he said gruffly.

Riker looked up, making full contact with the man. 'That's me! Who wants to know?'

'There's a call for you. You can take it through the back, it's more private there,' he said, as he pointed to a small, dark door at the rear of the bar behind the stage.

'Who's callin'?' Riker asked, but the barman didn't acknowledge the question, he just answered.

'I'll transfer the call to the extension in the hallway.'

Riker made little of it, and walked to the rear of the bar to answer the call. The booth was there in the hallway and Riker picked up the receiver. 'Hello. Riker here,' he said.

That was the last words he spoke before he slumped to the floor. He never felt a thing as the sharp blade delved deep into his body and upwards to his heart, while a strong arm and hand capped his mouth.

Riker was dead.

His body was removed from the hallway to a small room and propped up on a chair, his back facing the door. His soft hat was replaced on his head as his assailant waited patiently for his next victim.

Frank Gennero was beckoned by the barman. 'Your friend wants you. He's in the small office at the rear of the club. Please, be our guest.'

Frank waved to the barman, thanking him for his hospitality and then made his way along the black painted corridor.

He knocked on the door, then entered. 'Riker, you in here. Have you heard from Randall?'

Frank felt no pain. He was dead in two seconds, and fell flat at Riker's feet.

Almost immediately, two heavy bouncers appeared and dragged the two bodies outside to the alley where they were dumped in the clear, plastic-lined trunk of the waiting vehicle.

No one spoke as the car drove off. The only sound was the screech of tyres as the black Sedan bounced over the ramp from the alley and joined the main thoroughfare.

Chapter 20

S teve waited patiently across from the precinct for Lieutenant Chandler to appear. He wanted to know how the meeting with Riker and Gennero went and Chandler's opinion of the fire at Rusty's breakers yard. There were other questions that continually ran through Steve's mind, and as he waited he recalled them.

1. Claire Monroe had come to him, offering him a case, but would only proceed on a "NEED TO KNOW BASIS." Steve didn't understand that as she hadn't given him anything to start with, and the memory of losing Maria because of Karen Rosenberg was just too painful. Karen too had imposed the same condition when she hired Steve and not only was she dead, but many others too; others that didn't need to die.

2. So he hadn't taken her case and yet five minutes after leaving him she was dead. Someone had followed her. Someone knew what she knew. Someone knew about him and his meeting with Claire.

3. Who was the caller on the telephone who never identified themselves on that fateful night when Claire Monroe died?

4. Six months of nothing, then an attempt made on his life by the same hit and run method, no doubt by Riker and Gennero, and who probably brought poor Rusty's life to an end.

What was next? He wondered, or, more importantly, who? Steve realised his life was not safe. He was a loose end and loose ends normally only ended one way – dead.

Something big was brewing, and Steve hoped that Lieutenant Chandler had enough initiative to reopen Claire Monroe's case, and if not then that was his next move. Pressure Chandler into helping him solve the mystery.

Steve recalled Jimmy Malone's article in The Times, recording the fire at the breakers yard and Rusty's death. Steve, like Chandler, didn't like the press, and Malone was no exception, but the thought crossed Steve's mind that if Chandler took no action then maybe a "tip-off" to Malone, just to get the ball rolling, might be no bad thing. One thing for sure was Malone had many connections, and once running with a story was like a dog with a bone, especially when he sensed a scoop.

Chapter 21

Jimmy Malone's telephone rang. The New York Times' offices were busy and noisy as usual.

'Malone,' Jimmy's voice answered.

'Don't ask any questions, Malone,' the voice said. Just listen. You want a scoop! The fire at Rusty's breakers yard, three days ago! You were there. Old Rusty died in that fire! It was no accident, Malone. I'll give you a name … Claire Monroe killed six months ago, supposedly hit and run, I think you'll find out otherwise.'

'Okay, who's callin'?' Malone replied, whilst waving his arms to a colleague to listen into the conversation on another handset.

'Maybe start your enquiries in the Justice Department. I'll give you another name, Malone. Riker …'

The line went dead.

The call was too short for Malone to ask for more information. There had been no request for money, which in itself was unusual. Just a pure and simple lead.

Jimmy Malone sat at his desk. He read the names on his pad.

Claire Monroe – hit and run

Rusty – killed in fire

Riker – Department of Justice

Malone recalled the scene at Rusty's, but it just appeared to be a careless, tragic accident. Now, however, his suspicions were aroused.

Steve hung up the handset in the phone booth. Maybe Malone of The Times would act and create enough smoke on Claire Monroe's case to allow Lieutenant Stuart Chandler to reopen enquiries and have her death and that of Rusty's fully investigated. He would wait, and hopefully Malone would act.

There was no sign of Lieutenant Chandler, and, confident that he had started the ball rolling, he concentrated on another score he had to settle. He wanted to locate Riker; he certainly wasn't finished with him, and so headed back to the bar where he had first encountered his two adversaries, hoping they may reappear. Maybe someone in the bar knew their whereabouts, or maybe provide some useful information?

Chapter 22

Detective Sergeant Johnston could not uncover any information on Riker or Gennero. No one at the Department of Justice had heard of them, and even checking driving licence records drew a blank. Johnston tried various other lines of enquiry, but on each occasion hit a brick wall. Whoever the two men were that he'd escorted from Steve Donaldson's apartment and were interviewed by his boss, had just seemed to vanish into thin air. Something was very odd about this whole case which made him more determined to investigate further, but first he would bring his boss, Lieutenant Chandler, up to date.

'What d'ya mean …. nothin'?! They work in the Justice Department,' Chandler stated flatly. 'I mean, you saw their shields, same as me.'

Johnston hesitated before replying. 'Well, Lieutenant, they sure as hell don't work there now, and its disturbing how nobody has even heard of them.'

Lieutenant Chandler reflected, then shook his head. 'Get Donaldson. He knows more than he's letting on. After all, he was the one who tipped us off about Riker and Gennero.'

Johnston held his own council but departed to track down Steve Donaldson, inwardly praying that the job would be much easier this time.

It was three days before Frank Gennero and Riker's bodies were discovered. They were found washed up on the banks of the East River, their faces disfigured and almost unrecognisable, with all personal identification gone, but the fact that they had been questioned by New York Police Department earlier solved that issue.

'Okay, Johnston, so nobody has heard of these two characters in the Department of Justice; well, we'll see about that,' Chandler exclaimed, as he picked up his direct line and made a call.

Chapter 23

Steve read Jimmy Malone's article in The Times about the two homicides that had been fished out of the East River. Their identities had been withheld, but Steve's intuition brought the names Riker and Gennero to mind. He had to have his suspicions confirmed, however, and there was only one person that he knew of who may just give him that.

Steve made his call from a phone booth on 48th Street. 'Hi, Lieutenant, Donaldson here. Can you confirm something for me; the two bodies fished out of the East River this week, were they Riker and Gennero?'

Silence reigned on the line as Chandler didn't answer.

'I'll take that as a yes then, shall I?' Donaldson replied. 'That's four people dead, Lieutenant. How many more will it be before you reopen Claire Monroe's case?'

'Now Donaldson, you listen to me, I want you in here, now,' Chandler shouted. 'Right now, you hear!'

Lieutenant Chandler was wasting his time. He was talking to a dead line.

'Johnston? Johnston!' Chandler shouted.

'Yeah, Lieutenant?'

'Get that son of a bitch Donaldson in here. Find the motherfucker now.'

'Will do, Lieutenant, as soon as possible.'

'No, Johnston … now … immediately … today, not tomorrow … today.'

Lieutenant Chandler's raised voice was at screaming pitch. 'He knows about Riker and Gennero, and a lot more besides. I want him, Johnston.' Chandler shook his head. 'Why is it, every time Steve Donaldson gets involved with anything, it seems to grow arms and legs?'

Johnston didn't reply, he just made haste to carry out his orders. It was going to be another of those awful days when his boss would ride him and the department for every indiscretion.

Johnston could still hear his Lieutenant's voice rambling on to some poor sod like himself, taking the flak on his other line. Once again, he heard Chandler's handset bang down.

***

Steve put more money into the phone booth machine, dialled and let the tone ring out. The line went live.

'Malone!' Jimmy answered.

'Just listen,' Steve said.

Malone had pen and paper to hand as an automatic reaction.

'The identity of the two bodies fished out of the East River are Riker and Gennero – Frank Gennero …'

'Hey! You the guy that gave me Riker's name before; Justice Department, wasn't it?'

Steve didn't confirm Malone's statement, instead he just continued with his information he was giving to the reporter. 'There's a link to the murder of Rusty.

You know the fire at the breakers yard? You were there, Malone, I saw you and I've read your article.'

'Hey! Who's this talkin'? Give me somethin'.'

Steve paused. 'Okay, Malone, Rusty was murdered. That fire was no accident and I guess Riker and Gennero are the culprits. They also took out Claire Monroe six months ago – hit and run, but the case is supposedly closed.'

'How d'ya know all this?' Malone said, his mind racing, his pen making notes on his pad.

'Because Riker and Gennero attempted a hit on me. They assumed I knew about Claire and information on someone big.'

'So, did you take them out?' Malone asked, wanting more information.

'No, I didn't, Malone, but I guess somebody did, 'cause they sure are dead.'

'You have proof of that?' Malone pressed.

Steve paused. 'In a word … no. But I suggest you try the Justice Department for confirmation and if that draws a blank, try Lieutenant Stuart Chandler of Manhattan South. He's been workin' the case.'

'Okay, bud, can we meet?' Malone answered, but the line was dead.

Jimmy Malone sat at his desk. He stared at the two names of Riker and Gennero on his pad and thought about how he remembered the junkyard man, Rusty, or what was left of him. Slowly, he picked up his handset, and requested his switchboard operator to connect him with Lieutenant Stuart Chandler of the New York Police, Manhattan South. He waited while his call was put through.

'Chandler,' Stuart answered.

'Lieutenant Stuart Chandler?' Jimmy said.

'That's right,' came the confirmation reply.

'Jimmy Malone, The Times,' Jimmy said, introducing himself.

'I don't speak to the press,' Chandler replied, about to hang up.

'Is it true that the two dudes fished out of the East River this week are Riker and Gennero from the Justice Department?'

Chandler went berserk! 'Who the fuck told you that, you little shit?'

'So, it's true then? Malone stated flatly.

'I didn't say that,' Chandler replied, but Malone had hung up.

Chandler stared at his handset. Motherfucker, son of a bitch!' he exclaimed. 'Johnston! Johnston! Get in here,' Chandler shouted.

'Anything wrong, Lieutenant?' Johnston answered, now standing before his superior.

'I've just had a call from that creep Malone of The Times. He could tell me that the two stiffs we fished out of The East River were Riker and Gennero.

'How does he know that, Lieutenant?' Johnston said.

'Could also tell me they worked for the Department of Justice,' Chandler said, ignoring his sergeant's question.

'So who, Johnston, do you think would give him that information?' Chandler said.

'Well, I …' Johnston started.

'Well nothin', Johnston,' Chandler interrupted. 'I'll tell you who, Mr Steve bloody Donaldson, that's who. Have you located him yet?' Chandler shouted.

'No … well, he's just disappeared. He's not at his apartment, or his office; we have both addresses under surveillance, and …'

'Oh! Poof!! Just up and disappeared in a cloud of smoke, I suppose! Now, you listen, Johnston. Find him, you hear. You've a whole department at your disposal, and yet he can't be found?'

'Lieutenant, we've been here before with Donaldson. If he doesn't want to be found, he won't be. He's got specialised skills and …'

'Out. Get out. Specialised skills my ass. Get out and find that son of a bitch.'

Johnston took the flak and departed, leaving Chandler fuming once again.

Chandler sat at his desk. All this over a hit and run of a young woman six months ago. Could Donaldson be right? Could there be more to this than it first appeared?

Stuart Chandler sat quietly, trying to still his mind, then reflected over the chain of events so far.

Claire Monroe, killed in a suspected hit and run. Then nothing for six months, then an attempt made on Steve Donaldson's life – same method, and Steve was the last person to see Claire Monroe alive.

The vehicle used in both incidents found in Rusty's backyard.

Donaldson is abducted by two men posing as agents Riker and Gennero working for the Department of Justice, but Donaldson escapes. Rusty ends up dead in a mysterious fire at his yard and Riker and Gennero are fished out of the East River, stabbed to death, then shot in the head like a contract killing by the mob.

Obviously Donaldson knew more than he was telling. Maybe more information on Riker and Gennero would explain that. Chandler considered the facts. There was more to the Claire Monroe incident than he'd given credence. He therefore summoned Johnston and once again instructed him to find out more about Riker and Gennero. That surely would be the starting point. The common factor that linked all these events.

'That's just it, Lieutenant. There appears to be no record of any Riker or Gennero at the Department of Justice. There's nothing in driving licence records either. No social security numbers – nothin'. In fact, Lieutenant, in short, Riker and Gennero don't exist.'

'Well, who have we got down in the morgue, Johnston – Laurel and Hardy?'

Johnston was speechless; he couldn't answer his superior.

Chandler just glared at his officer.

Chapter 24

Chandler's telephone burst into life. Both men just stared at the instrument. Stuart Chandler picked up and listened to the voice on the line.

'Lieutenant Stuart Chandler?' then paused for confirmation.

'Yeah! Who's calling?' Chandler answered.

'Never mind! This is not a warning, Chandler. This is an order.'

'I beg your pardon, who is this?' Chandler asked, now glancing over at Johnston.

The voice on the line continued. 'I'll say this only once, Chandler. Back off on the Claire Monroe case, and forget about Riker and Gennero. They are no concern of yours.'

'Hey, who is this?' Chandler interrupted.

'We're investigating certainly two murders, maybe even three, or four and …'

'Listen, you jumped up son of a bitch' the voice interrupted.

'Back off! You have other cases. Drop this enquiry if you know what's good for you.'

'You threatin' me and my department?' Chandler retaliated.

'There's no threat Lieutenant, but if you value not just your career, but your life, do as I say.'

'You son of a bitch, who dy'a think you're talking to?' Chandler replied.

'I won't warn you next time, so close your enquiry.'

The line terminated and Chandler just stood there, holding the dead handset. He turned to his sergeant. 'Johnston, you've seen this Claire Monroe's file, anything there unusual? Anything that would cause all this interest?'

Detective Johnston recalled his memory. 'Nothing comes to mind, Lieutenant, but if Steve Donaldson is involved you can bet your ass he's stumbled onto something and given all the incidents so far, if they are connected appears to be something big.'

'I agree Johnston. We've just been told by that last call to back off all those cases. Now, remember who told us exactly that recently?'

Johnston thought for a moment. 'Riker did, when you had him in your office,' he said slowly.

Exactly, Johnston. And yet Riker is dead.

An orange light flashed, indicating an internal call from his captain. Chandler listened to the matter-of-fact voice of his superior and attempted to interrupt, but the call had been terminated.

Detective Johnston eyed his Lieutenant, an anticipated expression on his face. 'Just been instructed in no uncertain terms that we have to drop the Claire Monroe case. He didn't even know we were working on it, but whatever his reason we've to keep it logged as a hit and run.'

'But ...' Johnston broke in.

Chandler raised his hand. There's more,' he said. 'Regarding Riker and Gennero! There has to be no further investigation regarding their murders. We've to chalk it down to a gang murder; be grateful that those scumbags are off the streets.'

Johnston was dumbfounded and his face showed it. 'Did the Captain give you a reason, Lieutenant?'

Chandler shrugged his shoulders. 'He just ordered us to shut these cases down. He said they were no big deal! We had other cases to work'.

'I don't understand,' Johnston replied. 'I mean there are four homicides that may be linked and we're to close down the investigation?'

'Yep,' Chandler said. 'It doesn't make sense.'

'Of course, Lieutenant, had our friend Donaldson been taken out then maybe Riker, Gennero and Rusty would still be alive,' Johnston stated flatly.

Chandler's mind was working overtime. 'Tell him I want to meet him. Give him a tickler that officially we've been instructed to close all these cases down, but remind him that I'm a stickler for detail; he'll understand that, and privately don't want to close our enquiries. Tell him I need his help to stay in the game. Tell him I'm prepared to work together on this one. Tell him that, Johnston.'

Detective Johnston turned to leave, when Chandler spoke again. 'Oh! And Johnston, keep all this between ourselves and don't share it with, or use any of the department services; just find him and arrange a meeting away from here.

Johnston nodded. He did not like the sound of what was going down.

Chapter 25

Steve was working late. First he saw the silhouetted outline of a figure outside his dimpled glass office door. Quickly he retrieved a newspaper from the waste bin and hid his .38 underneath.

The knock on his door was quiet but firm and Steve hesitated before replying. 'Come in,' he said, his hand in readiness to grab his gun.

The visitor entered and Steve exclaimed 'well, well, Detective Sergeant Johnston, to what do I owe this pleasure at this late hour? Come to arrest me?' he said, smiling and holding out his arms and hands for Johnston to cuff him.

The detective sergeant smiled. 'Listen, Donaldson. The Lieutenant wants to meet you but in an unofficial capacity, so it can't be at the precinct.'

Steve listened as Johnston explained that Lieutenant Chandler and his department had been instructed by an unknown higher authority to shut down the cases of Riker and Gennero and to close any further enquiry into Claire Monroe's hit and run.

Johnston continued before Steve could ask any questions. 'You know what he's like, Steve. Doesn't like to be told what to do and how to run his department. Bit like a patient telling a doctor what illness they have. He's a stickler for detail, you know that.'

'Yes, I remember,' Steve said, and allowed a small smile to escape.

Johnston continued. 'So you can understand the fact that somebody who he doesn't know is ordering and threatening him to close these cases has the opposite effect. Even our Captain has been nobbled, so there'd be no help from that quarter.'

'So where do I fit in?' Steve asked. 'Does he want me to trace who is threatening him and his department?'

Johnston hesitated. 'That would be helpful but let's face it Donaldson, you brought the Claire Monroe case to light which in turn brought these two Justice Department goons, Riker and Gennero, to the Lieutenant. Riker also threatened him. I can assure you he didn't like that. The Lieutenant had dismissed the Claire Monroe enquiry. We have too many current cases to handle and a hit and run six months ago just doesn't cut it.'

'That was until he was threatened and ordered to close the enquiry down,' Steve said.

Johnston nodded.

'So, what do you or Chandler know?' Steve said, hoping for some new facts.

Johnston shrugged his shoulders. 'That's not for me to discuss. The Lieutenant wants a meet. You name the time and place. He … we … believe you, Donaldson, have stumbled unintentionally into something big. Our hands are tied officially, but you're a free agent. You can work independently, but with us, if you see what I mean…?'

Johnston paused, then added. 'Unofficially, of course.'

Steve digested all he heard. 'What's in this for me; how do I get paid, my expenses and costs don't just take care of themselves.'

Johnston chose to ignore the question. He was not about to debate something he had no authority over. 'Are you going to help the Lieutenant or not?'

Steve sat back in his old swivel chair. 'Okay, Johnston. Tell Chandler I'll meet him tomorrow morning – 6:00am sharp at Rikki's Café. It's on Mulberry Street.'

'Why there?' Johnston asked.

'Because I trust Rik and besides, Maria and I used to go there, so I'm known. There won't be any interruption and Chandler and I can talk freely.

'Oh, and Johnston, tell Chandler to come alone. No offence to you, but we don't want it to look like a convention.'

'Till tomorrow,' Johnston replied. 'The Lieutenant will be there, Donaldson, just make sure you are,' he said, then departed.

Steve heard his footsteps disappear along the corridor and eventually out of earshot. 'Maybe, just maybe, we're getting somewhere at last,' Steve said out loud to himself, his head nodding; his mind racing.

He switched out his desk lamp, sat a few moments then made his way home.

Chapter 26

Johnston reported back to Lieutenant Chandler and relayed his conversation with Steve. 'Said you'd to meet him at Rikki's Café on Mulberry Street, 6:00am sharp, tomorrow morning. Also said you to go alone and not crowd him.'

Chandler nodded. 'Better that way,' he said. 'Anyway, I can fill you in with any details you need to know. Better if you're not seen to be involved with all of this in case it all goes belly-up.'

Johnston was grateful for his Superior's consideration as he didn't feel relaxed working outwith the department or his Captain, even although he wanted to assist his Lieutenant.

'You know I'll do anything I can, Lieutenant. All you have to do is ask.'

'Thanks,' Chandler replied. 'I appreciate that, Johnston. Now you'd better keep on top of those other cases we're investigating, if we are to play the game. We at least need to make it look like we're obeying instructions and doing our job.'

Just then their Captain appeared. 'Got a call from the friggin' DA's office regarding those two stiffs in the morgue; I hope you're terminating your investigations as instructed.'

Chandler hesitated. He would like to have come clean with his superior, but decided to keep everything under wraps meantime. 'Yeah, Captain. Can't say I like it or understand it all, but hey! I've enough on my plate already,' he said, pointing to a stack of pending files on his desk.

The Captain paused, then added 'anything you need to ask me on these other cases, Stuart?' he said, nodding his head towards the files on Chandler's desk.

Chandler shook his head negatively. 'Hey, Captain, if I need anything you'll be the first to know.'

'Fine,' the Captain replied, 'but remember Stuart, our budgets are limited.' With that last comment he departed, leaving Johnston and Chandler sniggering.

'You know, Johnston, this whole friggin' case stinks. All started with a hit and run on Claire Monroe, then its old Rusty the junk man and finally Riker and Gennero, obviously all taken out for something they knew. Normally those assholes at the DA would be pleased to have proof against Riker and Gennero, but now its "close it down". Drop all investigations. What has Donaldson got us into this time?'

Johnston listened, then returned to his duties.

Lieutenant Stuart Chandler drummed his fingers on his desk.

He focused his thoughts on recent events. Somebody had tipped off that little shit Jimmy Malone of The Times. Malone was a skilful journalist and could smell a scoop before it hit the department desk. Maybe on this occasion he should break with tradition and involve him on a strictly unofficial capacity, 'cause one thing was for sure, he'd need all the help he could muster, and

Malone's outside ears would be helpful. Chandler sat there and quickly changed his mind. Inwardly he knew he couldn't trust the reporter.

Chandler browsed through another couple of cases on his desk. He would need to keep abreast of them if he were to convince his Captain he had dropped the Claire Monroe enquiry, to say nothing of the deaths of Riker, Gennero and Rusty, who were still lying in the morgue.

He and Johnston would require to be discreet if they were to keep any information of these cases away from the squad and their Captain.

It would not be easy.

Next morning at 6:00am Stuart Chandler found himself standing under the awning of Rikki's Café on Mulberry Street. It was cold, as the early morning air had not yet lifted from the city. The refuse truck had yet to pass and the rubbish bags and bins were still on the sidewalk from the previous day's activities. Chandler cupped his hands and blew his hot breath into them. He peered inside the glass doorway of the café, but all was in darkness and Chandler was becoming impatient, when a voice spoke to him from behind.

'Good morning, Lieutenant,' Donaldson said, tapping his shoulder.

Stuart Chandler checked the street once more, then followed Steve inside.

'So, how long have you been here?' Chandler asked.

'Oh, long enough. Rikki let me in the back door, but I had to check you were alone.'

'Still don't trust me, Donaldson, eh!' Chandler replied.

Steve eyed the Lieutenant, but didn't reply.

They were the only customers and Rik himself stood at the counter.

'Coffee and doughnuts please,' Steve shouted, as he led Chandler to a quiet booth at the rear of the café.

Rik brought steaming hot coffee and a plate of doughnuts. 'Hey, Steve, your friend here. He a cop?'

Steve smiled at Rik. 'No, he's just helping me on a case. A bit hush hush, Rik. Listen, we're not here, okay? Just you keep the coffee comin'.'

Rik glanced at Chandler. 'Looks like a cop to me,' he muttered, before returning to his counter and continued with preparation for the onslaught of the day ahead. Steve smiled.

'Do I look that conspicuous?' Chandler said, removing his soft, narrow-brimmed hat and revealing his greying hair. Again, Steve smiled.

'Yeah!' he whispered, 'yes, you do, but people around here can spot you guys a mile off, but don't worry, Rik's all right, he won't say anything.'

Chandler nodded. 'I assume Johnston filled you in?'

'Not really,' Steve replied. 'Said you needed my help, said he couldn't discuss anything, but he did tell me that someone has instructed you and your department to cease investigations into the cases of Riker, Gennero and Rusty, not to mention Claire Monroe. I assume Johnston is with us on this?' Steve said, sipping his coffee.

'Yeah! But unofficially, just like me. It's only the three of us; even our Captain can't be included.'

'Who has that kinda clout, Lieutenant?'

'Don't know, but our Captain received a call from the DA's department, so someone high up is pulling the strings.'

'So, if the cases are closed officially, how do you expect you and Johnston to acquire information?' Steve asked, feeling that he already knew the answer.

Chandler sipped his coffee and selected a chocolate-covered doughnut,

'That's where you come in, Donaldson, after all, you started all this with this Claire Monroe business and anyway, you being a loner should be used to uncovering information.' Chandler paused. 'The only difference this time is that you'll have my help and Johnston's. Of course, you can't just ring up and speak to either of us,' Chandler said, then added, 'but that's par for the course for you, Steve. So the real question is, Steve, what do we know so far? Tell me,' Chandler said, as he bit into his chocolate doughnut. 'Hell! That is good,' he said, his words muffled as he savoured the sweet, delicious taste in his mouth, and munched its contents, before wiping his lips with the back of his hand.

Steve bent forward so that he could speak quietly. 'First off! Claire Monroe came to see me just over six months ago. She wanted me to take her case, but on a strictly "need to know basis".' Steve held his hands up in inverted commas. 'I don't know why she insisted on that, but I was so full of remorse after losing Maria in the Rosenberg case, that I dismissed her. Suppose I felt too many deaths in that case could have been avoided, especially Maria's,' Steve said. 'I felt obligated, used and abused.'

Lieutenant Chandler understood, after all, he'd arrested Steve for murders and rapes of which he was innocent, but he could understand Steve's reluctance to get involved under such a condition. Chandler also reflected that if it hadn't been for Steve's perseverance, Michele Salvadori would probably still be alive and wielding all sorts of vendettas that would keep his department so busy it'd make their head spin. So Steve's intervention had helped the city remove a real mobster from the streets, whose organised crime machine had been halted in many areas.

Chandler now also wished Steve had taken the case because if they were to proceed positively it was obvious that whatever Claire Monroe knew was the key.

'What else have you got?' Chandler said.

'Well, as I told you, Riker and Gennero attempted to take me out, using the same method and by all accounts probably the same vehicle. They had waited six months, with no other action against myself until after the attempt on my life. Then I discovered the car at Rusty's yard, ready to be crushed. They abducted me … why? I suppose to find out what I knew, or how much Claire Monroe had told me. I escaped capture. They took their revenge out on Rusty, probably to find out what info he'd given me.'

'Hence the fire,' Chandler interrupted.

Steve nodded. 'Exactly,' he said. 'However, allowing me to still be on the loose obviously displeased somebody, because somehow they ended up dead and you guys fished them out of the East River. You and your Captain have been threatened and now your department has to close any enquiries into these murders.'

Rik approached. 'You guys need fresh coffee, or anythin'?'

'Thanks Rik, a new pot would be appreciated,' Steve said.

Rik glanced at Chandler as if there was anything else he wanted, but Stuart Chandler just smiled at the café owner and nodded, signifying coffee would be fine. Rik departed.

'There's something I haven't told you, Lieutenant,' Steve said.

Chandler's eyes narrowed, the lines on his forehead meeting in the middle above his nose. 'Okay, hit me Donaldson, what else have you got?'

'Well, the first time I met Rusty and discovered the dark green Ford Sedan sitting there waiting to be crushed, I had a discussion with him in his office and let's just say, after some gentle persuasion, I saw a file with Riker's name on it. There was also another name scrolled at the bottom, but I didn't get the chance to read it and by the time I returned to find out more, well …' Steve paused. '…. the whole place was on fire and Rusty was dead.'

Steve did not tell Lieutenant Chandler that Rusty had whispered in his ear before he met his maker. That information would keep, meantime.

***

Lieutenant Stuart Chandler summarised the facts. 'So, Claire Monroe came to you, wanted you to take her case, but on a "need to know basis". You turned her down. Immediately after departing your premises, she was the fatal victim of a hit and run. All standard procedures followed for a RTA. No need for fingerprints as identification was available on the body. No need for further investigation either, until of course you poked your nose in Donaldson, which is not unusual for you, but given the fact that nothing had happened, no intimidation or anything, not even any contact until, of course, you were targeted as another hit and run. The fact that they failed unearthed a whole investigation on your part.'

'Yeah!' Steve interrupted, 'but just consider this. I was, on the face of it, not a threat. I knew nothing as I didn't take the case, but Riker and Gennero didn't know that. The fact that Claire was dead, their mission complete and that I didn't pursue any further enquiries, should have been enough. So, my guess is that's why I was left alone. They, whoever *they* are, didn't want to arouse any connection to Claire's death, and so left it for six months. But also consider, Lieutenant, the fact that I did nothing was not enough, they had to be sure. I, Lieutenant, was a loose end, and loose ends have to be dealt with sooner or later. Riker and Gennero are just pawns in a bigger picture. They ultimately failed in not eliminating me, and so became loose ends themselves. Your guys fished them out of the East River, but somebody does not want your enquiries to go any further, hence all the heat you and your department have received. Do you or did you find any info on them in the Department of Justice?' Steve asked, picking for more information from Chandler.

'Well, that's just it, Steve. There's no record of them being employed there. No driving licence records; in fact, they don't exist. Nobody's heard of them anywhere and yet Riker had enough balls to threaten me to my face in my office, so he's obviously been very confident that he would be backed up by a superior. Who, or where that person is, well, it's beyond my jurisdiction and now that the department has closed these cases no one can access any details whatsoever. But you, Steve, you can operate outwith my restraints. You can, and have, the time to break this down, and I want to help, but unofficially, you understand? I don't know where you start with Riker and Gennero gone,' Chandler said, 'but I'm sure you'll figure something out.'

'So, how do I contact you?' Steve said. 'Or do I operate through Johnston?'

Lieutenant Chandler paused in thought, then, with inspiration, 'Let's use the code name Jericho. That way, I'll know it's you,' he said.

'And the walls of Jericho will come tumblin' down,' Steve added.

They drank their coffees and talked about generally putting the world to right.

'You miss Maria, Steve?' Chandler asked, changing the subject.

Steve nodded. 'Very much, Lieutenant. If it hadn't been for her, I may well have spent jail time as it was down to her, and of course her father too, who kept me out of your clutches. You met my first wife Gill, well she was fabulous, but I guess I used up all her patience and love when I was commissioned overseas. The missions changed me and my family life suffered. When you're a marine in Special Forces, Lieutenant, it's not like any other job. It takes over your life.' Steve fell silent as he reflected on his memories.

'Hey, I've got sympathy, Donaldson. You've been on the Force, it commits you, eats you up. Wife, family, they all suffer; they don't really understand. Nine to five doesn't exist.'

Steve didn't respond.

'Okay, that's it for now,' Chandler said, standing up. I'll look forward to hearing from you, Jericho,' he whispered in Steve's ear.

'And how will I know you if you want to contact me, or want to pass on some information?' Steve said, staring into the Lieutenant's face.

'Oh! Hell, I don't know!' Chandler replied. He had not thought that he or Johnston would be parting with any information. Chandler thought for a moment. 'How 'bout Rubber Duck?' he said, without really thinking the phrase through. Both men laughed.

'I like it,' Steve said. 'Rubber Duck calling Jericho,' he teased.

There was a silence between them. Each knew this case would not be easy.

'Let's catch this son of a bitch,' Chandler said. 'I want this motherfucker who thinks he's so untouchable.' Chandler turned to go. 'By the way, Steve, was it you who gave Malone his lead?'

Steve just returned Chandler's stare, but didn't answer, or acknowledge the question, and with that, Lieutenant Chandler checked his watch and without further comment vacated Rikki's Café.

Steve sat down. 'Hey, Rik, how about another coffee and a JD to go with it?'

'Bit early for that,' Rik replied.

Steve shrugged his shoulders. 'What does it matter what time of day it is? Rik, just pour one and bring it over.'

Steve sat still. He recalled the name Rusty had whispered in his ear before he died. 'Bob,' he repeated to himself. Could he be Mr Big, Mr Untouchable?'

Chapter 27

B ack at the precinct, Lieutenant Chandler brought Sergeant Johnston up to date.

'You are kidding me, Lieutenant, right? I mean, you and Donaldson …, Johnston paused in disbelief. 'Rubber Duck and Jericho? Do you guys think this is the movies? I mean, Humphrey Bogart's not going to come walking in here and shoot off some line from the Maltese Falcon. I mean, are you mad, Lieutenant? I mean, the Captain told you to drop these cases, the friggin' DA has too, and oh, that guy Riker, he warned you, don't forget about that and …'

'And what, Johnston? Riker is lying down there in the morgue on a slab. He felt safe when he threatened me and now he's dead. Are we just to roll over, just because of a few threats?'

'Lieutenant! Lieutenant, this is different, the Captain's obviously …'

'Obviously what, Sergeant?' Chandler interrupted. 'I think the word you're looking for is scared. Anyway Sergeant, we have Donaldson working on the outside and you know as well as I do he'll come up with something, and, I suspect, someone, I …'

'Lieutenant,' it was Detective Sergeant Johnston's turn to intervene. 'Ah don't like it. Not one bit. Think of your reputation, Lieutenant, think of …'

Lieutenant Chandler raised his hand. 'In or out, Johnston? I need to know.'

'I … I ...' replied Johnston.

'In or out?' Chandler repeated. 'Come on, Johnston, in or out?' He shouted again.

Johnston had served under Lieutenant Chandler for more years than he cared to remember. He had been taught well; in fact, everything Johnston knew he had learned from him, and he had a lot of respect for his superior, but this was different. If he said yes to him, he'd be working outside the department and without its back-up, or indeed authorisation from even his Captain. If he said no, then his Lieutenant would be on his own and there could be an awkward atmosphere between them.

'Well Johnston, what is it to be?' Chandler pressed, his tone of voice determined and assertive. 'Johnston, answer me, or so help me I'll …'

'In … Lieutenant. In, goddamn it.'

Lieutenant Chandler smiled, grateful that he had another player on his team.

'Do I call you Rubber Duck too, Lieutenant?' Johnston said, as a smile broke out across his face.

Lieutenant Chandler started laughing. 'Don't even think about it,' he replied.

Just then their Captain walked in. 'Don't think about what?' he said.

Both Johnston and Chandler just smiled.

***

Steve arranged a meeting with Jimmy Malone of The Times. He, like Chandler, didn't have much time for the press, but he needed another pair of eyes and ears out there, and besides, he had already whetted Malone's appetite for a scoop.

The only danger was that Malone being press may exaggerate his information and print it without substantiation, which would only alert the people or persons organising their cover up. Steve wanted Malone's help, but in a subtle way. All the cases linked with Claire Monroe were to be closed; even his own attempted murder was not to be followed up.

Who would have that much power to influence the DA's office? It obviously went way above the Department of Justice, but there was no proof.

Was Claire Monroe having an affair that went wrong, which cost her her life, or was it that she had stumbled onto something? Whatever reason, she was dead now, so there was no hope of finding any information from that source. Randall was the other name he'd read on Riker's file at Rusty's junk yard. Who was he? Was he the name with the power to sanction and control the DA's office, Justice Department and police? Steve didn't know who Randall was, but he suspected he was just another pawn on the table; after all, he couldn't see Mr Big's name appearing on a document in a junk yard.

Malone arrived on time and brief pleasantries over, Jimmy recalled Donaldson's involvement with the Rosenberg case and the fact that Steve used to be on the force.

The two men walked through Central Park, Malone for once listening without interruption. Jimmy eventually spoke. 'So, who 'd'ya think in the DA's department is pulling the strings? Do you think the Mayor is involved?'

Steve shook his head negatively. 'Don't know, Malone, but one thing is for sure, it's someone with a lot to gain or lose; also it's someone with unquestioned authority. As to who has that kinda power, I don't know, which is why I'm enlisting your help. Could you print a headline feeler to see what reaction it has and maybe fetch a response from a source we haven't thought of?'

'You mean, print a deliberate lie!' Malone answered.

'Well, you newspaper guys do that most of the time anyway, just to boost your sales.' Steve smiled at Malone.

Jimmy Malone appraised Steve. 'Suppose I could do that. Question is, will my editor approve? The last thing the paper needs is a lawsuit for slander, especially when we can't substantiate any of this. Is there no one on the force that can help?' Malone asked.

Steve did not want to compromise or divulge Stuart Chandler's involvement, so simply answered 'No!' then added, 'And as far as I know, nobody there has linked all the crimes together.'

'Well, there you are, Donaldson, you once worked on the Force, you must have connections; contact them, get the investigation reopened, tell them what you've told me and I'll keep my eyes and ears open.'

Malone made the suggestion, thinking he'd found a way forward and also an inroads to how the New York City Police force were reacting in a case that the public should be aware of and he and his newspaper could be first in line for the scoop.

Steve did not want his undercover arrangement with Stuart Chandler to be blown and so remained silent.

Malone and Donaldson parted, each feeling somewhat bemused; nothing had been gained from this meeting, but nothing had been lost either. Malone, always the hungry dog, would need to convince his editor to allow him to spend time on the case with the information he'd received and Malone knew his boss; any article printed would require to be accurate to avoid a lawsuit. Newspapers took chances, but only when the sales and publications outweighed the possible consequences. To proceed on a hunch from a PI was no sure thing. Malone knew he'd need to play this story close to his chest. After all, he had more to lose personally than Steve Donaldson if his paper was sued.

Chapter 28

Detective Sergeant Johnston's enquiries were discreet, but he found it nigh impossible to gleam any information on his own without the coordinated help of the team he worked with at the precinct.

He was sure other detectives sensed that he and Lieutenant Chandler were hiding something.

How had Riker and Gennero's records just disappeared? Who was pulling the strings that could influence the DA's department and instructing the NYPD to close these cases and cease any further enquiries.

What was the common denominator that linked Claire Monroe, Riker, Gennero and Rusty, apart from the fact that they were all dead? His Lieutenant was correct. Steve Donaldson, for whatever reason, had become a loose end and obviously given the attack on him had to be dealt with. Who had that kinda power?

Johnston pondered on the word "power". The Mayor, The Chief Commissioner, Senators, certain Italian families with influences throughout the justice system. They all had power.

Since Michele Salvadori's death, many of his and associated members, or soldiers as they were known, had been arrested, some of whom were singing from the pressure by the FBI and CIA and especially when bribed with the Witness Protection Program.

Was that what Claire Monroe knew? Did she have information on someone big in organised crime? Is that why she wanted to enlist the help of a PI, rather than go through normal channels? It was a maze and Johnston felt troubled.

He decided he couldn't work like this. He would come clean and inform Lieutenant Chandler that he'd changed his mind about working on this caper.

Chapter 29

Down at the City's Morgue, Charlie O'Brien was working on his subjects when the call came in.

Being a Coroner, his work schedule was immense. He was always being pressed for results by detectives who needed his analysis for their investigations and there were always plenty of subjects to work on.

Charlie answered the wall handset in his Irish New York accent. 'Coroner,' he said. 'O'Brien speaking.'

'You have two bodies there; Riker and Gennero,' the voice said. 'There's no requirement for any further analysis on them, O'Brien. So just process them in the normal way and don't spend any more time on them.'

'What d'ya say?' Charlie replied.

'Accidental deaths; drowning or whatever, but no more investigation, okay?'

Charlie stared across the room at the two dead bodies that lay on steel trollies. Riker and Gennero, he thought. Well, at least he now had names for the deceased.

'Who's callin'?' Charlie asked, very matter of factly.

'That's not important,' the caller said. 'Just you process these two as accidental deaths. There will be no follow up. No investigation. In fact, the case is closed.'

Charlie was dumbfounded. 'But these two guys have been stabbed, to say nothing of the fact that they both have been shot in the head. Not much accidental death with that,' Charlie said.

There was silence at the other end of the line. 'Charlie O'Brien, you not got enough on your plate down there?'

'Well, yeah, of course, but these guys …'

The voice interrupted Charlie. 'Well, we have all the info we need, so just tag them and bag them, okay, and Charlie, do it. Do it now.'

Charlie O'Brien stared at the handset, a puzzled frown on his face. He normally complained about his workload and the pressure he received from detectives and was always working against the clock; always having to provide enough evidence for crimes to be solved and hopefully the perpetrators brought to justice. Now he was being instructed by a senior authority to stop his enquiry; tag and bag two dudes that obviously had been murdered. Professional hits, which in itself narrowed the possibilities and yet he was to report them as accidental deaths.

Charlie replaced the handset and walked back to the two bodies of Riker and Gennero. They at least had names now instead of their usual tagged numbers tied to their big toe with luggage labels.

Charlie re-examined both bodies visually, then re-zipping their bags pushed their trollies together for his assistant to process.

He was doing just that when he thought of Lieutenant Stuart Chandler. He knew these two dead schmucks were his case. Had Chandler also been instructed to close his investigation? Charlie thought the matter over.

He couldn't see the Lieutenant just accepting an instruction like that, which was obviously so wrong. After all, Stuart Chandler was normally a stickler for detail.

Charlie walked to his office, picked up his telephone and made the call.

Stuart Chandler listened to Charlie sprouting on and on, then eventually interrupted him.

'Charlie, we've been instructed to put this case to bed, so there will be no further action from this department, so I suggest you do as you've been told, because right now there's no option but to comply.' Chandler did not want to come clean with Charlie O'Brien of his involvement; the fewer people who knew that he and Johnston were working with Steve Donaldson the better. Besides, if the word got out there would be hell to pay, and probably the end of his career, not to mention his life. Whatever was going down, people were dead and he did not want to join that brigade.

Charlie O'Brien was still unhappy. He did not like being told how to do his job, and so spoke calmly into the telephone. 'Okay, Detective, but I still don't like it.'

'Hey buddy, what d'ya say we meet for a beer later? Get it all off your chest,' Chandler said, hoping that Charlie would take the hint.

Charlie realised that Lieutenant Chandler was not prepared to divulge anything on the phone. 'Okay, Lieutenant. That'd be great.'

'Say Chelsea's Bar on West 45th, 7:00pm?'

***

7.00pm arrived and Charlie met Chandler and Johnston at Chelsea's

119

'So, what's the beef?' Charlie said, in his strong Irish New York accent, as he settled down with his beer.

Stuart Chandler glanced at Johnston, then spoke, his hand thumbing the table. 'Charlie … we … don't actually know. We've been told just like you to put our investigation of these murders to bed, including a hit and run on a Claire Monroe which occurred six months ago. We don't know how they're linked, but the fact that the Monroe incident has been mentioned obviously tells me they are.'

'Who was Claire Monroe?' Charlie asked, unable to recall the incident.

'Oh, just another statistic, or it appeared to be. Just another RTA never followed up and at the time no reason to either.'

'So, what's the link with Riker and Gennero? O'Brien asked.

Chandler shook his head negatively. 'We don't know Charlie, but we suspect that Riker and Gennero are the two dudes who killed her and we have reason to believe it was no accident. The fact that they too are dead only increases our suspicions.'

'So, you guys have to bury this one,' Charlie said, then fished in his pocket. 'Maybe this can help you. I don't have a clue what they mean. Found them in the lining of Riker's coat pocket. Brought it along before they bagged his belongings, 'cause what you're telling me is someone's toes are being tread on and that someone will stop at nothing to prevent any other enquiries into the matter.'

Chandler read the numbers on the yellow tab. '3433 175 BOB. What are they?' he asked.

'Don't know. They don't ring any bells with me.'

Chandler re-read them. It didn't look like a telephone number. 'Could it be a laundry ticket?' he ventured, maybe when the coat was being cleaned and it's gone unnoticed.'

Charlie O'Brien shrugged his shoulders. 'Could be! Hey, you guys are the detectives, you figure it out; I mean, I've enough to do tellin' you people when and how the stiffs die without working out friggin' motherfucker numbers.'

'Who else knows about these, Charlie?'

Again, the coroner shrugged his shoulders. 'Nobody, I guess! The items listed were one coat and the contents of its pockets were also listed, but no number or ticket was recorded.'

'I'll keep this,' Chandler said, as he put the label with the numbers inside a polythene sample bag. 'Tell nobody about this, Charlie, okay?'

'You got it, Lieutenant. Anyway, I must be off. If I can be of any further assistance, Lieutenant, just contact me. Like you, I hate being told how to do my job and am certainly not happy with loose ends, especially when I'm told to close a case which by all accounts is far from over.'

Chandler nodded his agreement. The three shook hands, then Charlie O'Brien drained the last of his beer and was gone.

Chandler and Johnston sat for a moment. The numbers Charlie had given them didn't mean anything, and nothing came to mind.

'What d'ya think we should do now, Lieutenant?' Johnston said, scratching his forehead.

'I think we need to speak to Jericho.'

'Jericho,' Johnston echoed, 'who's Jericho?' he asked.

'Jericho! You know, Donaldson. He may have some more information for us and maybe we should tell him about the numbers found in Riker's coat.'

Johnston shook his head. This was becoming like a movie, and so mimicked his superior. 'Contact Jericho; Rubber Duck wants a parley.'

Chandler frowned. 'Listen, Johnston. You're in now, so get with the programme if you want to keep your badge.' Chandler's voice was sharp. It was evident he didn't care for mockery, just as he didn't care for some smart ass in the DA's Department jerking his chain.

Lieutenant Chandler and Detective Sergeant Johnston sat for a while summarising Charlie O'Brien's discussion.

'What do you think these numbers mean, Lieutenant?'

Chandler shook his head. 'I don't know, Johnston; laundry code, something like that. Maybe somethin', maybe nothin' significant.'

'What do you think Jericho will make of it then?' Johnston said, attempting to hide a snigger.

Chandler drew a wicked look at his sergeant. 'You'd do well to remember that you're involved too, Johnston,' he said dryly.

Both detectives returned to the precinct when the call came in.

'Ah! Lieutenant,' the duty desk officer yelled. 'Call for you!'

'Yeah, who is it?'

'Don't know exactly; goes by the name Jericho, or something.'

Chandler hurried to his office and picked up the handset.

'Hello!, ……Hello! Jericho'

'Need to meet you' Steve said. Then the line went dead.

Lieutenant Chandler understood the need for caution; none of them could take the chance in case the line was tapped. After all, whoever had the power to shut down murder enquiries could certainly have the authority to tap a telephone line.

Chandler's line rang again. Cautiously he lifted the receiver.

'It's me,' Jericho.

Chandler was not slow and spoke evenly but clearly. 'Rubber Duck has a number. Its 3433 175 BOB. Found in a coat pocket. Hope you get this.' It was Chandler's turn to terminate the line between Rubber Duck and Jericho.

***

Steve had written the number given on his hand. It didn't make sense. 'Found in a coat pocket,' he repeated out loud to himself as he stared once more at the digits and name. Chandler obviously gave them for him to check out, but as to what they were remained a mystery. The numbers could refer to anything. Maybe even a laundry ticket, if found in a coat pocket, or even a safety deposit box, but Steve dismissed that option; Ricker was not the type to have that. So, the numbers could refer to anything and who was BOB?' He'd recently heard that name only once before and the man who whispered it had died.

Steve stood in the phone booth. He'd expected more info from Stuart Chandler, but also realised Chandler, like himself, was limited to telephone discussions. Anyway, he did have Jimmy Malone working with him and just as he didn't tell Malone about Chandler's role he would keep Malone's name away from the Lieutenant meantime.

Steve searched his memory. He had seen a set of numbers before, but where?

Chapter 30

Steve made his way towards Rusty's junkyard and once again wondered what Claire Monroe had been involved in. He wished he'd taken her case, but it would have made little difference as the hit and run on her would have happened anyway.

He arrived at the entrance to Rusty's junkyard. The police and fire-marked crime scene tapes strung out its front and along its perimeter. He could see the remnants of the burnt out Portakabin, its windows blown out but their grills still intact.

Steve expected the whole Portakabin to have been destroyed given the ferocity of the fire, but being made of steel it had survived. He wondered about the inside of the 'kabin and more especially its contents. He knew he would need to check them out. He decided he would return later to the site after dark and make his own investigation.

Night fell over the City that never sleeps and as city life began for some, Steve cautiously returned to Rusty's yard. Checking that he was unobserved, he ducked under the security tapes at the rear of the lot and removed a half-dislodged corrugated iron sheet from its housing and entered holding his flashlight, shielding its beam with his left hand, hoping it would not attract attention. It seemed to take forever as Steve made his way towards the silhouetted shape of the burnt out Portakabin and once there stood quietly for a few moments, making sure there was no one else around. He strained his well-trained ears for movement, then slowly slid from the shadows and with one powerful shove opened the door to what had once been Rusty's office. He beamed his flashlight across the interior. It was a mess. Debris everywhere, with the broken vodka bottles shattered on the floor, the spirit contents very little as Rusty had consumed most of the liquor, and Steve could imagine the destruction the fire would have caused had that not been the case. Steve moved forward, treading carefully, feeling and hearing the broken glass underneath his feet. He scanned the 'kabin with his flashlight and there it was, lying face down – the old green metal filing cabinet.

Could he be lucky? Could its contents still be intact? Steve moved towards it. The cabinet was solid and seemed to be welded to the floor. He had to upturn it, but how? He certainly did not want to attract attention with too much noise, and so attempted to wedge it at its base with a piece of wood he found while lifting it backwards. His flashlight still lit lay on the floor, giving limited light as Steve mustered all his strength. Slowly, inch by inch, the cabinet raised and eventually stood upright. Steve was perspiring with the effort, his arms and hands sore and took a few moments to gather himself. It had been some time since he had lifted a dead weight but now the green metal filing cabinet stood upright, staring back at him. Its drawers were all closed;

then Steve noticed the bent key in its lock. It had obviously been in the locked position when it fell and its key had bent over when meeting contact with the floor.

Steve groaned. He must gain access to the filing drawers if he was to obtain Riker's file. The thought then occurred to him; a simple thief would just bust the drawers open and not care what damage he would do. Steve picked up his flashlight and rotated its beam around the 'kabin and allowed it to come to rest on an iron bar with a flattened chiselled end. Quickly he prized it into the top drawer joint and using its length as a lever quickly sprung the drawer open. The file he was after was not there, so he returned it to its closed position and repeated his method to the second top drawer. It gave way more easily this time, as the overriding lock had been broken on his first attempt.

Steve's eyes scanned the drawer's contents and there it was in bold, black marker ink, capital letters – "RIKER."

Steve rescued the file from the cabinet and brought his flashlight towards the file. He scanned the name at the bottom of the page – "Randall" … There was a number beside it – 3343 571 ~~BOB~~ 202.

'Hey! Anybody there?' the voice said. 'Who's in there …? Police! Come out, hands up. This is a restricted area,' the patrolman shouted, as he aimed his powerful flashlight inside, illuminating the Portakabin. Steve heard his heavy footsteps approach. He had no choice, so crouched down on his knees next to the door.

'Okay, buster! Out you come,' the officer shouted, unholstering his handgun. 'Don't make me come in there and get you,' he yelled.

Steve could see the shadow of the officer's frame and the gun he was holding. Without hesitation, Steve attacked and after a few moments rendered the patrol-man unconscious.

Another flashlight caught him from the parked cruiser at the edge of the yard. Steve didn't hang about. File in hand, he ran off towards the rear of the yard and wedged himself through the gap he'd made in the corrugated sheeting. He ran, then conscious of pain in his left leg, started limping, but he had his file, that was all that mattered.

Chapter 31

Within minutes Rusty's yard was surrounded by police vehicles, their emergency lights illuminating the darkness, as once again Rusty's yard was sealed off and became a scene of activity.

'Bailley's been hurt, get an ambulance,' Jackson, his partner, shouted. 'Hold on, buddy, you'll be okay,' he said.

Bailley was conscious now. 'Where is that son of a bitch, my legs hurt; hit me like a bloody train,' he whispered, as his face started draining of blood and nausea set in.

Flashlights beamed over the entire yard as a search for clues and the intruder began.

'The only thing we got, Lieutenant, is a flashlight that was left behind on the floor. It still works and we've bagged it. God knows what anybody would want in a place like this. It doesn't make sense, unless it was kids mucking around.'

'It was no kid that attacked me,' Bailley said, regaining his strength. 'Gee! I'm sore. Friggin' son of a bitch.'

'Let me see that flashlight,' Chandler said, as he inspected the bag. 'Get this downtown for prints,

Johnston. But I doubt you'll find any,' Chandler said, eyeing his sergeant with a silent instruction.

Johnston was quick on the uptake. 'You can't be serious. We can't tamper with evidence,' he whispered.

'Yeah, check it out, Sergeant,' Chandler said out loud to impress others, then whispering to Johnston, added, 'Make sure any prints on that flashlight are wiped. You got it?'

'But Lieutenant, we can't … we …'

Chandler bent close to his officer's ear. 'You're in this with me all the way. If there are prints on there, 5 to 1 says they'll be Jericho's and we can't have them recognised.'

'This is madness, Lieutenant,' Johnston whispered furiously. I'll lose my job!'

'You'll lose a lot more than your job, Johnston, if you don't do as I say. Now, just do it. Listen, if it makes it any easier, my life is on the line too. There's something rotten here, I can smell it and our first lead is hopefully with our friend Jericho. Get a message to him to contact me.'

'Ah! Lieutenant,' a voice shouted, holding up his press badge.

'Second time something's happened here,' Malone said. 'This was Rusty's yard. He died in unpleasant and suspicious circumstances, so what's the story this time?'

'Get out of my face, Malone. You're not wanted here; besides, there's nothin' to tell, just some kids mischief-making.'

Jimmy Malone smiled. 'Oh! You and I know it's much more than that, Lieutenant, and Steve Donaldson does too.'

Lieutenant Chandler brushed him aside and vacated the scene without further comment.

Chapter 32

Back in his apartment, Steve settled down with a large Jack Daniels and read Riker's file. There wasn't much information to go on, just the description of the dark green Sedan, the scrolled signature "Randall" and of course the number beside it – 3343 571 ~~BOB~~ 202.

Steve read the number out loud. BOB was scored out, why? And who was Bob? There were other details of vehicles in the file, obviously all previous assignments for crushing and each had a large red marker pen cross and a tick across the page, which Steve assumed was Rusty's method of signifying when a job was completed.

Steve sipped his Jack Daniels. He required more information. He realised both he and Chandler were restricted to speak freely on the telephone, but he would need to arrange a meeting with him to discuss the next move.

Steve wrote a note, finished his drink and retired for the night.

Next morning, fully refreshed, he headed for the precinct in Manhattan South. There was an elderly lady entering the precinct and Steve asked her politely if she would hand his note in at the desk.

The duty officer listened to the old lady's complaint and took some particulars, more as a record than action. The elderly lady then passed Steve's envelope to the duty desk officer, who casually handed it to another colleague, along with the rest of the morning mail.

The mail was now being sorted and opened, and although Steve's envelope was addressed to Lieutenant Chandler, it was opened by mistake.

There was an outcry from the officer. 'Hey, listen fellas, some crank put this in the mailbox.' The officer held the note high with outstretched arms and read it out loud to the rest of the crew in the precinct.

'THE WALLS OF JERICHO ARE FALLING DOWN. NEED A RUBBER DUCK TO KEEP AFLOAT.'

They all had a good laugh, even though they couldn't understand it. That was all of them, except for Lieutenant Chandler and Detective Sergeant Johnston. They eyed each other quietly, realising Donaldson wanted a meet.

Chapter 33

Lieutenant Chandler found himself back at Rikki's the following morning, at the same table in the rear of the café. Rikki remembered him and served coffee and iced doughnuts before contacting Steve, who appeared an hour later.

'Okay, got your message at the precinct, caused a bit of hilarity,' Chandler said, then added 'You struggling with this one, Steve?'

Steve nodded. 'There's no lead, nobody talking.' Steve paused, then added 'Even attempted to get Jimmy Malone of The Times to see if he had any further info on Riker and Gennero's deaths. I didn't mention Claire Monroe of course,' Steve lied.

'You haven't told him anything?' Chandler said, butting in. 'I can't stand that little shit; always pushing his friggin' nose where it's not wanted.'

Steve fell silent.

'Any more thoughts on the numbers I gave you,' Chandler said, as he then uncharacteristically rambled on about Charlie O'Brien and his workload. It was five minutes before Chandler realised Steve was still silent, and the penny dropped.

'You did,' he shouted at Steve. 'You gave Malone information, you stupid son of a bitch; what were you thinking? It's hard enough Donaldson, without that son of a bitch in my face.'

'He knows a lot of people Lieutenant,' Steve said, attempting to defend his decision to involve Malone.

'He's a goddamn reporter Donaldson. The lowest of the low. He'll stop at nothin'! Nothin' to get a story,' Chandler paused, 'No matter who he hurts in the process.'

Steve remained silent for a moment, then spoke quietly. 'If he prints anything, Lieutenant, whoever is behind all this has enough influence to deal with Jimmy Malone; I mean, let's face it, whoever is behind all this has connections. The DA Department has been warned off! Your Captain too, probably his superiors, not to mention your good self, so, I don't think we have to worry about Malone and his newspaper. Anyway, it may flush out whoever we're up against 'cause right now our enquiries ain't going anywhere and the longer we wait, the harder it will be to make a case.'

Chandler considered Steve's comments. 'Okay! Okay, but watch that two-faced motherfucker Steve, because I'm watchin' you, understand?'

Steve smiled. 'Okay Rubber Duck,' he said.

Lieutenant Chandler was not amused. 'Now you listen to me, Donaldson. I'm risking my career here, all because of you; me and Johnston. We're going behind our superior's back, all because you've raised a hornet's nest over some broad who'd only proceed on a "need to know basis". Well, Mr Private Eye, let me spell it out for you, this is not a game, people's lives are at stake and one of them could be mine.'

'Hey Lieutenant,' Steve interrupted, holding up his hands as if under arrest, 'you're way too heavy, man.'

Chandler leaned across the table, so close to Steve their noses almost touching 'THIS IS NOT A GAME,' he repeated. 'IF I GO DOWN, OR JOHNSTON FOR THAT MATTER, THEN YOU GO DOWN TOO ... UNDERSTAND?'

Steve, being laid back, sat back in the booth calmly, after all he was used to pressure and had not been ruffled by Chandler's outburst.

Lieutenant Chandler calmed down. He knew losing it would not achieve anything and he was like Steve, he wanted now more than ever to resolve the case. ' It's not easy working without help.' He said.

'Hey, Lieutenant, I do it every day, welcome to my world.'

'Stop it, Donaldson. Stop it right now.'

Chandler was still bent forward. 'Were the numbers I gave you of any use?'

Steve shook his head negatively. 'You said something about a coat?'

'Yeah!' Charlie O'Brien, the coroner, has also been instructed to cease any further action on this. Tag and number Riker and Gennero and put the matter to bed. He found the number inside Riker's coat pocket, sewn into the lining. It's not logged on the contents sheet, therefore it's been, by all accounts, missed. You know Charlie, Steve, it goes against his grain to be told how to do his job. So he gave me the information. We think most laundrettes use a colour code as well as numerical identification for items and according to Johnston, the number is too long. So I think we can rule that one out. We also tried it as a telephone number, but each time we dialled it didn't register. Also, the name BOB at the end of the number doesn't make sense. I mean, who is BOB?'

Steve cast his mind back to the name Rusty had whispered in his ear before he died. 'Well, if this number was found in Riker's coat pocket, it must mean something, Lieutenant.'

It's like looking for a needle in a haystack,' Chandler replied. 'Okay, tell me! It was you who was in that Portakabin in Rusty's yard the other night – wasn't it?' Chandler asked, as he played with a beer mat in front of him.

Steve stared at Stuart Chandler. He did not want to admit the fact verbally and so shrugged his shoulders. There was a long pause between them, then Chandler spoke.

'Look, the number Charlie O'Brien retrieved from Riker's coat pocket must mean something?' I know you were there at Rusty's the other night, Steve, I even had Johnston wipe your prints off your flashlight, but even I can only do so much. So tell me, did you find anything in Riker's file that was in that old green cabinet?'

'Well, like I told you, Lieutenant, I remembered the name Randall on a document,' Steve said slowly.

'And?' Chandler pressed, wanting to know more of what Steve had discovered.

'Well, it was there just as I remembered, along with a number which is similar to the one O'Brien gave you, but I can't figure it out.'

'So what's the number you got, Steve?' Chandler said.

Steve glanced at the Lieutenant opposite him. '3343 571 BOB, but the name BOB is scored out and underneath were the figures 202.'

Chandler shook his head, attempting to figure out the connection between BOB and 202. 'Why Rusty scored the name BOB out and inserted the numbers is anybody's guess,' he said.

Steve paused, his mind staring at the digits before him. His eyes grew wide as he realised what he was reading with the numbers. 'Rikki, you got a Yellow Pages?'

'Yeah! Why?'

'Look up the area code 202,' Steve said, a soft expression of anticipation growing over his face.

Rikki thumbed the directory. '202 is Washington DC,' he said, allowing his words to travel across the room.

Steve now realised that Rusty had been given the code BOB as part of a contact number. B was the second letter of the alphabet, O was natural, B was repeated. So the number in Rusty's file read 3343 571 BOB, or possibly now 202. Steve mused over the digits and smiled at Chandler. 'Lieutenant, if you were dialling someone in DC, what would you start with?'

'Start with?' Chandler echoed. 'The area code, of course.'

'Exactly,' Steve responded. 'Don't you see, Lieutenant, the number in Riker's file at Rusty's yard has the name BOB, but at the end. Now, let's put BOB at the beginning and change it to 202. If it's a telephone number it would now read 202 571 3343. Now, compare that to the number Charlie O'Brien gave you that he found in Riker's coat pocket.'

'Lieutenant Chandler read out his number 3433 175 BOB.'

Steve smiled. 'Lieutenant, put BOB or 202 at the beginning and then read them from right to left, ie backwards.'

Chandler frowned; he looked puzzled, but carried out Steve's exercise. Pen and paper to hand, he slowly wrote:

BOB = 202

175 = 571

3433 = 3343

'So, 202-571-3343. If that sequence is applied, makes the numbers in Riker's coat match the one in Riker's file at Rusty's yard.'

Steve now had Lieutenant Chandler's full attention. Steve used the phone in the booth at the end of the café and glanced over at Chandler as he carefully dialled each digit. The coin accepted and processed; he heard the line ring out. He watched Lieutenant Chandler's face, his curiosity bounding, impatiently awaiting the result from Steve's call.

Lieutenant Stuart Chandler waited while Steve made the call from the phone booth in Rikki's Café. 'Any response?' Chandler said.

Steve just sat there. 'None,' he said, quietly and slowly.

'I thought you were talking to someone?' Chandler said, as he had witnessed Steve's mouth moving.

Just the opposite, Lieutenant. The line rang out but no response. I think we'll need to rethink this one.'

Lieutenant Chandler didn't fully believe his partner, but really had no choice but to go along with Donaldson's word. Anyway, he had the number now and could try the number himself and hopefully trace the person, or persons, behind it, and unlock numerous unanswered questions.

Lieutenant Chandler and Donaldson had gone their separate ways, each back to their offices. They both had work to do.

Two days passed and Chandler sat glancing over some other case files. His telephone rang and he answered, but it was his Captain, phoning in from another homicide.

'Better get down here, Stuart. Looks like we got another gangland murder.'

'Will do, Captain, where are you?'

'Between Baxter Street and Mulberry, China Town. Get more back up. I think we may need it. Oh! And Stuart, as soon as possible, okay?'

Chandler replaced his handset. 'Johnston, we got a job. China Town, usual fuck-up with the gangs. The Captain's already there. Get more back up. Let's go,' Chandler shouted.

'What about Donaldson, Lieutenant?'

'Forget him, Johnston. He won't go anywhere soon without contacting ourselves, besides, I still have that number and can try it later but right now our Captain needs us.'

The two detectives made their way to China Town, Chandler driving, his emergency flashing light now fixed to the roof of his car.

The Chung-Loewe incident had caused quite a stir. It all kicked off when two patrolmen following up a lead on a homicide entered a club on Baxter Street. By the time they identified themselves, automatic weapons had been discharged and a quick successive exchange of fire resulted in three dead and one of the officers critically wounded. Chung-Loewe's main man, Francis Wong, was amongst the dead and being a player of notoriety it could spark off another full episode of a gangland feud.

Chandler checked with his Captain. 'I'll wrap things up here,' he said, 'then Johnston and I can fill you in with the details.'

The Captain nodded. 'Do whatever, Stuart, but ah don't want this incident to start a war, God sakes; we have enough on our plates.' Then the Captain whispered, 'Get Chung-Loewe on your side; get him to promise no retaliation. If that takes some cooperation from the Department so be it, but you must get his assurance first.'

Stuart Chandler listened to his superior.

'Any questions, Stuart?' the Captain said.

Lieutenant Chandler hesitated. 'What about our budget, Captain?'

His captain drew him a look. 'Get outta here. Just fix it, Lieutenant.'

Chapter 34

General Bob Harris sat in his office on E Floor of the Pentagon, his fingers drumming on his large leather inlaid desk, the American Stars and Stripes flag displayed prominently behind him. He stared at the photograph which showed him receiving his first Purple Heart from the President. He had been younger then, tall and slim with a solid muscular frame. His hair was almost non-existent, nearly as close-shaven as his face, his cap worn proudly; its skip shielding his sharp, penetrating brown eyes.

Bob Harris had trained at the US Navy Base in Mississippi and had excelled in every task he was instructed to fulfil. He was recognised as a leader; someone, no matter what, managed to get things done and achieve results. Nothing phased him and no one stood in his way; his job and assignment always the priority, the load never too great.

Promotion after promotion came and he inherited the nickname Cleaver Harris, as he destroyed anyone, or anything, that stood in his path. There was a ruthless streak in him which frightened his fellow marines, but it was disciplined and he being different stood out from others around him.

His peers recognised his qualities and he served on countless overseas missions, both official and otherwise. His organisation skills and grasp for tactics saw him rise through the ranks at every level, and ultimately, General.

Cleaver Harris was ambitious and his position gave him power and wealth which fed his appetite and hunger for more, which consumed him in every facet of his life. The more he achieved, the more greedy and powerful he became. The good life over the years took its toll; his enjoyment of women, wealth, power and the vices they attracted saw him with a finger in every pie. He knew everybody and everybody knew him, his ruthless reputation preceding him wherever he went. Bob Harris therefore believed he was invincible and coerced others to do and carry out his bidding.

Over the years he had amassed his supporters, but of course also his enemies whom he knew and kept close and in the loop when it suited himself. On his climb of the ladder to success he had organised and built a fortune. Slush funds were set up using public money and hidden in offshore accounts. Contracts were carried out in an unofficial basis, unknown to his superiors. Funds and personnel were used to suit his personal needs and all while commanding the respect and ear of the President and the Joint Chiefs of Staff in the White House, who never suspected anything. Bob Cleaver Harris was, on the face of it, a well-respected, powerful General who didn't suffer fools gladly, and with his nickname and reputation, always impressed.

Bob stared at the picture and his memory of the day. A lot of water had passed under the bridge since then.

He decided to freshen up and after relieving himself, washed his hands and patted cold water on his face. The face he saw in the mirror was not the same, well-honed rugged face of that in the photograph on his desk and momentarily he stared at his own reflection. He was chubbier now, full in the face, his cheekbones bulged – his neck too, with all his good living and lifestyle. His hairstyle was the same, but its colour was grey and showed glints of silver beading, the true sign of his age.

He pulled the plain folded A4 sheet of paper from his tunic and re-read the threatening statement, the bold black cut out capitals embossing the white background:

MURDERER
RAPIST
TRAITOR
CAYMANS
I'LL GET YOU
YOUR TIME IS COMING

General Cleaver Harris held the letter in his hand. Someone was intimidating him. Was it someone close? The question was, who?

Cleaver wiped his brow with his handkerchief. The last name on his letter was Caymans.

'I wonder,' he said out loud to himself. He pressed the button on his internal line. 'Barbara, will you come in a minute, please.'

Barbara appeared, pen and notepad in hand. She had become Bob Cleaver Harris's secretary almost six months previously, after being recommended by Major General Gerald Shaw of the US Army. Barbara was attractive in appearance, with her green eyes and soft olive skin. Her shoulder length dark hair shone like black silk. Her attire was always conservative and business-like; her black suit, white blouse complemented by a single strand of pearls around her neck, which exuded a confident air of efficiency and pleasing attitude.

Today she wore her hair up in a chignon which suited her as it allowed her fine bone structure of her face to be appreciated.

'I'm going down to the Caymans for a few days. I need you to cancel my schedule this week, through the weekend. Is there anything particular that is urgent?'

Barbara checked her boss's itinerary. 'You're meeting Robert Nelson on Thursday. You know, the new Senator. He wants to discuss our military overseas expenditure …' Harris held up his hand, signifying Barbara to stop talking.

'I don't need to do that this week. Give him my apologies. Tell him I've been called away … or … something. Overseas expenses! Who the hell does he think he is?'

'Sir, you've already cancelled him twice before. He won't take "no" a third time.'

Cleaver Harris smiled. 'Dog with a bone, eh?'

Barbara also smiled, then offered a suggestion. 'Well, it may be prudent to actually meet him. Give him something to check. Fill his tray, so to speak.'

Cleaver allowed himself a smile, then laughing said 'That's what I like about you, Barbara. You know when we should all be singing from the same hymn sheet. Okay, I'll meet with him but bring the meeting forward to tomorrow. I want to be in the Caymans as soon as possible.'

Barbara turned to leave. Cleaver appraised her. She was smart, attractive and probably good company.

'Oh, Barbara!'

Barbara turned to face her boss.

'How'd you like to accompany me on this trip? We'll get to know each other better, so to speak. I promise no work, just a few days away.' Cleaver let his invitation hang in the air.

Barbara was obviously surprised and her hesitance in replying showed. 'Well, thank you, Cleaver … but …'

Cleaver pressed his invitation. 'Come on, Barbara, what d'ya say?'

Barbara stood, rooted to the spot. She could feel her cheeks blush. She did not want to cross her professional line, but also did not want to appear ungrateful; after all, she knew her boss was used to having his own way.

She hesitated momentarily. If she accepted and a more intimate relationship developed, then her career and professional position would become unattainable and so she composed herself and replied 'Cleaver, Sir, I'd like that and it sounds fantastic, but I do have family commitments this weekend and the arrangements have been made for some considerable time. Can I pass, please, although I'm very flattered you thought of me.'

Cleaver just sat there. He was about to assert his authority, then changed his mind. He hesitated, then replied. 'Maybe another time?' he said quietly, his dark brown eyes holding Barbara's stare.

Barbara broke off the contact between them, then said 'I'll rearrange Robert Nelson and make suitable arrangements for you in the Caymans.'

Cleaver Harris nodded his acknowledgement, but didn't utter a word.

Next morning, Senator Robert Nelson arrived. He carried his new leather briefcase and wore a plain dark blue three piece suit, white shirt and maroon tie; its Windsor knot tied impeccably. His face was tanned, his grey hair well-groomed, his blue eyes attentive but slightly strained. His nose was short and wore the indentation marks made by reading glasses with all the paperwork he embedded himself in.

Yes, Robert Nelson was efficient and carried an air of urgency and authority.

Barbara announced his arrival and after some simple pleasantries, Cleaver listened to the man before him.

God, he was a bore. A pen-pusher who produced nothing. Cleaver sensed the man's eagerness for detail. Details that Cleaver did not want to fully answer, and quickly realised Barbara's advice had been correct; listen to what he had to say, then give him plenty of work to check up on. Keep him busy and out of your hair and out of any really important issues you'd rather not discuss.

So Cleaver did exactly that. He fed Senator Robert Nelson small tasks that would involve his time and keep him busy with administrative duties. Tasks that really meant nothing but would keep the new boy out of Cleaver's space.

Cleaver was tired now and so brought his meeting to an end. He called Barbara. 'Have you made my arrangements for the Caymans?'

'Yes, General. Governor Gordon is expecting you.'

Cleaver nodded, pleased that Barbara had done her job. 'Sure you won't come with me?' Cleaver said, attempting to turn on his charm.

Barbara smiled, then blushed. 'I'm sorry, Cleaver, as I said ... family.'

'Well,' … Cleaver interrupted 'If you should ever change your mind … you … can ...' his voice trailed off.

Barbara smiled with her eyes then returned to her desk in the outer office to attend her duties and complete amending Cleaver's schedule.

The limo sped its way to the airbase; Barbara accompanying her boss, taking last minute instructions and documents that Cleaver had to sign. She watched Cleaver board his private plane. She knew she could have been there too, but there was a line she must not cross.

Cleaver sat back in his leather seat and strapped himself in, prepared for take off. The pilot had completed his checklist and everything was in order; all he required was the green light from the tower. The air traffic controller's voice came through his headphones, allowing take-off to proceed, and the aeroplane taxied lightly along the runway, turning on its axis, its engines throttling as power was gently applied. Vibrations shook the cabin noisily, then as the pilot released the brakes the aircraft thrust its way forward down the runway.

Cleaver took a deep breath as the aircraft became airborne, and the ground fell away beneath him. He was on his way now, his mind focused on his evening ahead. Who would accompany him? He was sure Governor Gordon would have arranged somebody suitable. He just hoped she had a sense of humour as well as a body.

Barbara eventually returned home and kicked off her black high heels and entered her kitchen, her stockinged feet appreciating the cold tile floor. She poured a Manhattan and sank into her easy chair, allowing the liquor to relax and calm her.

'It's been one hell of a day,' she said out loud to herself, inwardly relieved that her boss was on vacation for the next few days.

Chapter 35

Cleaver's jet landed and set down in Grand Cayman. The sun was shining and Cleaver was looking forward to his few days on the island and the usual hospitality of Governor Alexander Frederick Gordon.

Governor Alexander Frederick Gordon loved his position of office. He served the British Crown admirably whilst enjoying the splendour lifestyle an overseas Ambassador position gave him. He was a tall man, with dark brown hair perfectly parted on the left side, his short back and sides depicting the stiff upper lip expected of a Queen's Ambassador in one of her colonies.

His stance was rigid straight and he was a stickler for all things protocol, but also had the talent for discretion, especially if those discretions benefitted himself.

He had sharp eyes, a small moustache and ears that heard and knew about everything, and more importantly, everybody.

Although his surname was Gordon, he was not related to the famous General Gordon of Khartoum, but his middle name, Frederick, came from his mother's side whose father was related, albeit distantly to the Royal House of Austria, and Governor Gordon used that influence at every opportunity. His Christian name, Alexander, was given to him as a sign of a strong and proud individual and he lived up to his name admirably.

He had met Bob Cleaver Harris in 1952 at the time of the Korean War, and the two men had developed a mutual friendship for each other; Gordon with his influence and position stationed in the Cayman Islands and Cleaver building a reputation for himself and achieving fast track promotions. Cleaver's appetite for power and wealth always the priority, shared some of his spoils with Governor Gordon who proved to be very amenable and their partnership worked, as long as it suited Cleaver.

General Bob Cleaver Harris's actions were never questioned. He had the ear of the President, and any of his visits to the Cayman Islands were looked upon Cleaver keeping up good relations with the United States' allies from across the pond, which suited all, especially when one considered the benefits of creating offshore bank accounts, which suited admirably.

Chapter 36

Alexander Gordon's valet, Benjamin Whyte, showed Cleaver to his usual guest suite. Ben Whyte had known Cleaver for many years and had come to know what his guest expected of him. He therefore commenced laying out Cleaver's clothes; white dinner jacket, black tie and trousers. He also inspected and made sure his master's shoes were a mirror shine.

'Cocktails are at 5:00pm, Sir, as usual. Just give me a call if you require anything further,' Benjamin said, his quiet demeanour waiting for further instruction.

'Who's joining us tonight, Ben?' Cleaver asked. 'Anybody I know?'

'Oh! I believe the usual crowd, Sir, and there's a visitor from the UK, a Charles Smyth. I believe he's related somewhere down the line to Her Majesty.'

Cleaver smiled. 'What does he do?'

'Do, Sir?!?' Benjamin Whyte hesitated before replying. 'Eat and drink I think, Sir.'

'That's very good, Ben. I won't tell anyone what you said. Any women here tonight I should know about?'

'A few that will be good company, Sir.'

Again, Cleaver laughed. 'That will be all, Ben. I'll call if I need you.'

Ben bowed and departed, leaving Governor Gordon's guest to settle in.

Cleaver wished he could have persuaded Barbara, his secretary, to have joined him, but hopefully as Ben had intimated there would be another who would fulfil his needs that evening. After all, he had plans for the next day. Business that would need his attention with his friend Rodriquez, but for tonight he would party.

Chapter 37

Five pm arrived and Cleaver entered the large reception lounge, the usual dignitaries present and the usual formal introductions made.

Charles Smyth was of medium height, balding, and his plump figure borne out Benjamin's description. Cleaver couldn't help smothering a smile as he met the man and remembered Benjamin's comments. Cleaver listened boringly to the pompous asshole, full in the knowledge he'd require to be civil, but the reality of it all absurd, as he would normally have crushed this type of person without batting an eye. In his world, Charles Smyth was just about as useless as a human being could be. No use as a man; certainly not a worthwhile contributor but a sponger of the first degree. Cleaver Harris wondered how the mighty Great Britain and her sovereigns had built an empire with such hanger-on's and generally useless people who never earned anything, or even aspired to achieve. They just played the party and social circuit and lived off the backs of others and probably some huge inheritance. Cleaver listened to the man's ramblings and was pleased for the interruptions when dinner was announced.

Dinner over, the gentlemen present retired to the library for brandy and cigars where they continued talking of the international politics of the day. Cleaver was bored with the topics under discussion, especially since none of the present company would, or could, influence anything. They would take no action relating to their opinions. In fact, for the most part they were as much use as an ashtray on a motorbike.

Cleaver therefore excused himself, making his apologies that his journey was taking its toll, but in reality he had to free himself from such hypocrisy; besides, he had his eye on a lovely filly he had met during cocktails earlier that evening. They had made amorous eye contact during dinner and Cleaver certainly wanted to partake in some more of her relaxing company, and more to the point, hopefully into the small hours in the privacy of his suite.

That particular package came in the form of a tall, sexy brunette who turned all heads when she entered the room. Governor Gordon had been quick to introduce them and from the moment they shook hands and their eyes met, Cleaver Harris knew he was captivated by Carla Roebuck, and as usual, Carla knew it too.

They each felt the chemistry between them as they shook hands. Carla was used to receiving admiration from men, after all she was stunningly attractive which allowed her to attend social functions within the right and proper circles. Carla was indeed the true society play girl who never stopped until she secured what she wanted.

Cleaver and Carla were a perfect match in that regard and each recognised it would be a challenge of which one would be the master. Cleaver assumed it would be himself; he was confident in his ability to power over others. Likewise, Carla believed it was just a matter of time before Cleaver succumbed and she would dominate their relationship. She had never failed on the subject of men before, but for the moment she would enjoy the cat and mouse game that she would undoubtedly play.

'I thought you'd be more at home with your brandy and cigars, discussing politics or whatever,' Carla said, allowing a teasing smile to escape across her face, her gorgeous, tantalising eyes glinting, giving a green light but with just enough hesitance to signal that any advance would be on her terms.

Cleaver appraised the beauty before him. She was intelligent, beautiful, sexy, and ... an American like himself. 'Oh! You know, had a busy start to the week, then the journey down here from Washington; it takes its toll, besides, I needed a break. If I wanted to talk politics I could have stayed at home. Anyway, some of those stuffed shirts in there for the most part haven't a bloody clue what's really going on in the world. I mean, at the end of the day those guys play at politics, all in the name of what's good for their countries and the Western world, not to mention religion which is just another excuse to cause confrontation, especially in certain parts of the world where we should not be involved. Many young men are forced into combat not of their choosing, and of course, many of whom don't make it back home and some that do have life-changing injuries and their country disowns them. So, it's not for me to discuss these subjects with people who have no real idea.'

'Oh! You sound very serious,' Carla said. It was not on her agenda to have such a serious conversation; after all, she was a party animal at heart, a socialite and she not only knew it but loved her lifestyle. Thinking she had misjudged Cleaver, she turned to leave.

'Don't go Carla, please,' Cleaver said, standing up abruptly. 'We just met tonight; I apologise for being so critical. I came away to get away from all that crap, so please, may we start again on a much more sociable and lighter note this time? I promise no politics. We could steal ourselves away, just the two of us. What do you say? Cleaver smiled as he finished speaking. His eyes looked into Carla's sparking green eyes which signalled that their game had restarted.

'Another glass of champagne would be appreciated,' she said, raising her glass and draining its contents, her lipstick staining the rim.

Cleaver downed his drink and waved to the waiter. 'Two more of these please,' he said, while staring into Carla's beautiful face.

'Certainly, Sir,' the waiter replied, and was about to depart when Cleaver changed his mind.

'No! Make it a bottle and two fresh glasses, we'll be outside on the terrace,' Cleaver said matter of factly.

The waiter nodded his head and departed to attend to Cleaver's request.

Cleaver and Carla made their way to the terrace through the open French doors. Each stood side by side, looking out over the balcony into the black velvet night. Nobody spoke. Each waited for the other to begin. Carla was enjoying herself, but the night was still young.

Cleaver took the initiative. 'Tell me about yourself,' he said, now turning to face his attractive companion.

Carla searched the face of the man that stood beside her. She wanted to keep their conversation light and therefore was hesitant to discuss her past.

Cleaver sensed her reluctance. 'Come on, it can't be that bad,' he said. 'I bet you had a good upbringing, good parents, and have seen a bit of … shall we say …,' he hesitated, then added 'how the other half live.' Cleaver let his words hang in the air, hoping for a positive response and reply.

Carla smiled. 'There's not much to tell. I was born in America; my mother was an Italian immigrant and met my father, John Roebuck, while working in an embassy. She had secured her job through a mutual friend of a friend, so to speak. They dated a few times and their relationship blossomed. They had a brief courtship, then they married. I was born almost nine months to the day and they were so much in love and proud of me; their baby daughter. Then Father's career took off and he was sent to various parts of the world, my mother Helena and I following with him. So I, from a very young age, became aware of the social skills required, along with the different customs in different countries that my parents worked in. We, as a family, were never too long in one place to put roots down, but my education didn't suffer because I was … *am*, intelligent and my mother made sure I never missed out. As I grew, I learned to embrace the quality lifestyle I had become accustomed to, never taking anything for granted, grateful that I had two loving parents, whose love for each other was everything. I was happy, secured, loved; I was seeing the world, albeit it through an advantaged lifestyle, but hey! I still saw it, even although I wish at times we could really settle in one place, where one could have and make friends and bond with other families … you know, the usual stuff, but I suppose I also embraced the excitement of meeting new people. I learned to be able to judge their characters quickly and therefore grew up and matured early in life.

'The sad day arrived when my father took a heart attack and died. He was only 55 and although my mother and he had just over 30 years of marriage it broke her heart. Her soulmate was gone. She had me, but life wasn't the same and although Father had made sure we were well provided for she never really got over his death. So Mother died within a year of my Father, broken-hearted.

'I went through a traumatic period, Oh, I was financially sound, but I needed to accomplish a life. Friends around the world helped. I had the intelligence and had been groomed in the social niceties of life and found myself receiving invitations from all quarters and sometimes from would-be suitors, but I wasn't ready to settle down.

'The years have rolled by and I've played the social calendar. I've made my own life; some have tried to capture me,' Carla said, smiling as she recalled various men that had attempted to control her. 'Some would have given me a good life, children of my own all that jazz, but at heart I'm a free spirit Cleaver, and I choose to do what I want. Be with whom I want and suit myself. Life is less complicated that way.'

Carla paused. 'Maybe one day I'll meet Mr Right and decide to settle down, but for now I enjoy life. Take each day as the gift it is.' Carla sipped her champagne once again, leaving another lipstick stain on the glass.

'So how about you, Cleaver, you seem interesting. How did you get to be a General?' Carla said, standing to attention and offering a salute.

Cleaver smiled, then laughed. 'I just wish all my troops were packaged like you and with your intelligence.'

Carla smiled, her eyes glinting once more as again she sipped more of her champagne. 'So, what's your story, General?'

Cleaver hesitated. 'Nothing much to tell, really.' He sipped his champagne and listened to the soft gentle waves of the ocean as they descended upon the golden sandy beach. 'I never travelled,' he said softly. 'Well, not until I joined the Marine Corps.' Cleaver hesitated as he let his mind drift back to his boyhood and some hard times.

'My childhood wasn't easy. My parents had no money; my mom worked as a cleaner, a domestic. She worked hard and took jobs on, no matter how menial or how difficult. I used to help her in a laundry she worked in after school. I was lucky I guess; I didn't spend much time studying my lessons, but I've never flunked an exam yet, so I guess I had a natural intelligence and could pick things up quickly.

'I was always out on the street working on some scam where I could earn more money. Other kids followed me but for some reason I was always the one leading the pack. When other kids were broke I somehow still had cash. Don't know how to describe it exactly, maybe I was just a survivor. Anyway, I decided to leave home when I was 14. My mom and dad certainly weren't too happy but I knew there was a bigger world outside of my usual sphere and I wanted to find it.

'So, as I said, I left home, took various jobs where I could find them, then I saw an ad and spoke to the recruitment officer. I looked older than I was so I lied about my age and by the time the paperwork caught up with me it was too late; I had enrolled in the Marines.

'Life was hard, and looking back now I suppose fair; I mean, I now understand why training has to be rigorous and disciplined. Anyway, I had secured a roof over my head and three square meals guaranteed every day. It wasn't all bad. The real fact of the matter is that I excelled in the Training Corps. I majored in being elected Squad Leader. Men looked up to me; they relied on me. Not just on manoeuvres but with their personal problems.

'I, in short, believed in myself. There was nothing I couldn't do, or achieve, nothing impossible, and anything that got in my way I crushed. I always won, no matter what the odds, no matter what was at stake.

'My superiors recognised my abilities and through many missions I got the nickname Cleaver, 'cause anyone who stood in my way always got chopped.' Cleaver hesitated, then continued. 'You know Carla, one gets used to having one's own way and once one has built that reputation then it actually becomes easier, not because it is, but for the fact of other people's perception, what they expect to get. So I just imposed my will, got the job in hand done and nobody ever questioned my methods, just as long as the result was satisfactory. A job needing doing. Nobody wanted it; we'll give it to Cleaver Harris, he'll solve it, make it happen.

'You know, Carla, the strange thing is I did, time and time again. I succeeded where others would have failed. I received decorations from The President. I received promotions, and now, here I am, a pot-bellied, fat-faced general, with the ear of all the Joint Chiefs of Staff – to say nothing of the President, and yet although I'm not as physically fit as I was I'd crush anybody who stood in my way.'

Cleaver was now aware he'd got carried away blowing his own trumpet and fell quiet for a moment.

Carla had listened intently, but she too remained silent.

Cleaver now appraised her as he sipped more of his champagne. She was stunningly beautiful; strong, like himself, and he liked that. He studied her a moment longer, then turned his attention to the stars that now shone overhead.

'I hope I haven't bored you, or spoiled our evening,' he uttered quietly.

Carla stared at her gentleman companion. She, like Cleaver, was used to having her own way; she also had to win and had already decided that she was going to have Cleaver Harris later that evening. It was all just a matter of time.

The couple talked quietly now – general chitchat, admiring the view and the stillness of the night, except for the ends of the waves as they landed on the beach. They teased and tested each other in each moment, both enjoying the cat and mouse game.

Carla's beauty shone magnificently in her long midnight blue evening dress, with its low, revealing back, indicating she was not wearing a bra, and with her young, firm body and the sheer clinginess of her dress, showed her figure off to its full.

A double strand of oyster pearls hung around her neck, held by a solid blue sapphire and diamond clasp that had belonged to her mother, given by her father on their wedding day. Carla cherished the piece and wore it proudly. There was only one other piece of jewellery worn which was a clustered diamond bracelet, given to her by a former lover attempting to snare Carla. The relationship hadn't worked out but Carla kept the bracelet and tonight wore it over her long midnight blue velvet evening gloves which completed her outfit.

Alexander Gordon appeared on the terrace. 'You two enjoying yourselves? You seem to have been neglected by the rest of the company,' Gordon said, motioning his arm which held his glass towards the other guests chatting in the main lounge.

'Alex, we're fine,' replied Cleaver, glancing at Carla, and waiting for her to confirm her agreement.

'Absolutely, Alex,' Carla replied. 'Bob is such an interesting person; I don't really want to share him this evening, all his escapades an' all. Oh! I mean, I'm enjoying listening to …'

Alexander Frederick Gordon knew exactly what Carla meant and, slightly embarrassed by his intrusion, made his excuses to leave and re-join the main party and leave the couple to their own devices.

Carla and Cleaver laughed with each other once Alex Gordon was out of earshot.

'You'll have them talking about us,' Cleaver said, smiling.

Carla sipped more of her champagne. 'Is that right, General? Well, we'd better not disappoint them then. Shall we retire? I'm sure we can find somewhere more private to extend our evening,' she said, as a broad, intoxicating smile broke out across her face, her wonderful eyes dancing with devilment as she laughed out loud.

Cleaver Harris was not slow. Benjamin, his valet, was correct; there was good company here tonight and he, Cleaver, had certainly bagged a beauty.

Bob Harris thanked his host Alex Gordon for his hospitality and made his apologies for retiring early. 'The journey today has just got the better of me. I'll feel better after a good night's sleep.'

Alex Gordon glanced at his friend and at Carla. 'You two enjoy the rest of your evening. I'm sure you'll both sleep well.'

Carla smiled at Alex Gordon and bade him goodnight. She extended her arm and Gordon, being a gentleman of the old school, kissed her gloved hand.

He shook hands with Cleaver, then whispered in his ear. 'You lucky dog, Cleaver, but be warned. She's a handful.'

Cleaver smiled. 'I hope so, Governor, I hope so.'

Carla and Cleaver departed, leaving the usual crowd to continue their merrymaking. Both had another agenda on their minds.

Cleaver admired the woman before him. Carla looked radiant and sexy. The sheerness of her gown clung to every inch of her taut, fit body. He held her close; he felt her bosoms rise and fall as they kissed and embraced each other. Slowly, he unzipped the back of her dress and allowed it to fall gently to the floor.

Carla wore nothing underneath. There was no chance of any panty line to spoil the contour of her dress. Slowly, she stepped out of the garment, her only attire now being her silver high-heeled sandals, her long blue velvet gloves, her bracelet and, of course, her mother's pearl necklace.

They held each other, Cleaver savouring the moment as Carla took control and slid Cleaver's white dinner jacket off and untied his black bow tie, leaving the butterfly tails in position as she seductively undid his shirt buttons. Next, his braces were unshouldered and his trousers fell to the floor. Carla laughed out loud when she saw Cleaver's underwear, his boxer shorts bulging at the front with his erection. Cleaver smiled, as he was pleased he was ready to unfold the woman he now held.

'Hey, big boy,' Carla exclaimed, as she gently held his manhood; then, with a gentle squeeze, she released him. She removed her gloves and bracelet and stood, wearing nothing but her pearl necklace. Carla pushed Cleaver onto the top of the large bed as she took control, fondling and kissing his manhood, allowing her tongue to slide up and down, giving pleasure, as she felt his hardness increase.

Their lovemaking continued with Carla doing the bidding, until it was her turn to be on the receiving end, as Cleaver took over and kissed her between her thighs, allowing her juices to flow as he tasted her saltiness and womanhood in his mouth.

Cleaver worked his way up to her navel and then onto her breasts and erect nipples. Carla was moaning in satisfaction, and once again wrapped her fingers around Cleaver's erect membrane, guiding him as he entered and rhythmically thrust himself into her, their lovemaking bringing gasps of excitement as each in turn exploded into ecstasy as they savoured each moment, until both bodies were fully spent and they lay in each other's arms. Contented and happy, they fell asleep.

Two hours later, Cleaver was aroused by a gentle rhythmic sensation. At first, he thought he was dreaming, but then felt the ecstasy of Carla's tongue at his manhood. Cleaver responded and each gave pleasure to one another, followed by mad passionate love until, naturally fully exhausted they fell into a deep sleep.

Cleaver's body clock still woke him in the early morning and he reached over to touch Carla, but she was gone. There was no sign of her, except for the ruffled bedsheets where they had played the night before.

Cleaver checked his wristwatch. It was 6:15am. He was normally awake by 5:00am. Better get on with the day, he said to himself. He felt good as he remembered his previous evening with Carla Roebuck and hoped they'd meet again; after all, she was a very pretty filly.

Cleaver then focused his mind on Rodriquez Mahon who would be waiting for him at Seven Mile Beach. He picked up the telephone at the side of his bed. Instantly, Ben Whyte answered. 'Good morning, General. I hope you slept well. What can I do for you?'

'Thank you, Ben. Never slept better. Ben, I'll require transport, preferably by sea to get me to Seven Mile Beach. Can you organise that, please?'

'Yessir. What time does the General require transport?'

'I'd like to breakfast in one hour Ben, then leave after that. Is that enough notice?'

'No problem, General. I'll organise that, then I'll wait in the dining room and serve you breakfast.'

'Great, see you soon. Oh! Ben, you don't happen to know if Miss Carla Roebuck is still around?'

Ben Whyte fell silent. He saw plenty, but never chose to comment. 'I believe she went home about an hour ago, General.'

'Oh! Okay. Thank you, Ben.'

Cleaver hung up the line, then made himself ready for the day ahead.

Ben Whyte set up breakfast. He had seen Carla Roebuck sneak out of the Mansion House in the small hours. It wasn't the first time Ben had witnessed such goings-on, but true to his position and professionalism, he remained very discreet. After all, it was not his place to make any judgement on any of his superiors or their guests. Life had judged his people for generations and it would be a long time before that could, or would, change.

Chapter 38

Cleaver breakfasted, then walked sandal-footed along the timbered jetty towards the dinghy that Ben had organised. The sun was up and it promised to be another beautiful day.

He pulled the starter cord of the Mercury 1000 engine and headed north towards Seven Mile Beach where he had arranged to meet Rodriquez Mahon.

He let his mind reminisce of his night of passion with Carla Roebuck and a gentle smile broadened across his face while the sea spray softly brushed against him as his dinghy sped through the water.

Cleaver's sharp eyes scanned the beach before him. He had cut the engine, allowing the boat to drift and rock gently as he searched for his man.

A solitary figure dressed in long white cotton trousers rolled up to the knees stood up and Cleaver recognised the image of Rodriquez Mahon standing, waving towards him. Cleaver directed his dinghy, then, hauling it out of the water to rest on the sand, shook the outstretched, dark haired tanned arm of his associate.

'Good to see you, Señor General, no! Eh! You are well?' Rodriquez asked.

Cleaver smiled, still remembering his night with Carla. 'Very,' he replied. 'It's good to see you, Rodriquez.'

Rodriquez was puffing a large Cuban cigar and smiled at his visitor, showing off his multiple gold fillings which adorned his teeth. His black wavy hair and tanned pock-marked cheeks completed his look. He stroked his dog and its barking settled to a whimper before lying down. 'It's good to see you Señor Cleaver. When you arrive, yesterday, I assume you staying with that bastard Gordon at Government House,' he said, spitting into the sand.

'Yes. He's not so bad, you know. Treats me well, tends to my every need.'

Again Rodriquez spat in the sand. 'You only visit Señor; I here all the time. He has eyes and ears everywhere. We have to be very careful; besides, he's a pompous, fat-assed Gringo and I don't like him.'

'Am I a fat-assed Gringo, Rodriquez? Is that what you say about me?'

Rodriquez smiled at his friend. 'Oh, yes, Amigo, but you pay well and anyway, I like you.'

Cleaver chuckled. He liked the honesty of the man. He was like himself; friendships and relationships work, as long as the pay is good.

'Let's have some rum, Rodriquez, and you can bring me up-to-date with the latest shipment.'

Both men entered the small house. It was cool, its dark furniture simple and traditional. They sat in easy chairs, discussing pleasantries before getting down to business.

'So, when's the shipment due,' Cleaver asked, sipping his rum.

'Next week. Usual procedure. The boat will be checked by the Coast Guard, the overhead spotter planes; all of that. We can't go near till they've inspected her, made their report and certified her to proceed.'

'What about the merchandise, Rodriquez, how's that handled?'

'Ah, Señor, sometimes what you don't know can't hurt you and ...'

Cleaver's eyes narrowed. Had he misjudged the situation and his partner?

Rodriquez spoke. 'The ship has special compartments built into her. They can search all they want, but they won't find anything. Hey, even if they stripped her bare they would not find those compartments Señor. Good, eh!' Rodriquez laughed.

Cleaver was not so amused. He needed the money from the drug shipments to finance his offshore accounts and the small personal army he was building. The money from the drugs laundered through the Cayman Islands was perfect, but only if every detail was checked, and everyone did their job and no one became careless.

Cleaver had to forgive Rodriquez's lackadaisical approach. It was part of his charm and the attitude of his fellow countrymen, but Cleaver could not help but be concerned. After all, he had such a lot riding on these enterprises and he depended on people like Rodriquez's trained thugs, instead of well-oiled professionals who got jobs done with efficiency.

Both men sipped their rum and each drew on their Cubans. Silence fell between them, each in reality wary of each other.

Cleaver loved his visits to the Caymans. It had all the trappings of luxury without the chaos and congestion of Washington, and the company was pretty good too, well, the females that he enjoyed, anyway. Cleaver agreed with Rodriquez; Governor Alexander Frederick Gordon was a prick, but a useful one, for now at least.

Hours passed and it was time for Cleaver to return and catch up with his host, Governor Gordon. He paid Rodriquez his usual retainer and enough money to take care of any expenses that would be required for next week's operation; after all, he had to keep him sweet if his plan was to succeed.

Rodriquez watched as Cleaver walked slowly back to his dinghy. He was always pleased to see Señor Cleaver because it meant more money for him, but Rodriquez was smart. He'd also been taking an extra cut for himself, unknown to anybody. He knew the day would come when his situation could change and he'd need some form of insurance and security. Anyway, he was the one taking most of the risks and as he said earlier, what nobody knew couldn't hurt them.

Cleaver arrived safely back at the jetty where Ben Whyte was waiting. 'You all right, General?' he shouted anxiously. 'Governor Gordon was looking for you and was concerned when I told him you'd gone out on the dinghy.'

'Oh Ben, an old dog like me won't come to any harm. I needed space. Time to think. Clear my mind. Know what I mean?'

'Well, I suggest, General, you let the Governor know you're all right, then prepare yourself for lunch.'

Cleaver was thinking how boring that would be but didn't comment. He'd lunched with Governor Gordon before and realised he was more relaxed talking to Rodriquez Mahon than a set of stuffed shirts who sat behind desks.

Chapter 39

Lunch was the usual affair, with prominent guests from the local institutions based on the island, and although Cleaver always gleamed information on investment performances and the markets, he at heart was a military man and therefore had a different perspective on everything.

'Will Carla Roebuck be joining us for dinner tonight, Governor?' Cleaver enquired.

'Carla? Don't think so. I think she had a prior engagement,' Gordon replied; then added 'would you have liked to see her again? You both seemed quite compatible.'

Cleaver smiled at his host, then nodded. 'She's an interesting woman and I would have appreciated the pleasure of her company.'

Both men smiled at each other, then laughed as they sipped their sherry.

Cleaver rested that afternoon, reflecting on his meeting with Rodriquez and was pleased that his plans were going well.

Dinner time came and Cleaver, suitably attired, joined Governor Gordon and his guests for cocktails on the terrace.

Cleaver was conversing with an Independent Financial Advisor when a tap on his shoulder interrupted the two men. Turning round, Cleaver was delighted to once again gaze into the magical eyes of Carla Roebuck. Cleaver smiled, as did Carla.

'Let me introduce you, this is Johnathan …'

'Yes, we've met,' Carla interrupted hurriedly. 'Last year, wasn't it?' she added.

Johnathan smiled. His memory of Carla was not his best, and therefore excused himself, leaving Cleaver and Carla to their own company.

'Something I said?' Cleaver said, smiling at Carla.

'Goodness, no. Johnathan thinks himself big, but he's not; well, maybe he is in the financial industry but not in any other department, I can assure you,' Carla said, laughing.

Cleaver got the message and laughed too. 'Thought you had a prior engagement?' he said, inwardly grateful that Carla had chosen to join Governor Gordon's party.

'I did … but I heard you were still here and I really enjoyed your company last evening, so … here I am, General. Now … are you pleased to see me?' Carla said, as she stared into Cleaver's eyes.

Cleaver grinned. 'That's an understatement, I think.'

Dinner over, the usual cigar and brandy time for the gentlemen and small talk for the ladies saw Carla leave, but she didn't leave the Governor's mansion; instead, she made her way to Cleaver's suite where she pampered herself and waited patiently for her General.

After a while, Cleaver joined the ladies with the rest of his fellow gentlemen and was disappointed to discover that Carla had already departed. He lingered for half an hour, then made his apologies that he'd had a full day and an enjoyable weekend, but would retire early as he had some preparations to make before his return flight the next day.

Cleaver made his way up the sweeping marbled staircase and along the corridor to a small-annexed, short landing area where his suite was located.

He opened his door and was instantly greeted with the smell of Dior perfume. Cleaver moved cautiously towards the bedroom, the soft lighting that shone creating a calmness. He smiled when he saw Carla, draped across the large bed in a black, sexy, silk short slip, black silk stockings and high-heeled shoes. Her perfect makeup with her dramatic eyes completed her look.

'Well hello, honey,' she said teasingly. 'Thought I'd lost you to those fat heads downstairs.'

Cleaver smiled as he admired the view. 'I thought you'd gone home, otherwise Id've been up here much sooner.'

'Well! You're here now, Cleaver.'

'I trust I've not wasted my time?'

Carla thrust her head back and beckoned Cleaver to join her on the bed. He moved towards her, their faces inches apart, each smelling and sensing each other's sexual impulses.

Carla made the first move and slowly removed Cleaver's clothes and seductively kissed him, as each item fell to the floor. Their intimacy was building and Cleaver caressed and kissed her vaginal lips, allowing her juices to flow. He could taste her, and after working his tongue inside her, shared his experience by kissing her on her mouth, allowing her feminine womanhood to mingle with her lipstick lips, bringing ecstasy and making her body quiver.

Carla was astride him now, he inside her as she rode him. Her back arched as she thrust upon him. She kept the rhythm going till she orgasmed, then feeling the ecstasy, allowed Cleaver to come in her mouth, his eruption exploding into a full ray of sparkling colours and ending with Carla sharing his juices by kissing him first on his hairy chest, then on his lips as their lovemaking consumed them. Both bodies entirely spent, they lay in each other's arms, highly satisfied and pleasured.

When Cleaver woke, Carla Roebuck was gone. He observed the state of the bedsheets and his own discarded suit, shirt and tie. He chuckled quietly to himself as the fond memories of the night before returned.

Carla Roebuck was exceptional, Cleaver knew that. She was so promiscuous, so fabulous; yes, Cleaver thought, she was the best he'd ever had and Cleaver in his time had bedded many.

He glanced at his watch. He had a plane to catch. 'Bugger,' he said out loud to himself; another night with Carla would have been a dream, but his responsibilities and Washington beckoned, not to say least of all his adrenaline for power.

He never found out what the Cayman Island's mention on his threatening letter meant, but Cleaver knew he would. There was always a next time.

Chapter 40

The aeroplane touched down at Bolling Air Force Base and Cleaver, after a brief meeting with General Wheeler, made his way by private staff car to the Pentagon. He reminisced of his evening with Carla Roebuck and hoped he'd be able to repeat their companionship on his next visit. He also checked his diary, circled the 18th, and inserted the name "Rodriquez". That was the date the next shipment was due and Cleaver hoped it would clear Customs so that more funds from its proceeds could be made into his private offshore accounts.

Cleaver had set-up various accounts, each with their own legitimate business as a front, but in reality they funded missions and projects that suited Cleaver Harris. The drug and vice game ran hand-in-hand and the procurement of young girls to satisfy demand was high and, more importantly, profitable.

Cleaver's main goal however was to amass enough money and power to challenge the President, or anyone else who stood in his way, as his ambition was driven by his appetite for control.

'Good morning, Barbara; I trust you had a good weekend?' Cleaver said, smiling as he walked onwards to his office.

'Yes, thank you, Sir. Your mail is on your desk. I assume you enjoyed the Caymans?' Barbara said.

Cleaver turned. He admired his secretary. 'Oh yes, I did, thank you, Barbara,' he replied, smiling. He paused at his office door. 'You know, you should have accompanied me to the Caymans, Barbara, I think you would have enjoyed it,' he said with a smile on his face and a soft glint in his eyes.

Again, Cleaver paused as he mentally recalled his time with Carla and then quietly thought to himself, but I bet I wouldn't have had such a fantastic time.

Cleaver smiled at his secretary, then entered his inner sanctuary where the wood-lined panelled walls oozed more opulence than the standard office bay and now sat behind his large desk.

He was reading his mail, preparing himself for the day ahead, where his input and authoritative decisions would all be important within the realms of Washington.

Barbara knocked gently on his door, then rushed in. 'I almost forgot. This came this morning, special delivery, actually hand delivered by messenger. I signed for it on your behalf.'

Cleaver examined the envelope. There was no postmark, or any franking stamp to divulge who'd sent it. He was curious and opened it carefully while reading another memo on his desk.

He unfolded the long, white parchment paper. He did not expect to find the contents that were written there.

'Barbara, Barbara!' Cleaver shouted, running out to his secretary's office. Who gave you this letter? You say it was hand delivered?'

Barbara looked up, astounded at her superior's action. He was always cool, calculating and organised. 'What's the matter, Cleaver?' she said, standing up.

'You heard me, who delivered this letter?' he repeated, waving its envelope in the air.

Barbara shook her head. 'A messenger.'

'Yeah, who? What messenger? Where? Cleaver said, raising his voice.

'I ... I ... don't know, I mean ...'

'You signed for it, I presume?' Cleaver said.

'Yes, well, I did.'

'Well, who sent it? Who delivered it?'

Barbara searched her desk for the relevant paperwork. She found it and read the name under sender. She closed her eyes. This was not happening.

'Well?' Cleaver said, once again repeating himself. 'Who bloody well sent the letter?'

Barbara's mouth fell open. 'It's signed ... It's signed ... David Crockett.'

'David Crockett?' Cleaver repeated. 'From where?'

The ... The Alamo,' Barbara said, her voice dwindling to obscurity.

'The what? Barbara, I thought I just heard you say David Crockett from the Alamo?'

Again, Barbara closed her eyes, then nodded. 'That's what's on the paperwork,' she said, trembling.

'Let me see that,' Cleaver said, as he snatched the receipt out of his secretary's hands. 'Okay, okay. So, what was this David Crockett like? You saw him, yes? Describe him.'

For the third time, Barbara closed her eyes.

'Well, would you recognise him again?' Cleaver yelled.

'It was a … a … motorcyclist delivery.'

'So …' Cleaver replied, not appreciating the significance. 'So, he, or she, was wearing a helmet?'

'One of those with a visor which they kept down.'

'A helmet, a friggin' helmet, with a visor. You are kidding me, Barbara?'

Barbara started to shake uncontrollably now.

'You mean a messenger wearing a helmet with a visor just walked in here to the Pentagon, passed reception, security, all the way up here, without being challenged?' Cleaver's statement was ridiculous, just as ridiculous as his security. 'Barbara, call the security chiefs, I want them all in my office, right now, understand?'

Barbara didn't quibble. She just started dialling numbers, trembling as she did so.

'And get me Glen Randall … now,' Cleaver yelled.

'Yes Sir, yes Sir,' Barbara was in a quandary; this was not the time to respond to her boss by his nickname. She didn't know what to do first.

Cleaver returned to his office. He sat down at his large desk, spread the letter before him and re-read its stencilled words in capitals:

MURDERER

RAPIST

CAYMANS

TRAITOR

I'LL GET YOU!

YOUR TIME IS COMING!

General Bob Cleaver Harris sat back in his leather chair. Who, he wondered, would have the audacity to threaten him? Who had enough information to accuse him of murder, rape and a traitor to his country?

Cleaver searched his mind. The Caymans were also mentioned. Could the threat be from someone down there? He was puzzled. Cleaver considered Colonel Glen Randall, but then dismissed the idea. Glen was close to him, part of his inner circle, and would have much to lose if he came to harm.

Anyway, Colonel Randall in his opinion wouldn't have the balls to threaten him and anyway, it was not his style.

Glen, however, was the one person he'd known the longest. They had fought together as they both received promotions and Randall had stuck to Cleaver like glue and reaped the benefits of their close friendship.

Cleaver needed Glen. He charged him with tying up any loose ends that could threaten their private enterprises and to date Randall had been successful. He'd organised the hit on Claire Monroe. He'd also taken care of Riker and Gennero, so who could be threatening him?

Cleaver had to find out.

Chapter 41

In an office in the Pentagon, a red light flashed intermittently, indicating an incoming call on a direct line. Colonel Glen Randall answered but the caller remained silent.

'Who's calling? Identify yourself,' Randall said authoritatively.

Again, silence reigned.

Glen Randall knew only a handful of people had his direct number and when used the conversations were short and to the point. As the caller had not yet spoken he decided to hang up. The line went dead. Randall stared at the dead instrument for a few moments as it once again burst into life. Cautiously, he lifted his handset and listened. 'That you, Randall?' an unrecognised voice said.

'Identify yourself, this is a priority line.'

'I need paying,' the voice said.

'What!'

'You know, for Claire Monroe in New York.'

'Hell, who is this?' Randall shouted, now standing at his desk.

'Don't tell me you don't recognise me Randall! We need to meet!'

Glen Randall laughed into the handset. 'And who am I supposed to be meeting?' he asked, his mind crossing names off his list of contacts who had his number. Identify yourself!'

'It's Riker, Randall; Riker in New York. You do remember me, don't you?'

The name stung down the wire, but Randall gave no response. 'I don't know any Riker,' he eventually said, attempting to appease his mystery caller.

'You guys need to get your hands dirty; you've been too long behind a desk, getting fat and lazy with the good life.'

Randall listened carefully as his instructions were given.

'Come to New York, Randall. I want paying; meet me in Central Park at the Loeb Boathouse, Friday afternoon. Don't mess me about, just be there.'

The line went dead as Steve hung up.

Glen Randall sat back down in his high-backed leather chair. His mind was racing. Riker was dead. He'd paid and organised the hit on him and his partner, Gennero. He'd even read about it in a short article in The Times. Could this be a hoax call, he thought to himself; but if it was, how the hell did the caller get his private direct line? Had Riker given his name and number before he died? If so, what else did the mysterious caller know? Claire Monroe, obviously; her hit and run death of six months previous but the real question burrowed away in Randall's mind. What else did the caller know? He thought he'd covered all angles. The investigation into Claire Monroe's death and the deaths of Riker and Gennero were all generously paid for and closed down.

There was obviously a leak.

Reluctantly, Glen Randall lifted his handset and dialled.

Cleaver was deep in thought when his other line rang out, its piercing tone stunning the atmosphere of the room. Cleaver let it ring for a while, too shocked to take control and respond. The piercing tone continued, then, as if with an automatic reaction, Cleaver grabbed the receiver. 'Yeah?!

'Cleaver. It's Glen. We may have a problem.

Cleaver sat there, astonished, but had only one reply. 'Well fuckin' deal with it. That's what I pay you for!' he shouted. He then slammed the handset back into its cradle.

Glen Randall stared into his handset and dead line. He knew of Cleaver's reputation and knew he could be ruthless but instinct on this occasion told Randall all was not well in the Cleaver camp.

Maybe his caller had got to Cleaver too? Well, Friday wasn't too far away when he'd meet at Loeb Boathouse in Central Park. Until then he had some organising to do.

Chapter 42

Cleaver sat at his large oak polished desk. This was not the first threatening letter he'd received. Where was the breach, he mused to himself. Who and what information did the sender know? They knew him that was for sure.

Could his secretary Barbara be involved? After all, she handed him the letter; said it was from David Crockett from the Alamo. Cleaver allowed himself a small smile. 'Who the fuck's kidding who?' he muttered out loud.

In his mind, Cleaver dismissed Barbara's involvement as she could just have easily accepted his invitation to join him in the Caymans that weekend, and the sender of the letter couldn't have known that. Cleaver did not like loose ends. He had always made it his policy that there were none, not ever.

His mind travelled back to Grand Cayman as he thought of Carla Roebuck and the time they'd spent together. He also thought of Rodriquez and their meeting. Hell, both men had so much to gain and everything to lose, so Cleaver discounted him.

There had to be some other motive. Something he'd missed.

He then recalled Glen Randall's call that morning. He sounded panicked and he had just told him to deal with whatever it was. Slowly, Cleaver reached for his handset and was about to dial when Barbara knocked on the door and appeared.

Cleaver replaced the handset. 'Yes, Barbara?' he said.

'Colonel Glen Randall here to see you, Sir.'

Cleaver nodded, acknowledging her as Glen walked in.

'Coffee, tea?' Barbara offered.

Cleaver, anxious to hear what was so important, replied negatively. 'Oh, and Barbara, hold all calls; we've not to be disturbed … understand?'

Barbara nodded and departed, closing the door.

'So, what the fuck's up, Randall? What's so goddamn important that you've traipsed yourself over here?'

'Well, Cleaver, you were off with me this morning. You seemed in a foul mood and I thought maybe you'd had a call, the same as me.'

'Call? What call?' Cleaver said, sitting down.

'You … didn't get a call, Cleaver?'

'No, just you babbling about some problem.'

Glen Randall composed himself. 'Well, it maybe somethin' or nothin' but I received a call. The caller knew all about Claire Monroe, in fact, the caller identified himself as Riker, but as we both know, Riker is dead.

'So who's impersonating him?' Cleaver asked.

Randall shrugged his shoulders. 'Look Cleaver, I organised the hit on Riker and Gennero. Pulled the strings in the DA Department to shut down their cases and all investigations regarding their deaths. I'm reliably informed that this had been attended to; I mean, I can't understand who would have my private direct line number.'

'Unless Riker talked prior to his demise,' Cleaver offered. 'I mean, if you pay peanuts Glen, you get monkeys.'

Glen Randall resented Cleaver's remark. He had certainly not paid peanuts and as far as he was aware, Riker and Gennero had been taken out without the opportunity of discussion, but he said nothing to counter Cleaver's remark.

'Listen Glen, meet this motherfucker, pay him off – and you know what I mean by pay him off, don't you ...?' Cleaver paused.

'You mean permanently?' Glen answered.

Cleaver stared at his Colonel. 'No loose ends, Glen. Got it ...? Understand?'

Randall nodded. 'I'm supposed to meet whoever at Loeb's Boathouse, Central Park New York this Friday, and ...'

Barbara knocked on the door. Randall broke off the conversation with Cleaver.

Cleaver nodded, then added 'Attend to that Glen, okay?'

Colonel Glen Randall stood to leave, his meeting with Cleaver over.

'Yes, Barbara? Any more news on that message?'

Barbara's head bowed. 'Sorry ... no ... I ... I should have been more attentive. I should have checked ...'

Cleaver could see the pain on his secretary's face. It was obvious she felt awful letting her boss down over such a simple procedure. 'Barbara, don't worry, we may just have a lead on his identity. Now, what else am I scheduled for today? I think we should resume normal transmission immediately, eh!'

Barbara offered a small, grateful smile; she appreciated Cleaver's magnanimous gesture. 'Yes, right away, Sir.' She then deposited some documents on Cleaver's desk and departed.

Cleaver walked around his office. 'So, we have a player,' he said out loud to himself.

Chapter 43

Steve sat at his office desk. He had instructed Randall to meet him at the Loeb Boathouse in Central Park on Friday afternoon. He had no doubt he'd meet someone, whether it was Randall or not, was quite another matter. He knew no matter whoever he met he would be watched, then followed and then … Steve stopped short of thinking what may follow. He had to come up with enough bait to interest whoever met him. He needed more information if he was to snare and trap the big wolf behind all this.

Steve locked his office door, drew down the window blind; poured himself a large Jack Daniels, switched off the lights and sat back in his old swivel chair, his legs outstretched; his feet resting on his desk.

'Now old friend,' he said out loud, as he sipped and savoured the liquor. 'Let me relax and give me some answers.' The liquor found its mark and he set his mind free.

Chapter 44

Steve wandered through Central Park. It was daytime; the serious morning joggers all gone, leaving behind the usual dog walkers and the fashionable set; fanatics who were more interested in their appearance and what they wore.

He stood facing Loeb's Boathouse at the toe of the Lake and scrutinised the surrounding area for a suitable escape route. Would Randall appear himself? Steve discounted that thought. Probably send someone else to negotiate with him, with others there ready to take him out. After all, why should Randall expose himself when his identity could remain unknown?

To his right he observed the statute of Hans Christian Andersen and the pathway between his position where he now stood. Maybe he should have chosen another part of the park, but Loeb's Boathouse was a fashionable location, with its boating facilities and popular upmarket restaurant. It was public enough to diminish the risk of attack, besides, the meeting had already been arranged.

Steve realised he should have back-up and therefore would require to involve his unofficial partner, Lieutenant Stuart Chandler, or "Rubber Duck" which was his code name. He then had a brainwave.

Chapter 45

Malone picked up the receiver of his telephone. 'Yeah?' he answered.

'You ready for your scoop?' Steve said.

'Who's callin'?' Jimmy answered, pen now in hand.

'You know who's callin', Malone. Meet me here today, Loeb's Boathouse, Central Park … say one hour?'

Jimmy was about to ask another question, but the line was dead.

Steve approached the park from 79th Transverse along East Drive at the side of the Ramble. He joined the path that ran to the East side of Loeb's Boathouse and shielded himself behind a tree. He watched and waited patiently.

An hour lapsed when he recognised the familiar hat and gait of The Times reporter. Malone wandered slowly towards the boathouse, waiting for contact to be made.

The boathouse was busy and its fashionable restaurant was still in full swing, ever popular with its discerning customers. Other people were queuing to rent boats as well as some who were just relaxing and watching the world go by.

Steve observed Malone and although the reporter seemed to be alone the thought crossed Steve's mind that Malone may not be without company. Steve scanned the area. There was a stationary cyclist on a bridge who watched as Jimmy sauntered along the pathway, stopping every now and then searching for Steve.

The cyclist and Malone's eyes made contact with a negative shake of their heads, a brief movement that would go undetected by any passer-by.

Steve needed to speak with Malone but only on his terms and not along with a third party, and so decided to leave the park. He walked slowly away from his vantage point towards the statue of Alice in Wonderland, now leaving the Loeb Boathouse behind him. He joined a path that linked him to 5th Avenue and decided he'd take time out before contacting Jimmy Malone again. He found a bar, ordered a JD and reflected on his next move.

Two hours lapsed before Jimmy and his partner called it a day. Malone was angry. He'd arranged the meet. It sounded a worthwhile scoop and yet he'd met nobody. Had something untoward happened to his contact, or was this just a waste of time? Jimmy Malone thought the latter.

His telephone was ringing as he approached his desk. 'Yeah!' he shouted, not amused that he'd been on a wild goose chase.

'You should have come alone, Malone,' Steve said sternly.

'What! What! I *was* friggin' alone. And are you tellin' me you were there, but didn't meet me, you son of a bitch. Do you know how long I waited for you to show?' Malone pressed.

'I told you to come alone, Malone.

'Hey bud, I've more to do with my time than play hide and seek in the park all day.' Jimmy Malone hung up.

He was really angry now.

Steve redialled. The line rang and rang; it was obvious Malone was pissed off. He was about to hang up when the line connected.

'Yeah!' the familiar voice answered.

'It's me,' Steve said.

'Oooh! It's me, the fuckin' Scarlet Pimpernel,' Malone answered sarcastically.

'Listen, Jimmy. I have information that I think you'd be interested in,' Steve said, hoping Malone being a newspaper man would put his anger to one side and listen.

'You're kiddin' me, Donaldson?'

'You are kiddin' *me*! You take the piss, then still want to play …'

'Well, I ain't interested. Okay? You got that – NOT INTERESTED – capeesh?'

The silence between the two men was evident. Steve broke it. 'What if I told you there's a connection to the Pentagon?'

'What d'ya mean?' Jimmy exclaimed.

Once again, silence reigned, then Malone spoke. 'Okay Donaldson, you have one minute to expand on that, then I'm hanging up.'

Steve paused. He needed Malone and wanted to give Randall's name, but disciplined himself.

'Can't talk on the telephone. Meet me at Rikki's Café, Mulberry Street, tomorrow morning, 7:30am sharp. Oh! And Malone? Come alone.'

Malone was about to comment but the line was dead. He slammed the handset down on its cradle.

'Anything wrong, Jimmy?' a fellow reporter shouted from across the office.

Jimmy just raised his hand and waved a "no" to his colleague, but inside he was fuming.

Jimmy thumbed the Yellow, checking the address of Rikki's Café on Mulberry Street, then sat at his desk, his mind working overtime.

Donaldson had already given him details on the murders; now there was a link to the Pentagon – 'gee, this could be big,' he whispered to himself.

Malone listed all the names he had so far:

Claire Monroe – hit and run

Rusty (junk man) – died in fire – suspicious

Riker – professional hit and possible killer

Gennero – professional hit and the same

Steve Donaldson – PI, attempted murder, possibly by Riker and Gennero who are now deceased

Once again Malone thought of Steve. 'Son of a bitch, deserves all he gets,' he said out loud to himself, but inwardly Malone knew if Donaldson could provide the information then who the hell could tell where the buck would stop?

The following morning Malone stood outside Rikki's Café in Mulberry Street. He wore his usual short brimmed hat with its broad ribbon band, his sports coat covered at this hour with a raincoat which had deep pockets that held his notepad.

He turned when he heard the door open behind him.

'Mornin' Malone,' Steve said.

Jimmy didn't even smile, or return pleasantries with Steve, he just followed him inside and nodded towards Rik who was preparing coffee.

'So, managed to entice you, whet your appetite?' Steve said.

'Oh, that depends Donaldson. If the info is good and it checks out. Also, it depends on how much you want.'

Steve sat back, aghast. 'Money? Malone! I don't want money. God, I've misjudged you,' Steve said.

'Hey bud! Everyone wants money, even you, you son of a bitch,' Malone said, biting into his iced doughnut. He then started laughing while chewing. 'Hey, don't tell me you're putting your neck on the line for some dead broad that you didn't even know?

Steve stared at the newspaper man.

'Well, my, my, she must have been something, Donaldson. Is it your conscience that's bothering you, because if it is my friend then I suggest you get a new career?'

'An attempt was made on my life, Malone. That changed my perspective on the case. I mean, I'm just trying to find out who'd want me out of the way. It bothers me Malone that I could be targeted, all because this young woman spoke to me. As it happens, she herself didn't tell me squat, but whoever killed her doesn't know that, and whoever is at the top and behind all this certainly doesn't want any loose ends.'

'Oh, I suppose you're as clean as snow,' Malone said laughing.

'Well, no, but all these deaths: that is, Rusty, Riker and Gennero are probably down to me. I mean, I didn't actually commit the crimes, but because each of them spoke to me and I followed up the enquiry is why they are all dead.'

Malone wiped his mouth with the back of his hand and took a sip of coffee. 'Hey Rikki, good coffee,' Malone yelled. Rikki just nodded. He could see his friend's meeting was not progressing well.

'You're saying I'm some kinda schmuck?' Steve said.

'Well, ain't you?' Malone answered, holding his palms upwards.

'No I'm not Malone. Listen, you don't want the story, I'll find somebody else,' Steve said, then rose to go.

'Aw, Gods sakes, Donaldson. Sit down … give me what you have and tell me what you want me to do,' Malone said, his eyes wide, his smile broadening.

Steve resumed his seat. 'There was a number in Riker's coat pocket, didn't make sense at first, then I reversed the digits and they tied back to a guy named Randall whose name just happens to be in a file under "Riker" which was kept at Rusty's yard. Also, this number, when activated, is a direct line to the same person's office, and where do you think he works?'

Malone whistled. 'The Pentagon,' he said. Steve nodded. 'What else do you have, Donaldson?'

'Well, I'm supposed to be meeting this dude at Loeb's Boathouse this Friday. He thinks I want paying for info I have on Claire Monroe and the other murders that he's obviously organised, but in reality Malone, something much bigger is going on and I want to know what, then expose it.'

'So, how do you propose to do that?' Jimmy asked innocently, then the penny dropped. 'Oh no, Donaldson! I write the stories, that don't mean I'm in them.'

'Jimmy … hey, Jimmy … I haven't intimated anything yet, but I have to admit it's a great idea, you meeting whoever and obtaining the info first hand.'

'Hey! You, Mr friggin' private eye, I ain't doin' your dirty work, got it? If that's what this meeting is about then you can count me out, Donaldson. You know, you really piss me off. First, I wasted an afternoon in the park chasing the invisible man, and now you want me to be set-up as the schmuck. Well, listen to me, you mother-fucker, no story is worth my life okay, so let's just forget all this crap. Its bullshit anyway … murder, hit and run, the Pentagon; next you'll be tellin' me the friggin' President is involved.' Malone had completed his outburst and it was his turn to stand. As far as Jimmy Malone was concerned the matter was now closed.

Steve smiled at the reporter. 'Okay Jimmy, now sit down and we'll discuss our plan of how we're going to nail this son of a bitch and how you playing a major role will have a scoop of a lifetime, to say nothing of the accolades The Times will undoubtedly receive.

Malone stared back at Steve in disbelief. 'You ain't heard a word I've said Donaldson. I'm outta here.'

'I know you'll change your mind, Malone,' Steve said, tapping his teaspoon on the table.

'Oh?' Malone replied. 'And what makes you so sure of that?' he added.

Steve slowly lifted his head and stared a long look at Jimmy Malone. 'Because Malone, it is the scoop of a life-time but also because it'll please you … you being such a dedicated and powerful leader in your field with an unmatched reputation.' Steve paused, still holding his stare. He then gestured for Malone to retake his seat so that discussions of their plans could follow.

'So, tell me more about this goddamn bastard in the Pentagon,' Malone said.

Steve pursed his lips. 'Not much to tell, really. I know his name is Randall; I know he employed Riker and Gennero to do his dirty work. I believe he also authorised their demise – no loose ends so to speak – I think he'll meet me, or who he thinks is me, on Friday. He'll not take any action until he knows or finds out what I actually know and if there are any other sources involved that could threaten him.'

'What d'ya mean – who he thinks is you?' Malone said, feeling that his involvement was about to become a nightmare.

Steve glanced across the table at Malone, his head down but his eyes firmly and squarely looking up at the reporter. 'Because, Jimmy, he'll be meeting you. You'll be me. I'll brief you of what to say; give him a teaser, see what he offers, find out who else is involved. How much is he going to pay for us to go away?'

'How much he's gonna pay,' Malone echoed. 'You just said any loose ends and this guy Randall makes sure there are no loose ends.' Jimmy backed up his statement by cutting his throat with his forefinger.

Steve still stared at Jimmy. 'We can catch this bastard, Malone, but together. I need your help and for you, what a story you'll have, to say nothing of the feather in your cap with your editor.'

'What about the boys in blue? Why don't you take this case to them, after all, that's what they're paid for?'

'You disappoint me, Malone. I've as good as told you, this Randall has connections, he's, or someone, has nobbled the DA Department as well as the NYPD, so this investigation can only proceed by outside action.'

'Oh, and that's you and me?' Malone said, laughing. It wasn't a happy laugh, though; more a sarcastic response.

Steve eyeballed the man before him. 'That's right Jimmy, you and me.'

'You're fuckin' crazy, man. I mean, off the friggin' wall, outta your mind,' Malone said, the decibels of his voice rising.

Steve let him have his outburst, then spoke. 'Okay, Malone, will you help me? Will you be me on Friday? Will you help expose this fat-assed Pentagon son of a bitch? Will you, Malone?'

A moment's silence reigned, then Jimmy raised his hands. 'Okay, let's do business,' he said.

'Rikki – more coffee and doughnuts, please,' Steve shouted.

Chapter 46

Jimmy Malone had on more than one occasion risked his life for a story. His reputation preceded him wherever he went. Sure, he was disliked but his employers at heart loved him and always cut him enough slack; enough to hang himself, but Jimmy Malone always seemed to bring home the bacon, get the story and normally the lead that many of his fellow colleagues admired. So Jimmy, although never looking the part, always came up trumps. He was Jimmy Malone and in New York that was a force to be reckoned with.

The two men went head-to-head in discussion, Jimmy Malone listening in most part to what Steve had to say and bringing him up-to-date with all his information. Steve still did not inform Malone of Lieutenant Stuart Chandler's involvement, or Rubber Duck, as he was now known. He'd keep that one to himself meantime.

'Does Lieutenant Chandler know all about this?' Malone asked, as if reading Steve's mind.

'No,' Steve answered.

'Are you sure, Donaldson? You answered pretty quick, eh,' Malone said smiling.

'Listen Malone, Chandler's not involved, okay. If he was, do you think I'd be sitting here talking to you right now?'

Malone once again appraised Steve and then allowed a glint to form in his eyes. 'I suppose not,' he said, smiling.

Jimmy sensed Steve's request for his help was obviously to meet this Randall on Friday. He just assumed Steve would accompany him and he would be there, more like a witness of what was about to go down. So he asked Steve to go over the plan.

'Well, I want you, Jimmy, to meet this cowboy in my place. I'll fill you in on what to say and ...'

'Hey! Hey! Hold on. I thought I'd be there along with you, not on my friggin' lonesome. These guys kill people, you said that yourself. Listen Donaldson, I put myself out on the line before, but this is different. We're dealin' with a different type of animal who has the connections to take me out, then you, and guess what, there'd be no questions asked and not many at our funerals. I agreed to help and take part but I can't be you. Besides, they know about you, hence the hit and run attempt on your life. So either we meet this schmuck together or not at all.'

Jimmy now sat back. He realised he'd just explained how he really felt about the whole deal.

Steve allowed a silence to reign between them, after all, he would not win Malone over by attempting to coerce him by forceful reasoning. Instead, he began listing the points in their favour in the hope that Malone would change his mind.

'Listen one moment Malone, then decide. Firstly, the only people who met me were Riker, Gennero and Rusty, and each of them are dead.'

'That's three good reasons why I should pass,' Malone said.

Steve ignored the interruption. 'Second, Randall and his other colleagues don't know me from Adam, so that's got to be in our favour. Thirdly, Randall, or someone he'll send, will want to know their exposure and if there is anybody else with information. Fourthly, I don't think this Randall is the top dog and if I'm correct, a report of the meeting will go back to whoever is really behind all this. Finally, this all started with Claire Monroe but she's out of the picture. It's just loose ends that require some attention and nothing will happen on Friday.'

You think that Donaldson?' Malone said. If it is so simple then why don't you just meet them yourself?'

Steve considered Malone's reasoning. 'I just want to observe at this stage. And if Randall doesn't appear himself then he'll still not know me on sight. You, on the other hand, Malone, will not just be playing an active role in this little saga, you'll have your scoop with first-hand experience. Besides, the venue is the Loeb Boathouse and there are always plenty of people about. Randall, or anybody else for that matter, is not going to try anything in such a public place.'

Jimmy Malone thought over Steve's explanation and reasoning. The Loeb Boathouse was indeed pretty safe he thought. There were always plenty of kids, busy parents at the Lake. The Loeb Boathouse restaurant was also very busy since it had all been refurbished a few years before.

'Well Malone, what is it to be?' Steve said, sitting back in the booth.

Malone shook his head from side to side, then spoke. 'What time does this meet go down?' then extended his hand across the table.

Chapter 47

Chandler called his sergeant in. 'You heard from Jericho yet?'

Johnston shook his head negatively. 'Seems to have disappeared. Did you have any success with that number, Lieutenant?'

'Oh, I got connected but to who I never found out and I was reluctant to disclose my identity. Didn't want to bring any unnecessary grief down on the department.'

'Do you think you got through to this Randall character?' Johnston said.

'Possibly, but whoever it was didn't speak. Johnston, I want you to locate Jericho. I don't like the silence. I feel there's something going down and we're being left out of the loop.' Chandler was deep in thought and the more he thought, the more he felt that Donaldson had made contact.

'He needs us, Lieutenant,' Johnston now volunteered. 'I think when he has anything he'll be in touch.'

Chandler nodded. 'I hope so, but he should be reporting anyway. I mean, we gave him that number; it connects to someone, Johnston, and I want to find out WHO.'

Johnston just stood there waiting, thinking his Lieutenant had more to say.

'Well, Johnston, get to it, don't just stand there.'

Chandler looked at his desk. Other cases were piling up. The DA had been pressing his Captain for results and yet he was struggling to solve them. He knew his mind was too preoccupied with the Claire Monroe case and wished inwardly that he'd never heard her name.

It was Thursday, late afternoon when Chandler's line rang. He picked up the receiver. 'Yeah?' he said.

'It's me, Jericho. Can you speak?'

'Where the hell have you been?' Chandler replied, raising his voice.

'Can't speak on the phone,' he said. 'Okay? Meet me at our usual venue tonight ...'

'Jericho,' Chandler whispered into the handset, but the line was already dead. Chandler checked his watch. He still had a few hours before he met Donaldson. 'Now, where was that bloody number,' he whispered to himself.

Chandler located the number and dialled. He let its tone ring out and was about to hang up when the line went live. He didn't speak, he just waited for a response.

Glen Randall eventually spoke. 'That you, Riker? Tomorrow afternoon. Loeb Boathouse, Central Park, as you said. You'll be paid as promised.'

Colonel Glen Randall disconnected the line; the conversation over.

Lieutenant Chandler sat at his desk. "Riker", the voice had said, but Riker was dead. And what was this about a meeting at Loeb Boathouse the next day? Chandler only had one explanation. Donaldson. He took some time out bringing himself up-to-date with the cases and got an update on the Chung-Loewe situation, then took a few minutes before grabbing his hat and coat and headed for Rikki's Café.

'Lieutenant,' Johnston shouted. 'Where you goin'?'

But Chandler didn't acknowledge his sergeant he just kept walking, leaving Johnston dumbfounded.

It was early evening and Steve was on his third cup of coffee when Chandler arrived.

'You've been conspicuous by your absence, Jericho,' he said mockingly, then added before Steve could reply, 'so, where have you been and what have you been up to, you son of a bitch.'

Rikki served Chandler a coffee.

'I assume you've dialled the number?' Steve said, watching the angry expression on Chandler's face.

Chandler shook his head. 'Are you supposed to be Riker, Steve? Is that it? You know that whoever answered that phone is aware Riker is dead.'

Steve listened but just shrugged his shoulders.

'And what's this about a meeting at Loeb's Boathouse tomorrow, eh? Start talking Steve, or so help me I'll …'

'You'll what?' Steve interrupted. 'Listen Lieutenant, I got through to the Pentagon, a direct line. The person who answered that call is prepared to meet me, or somebody that he thinks is me.'

Chandler was confused. 'I also rang but the guy who answered called me Riker and you know as well as me, Steve, that Riker is dead.'

Steve nodded. 'I told him I was Riker and that I needed paying for the Claire Monroe hit, which I thought would shake him up a bit, considering he probably had already paid Riker for that hit, and then paid again to take Riker and Gennero out. He'll assume it's me 'cause they did attempt a hit on me; I told you that, which would never have happened if Claire hadn't come to me on that fateful night. This person knows I'm not Riker, Lieutenant but he's playing along. I'm a loose end he's got to tidy up.

Lieutenant Chandler was silent for a moment. 'You do know that was a Pentagon number that I dialled?' he said, sighing.

Steve nodded. 'I already figured that one out. So, who are we dealin' with, Steve – who?' I mean, all this cat and mouse game, it's getting to me. These guys at the Pentagon have more power; more jurisdiction than I have on my little finger, and maybe that's unfair, but so is life.'

'So, what are you sayin', Lieutenant?' Steve asked, now sensing that Chandler may be about to bail.

'Am just sayin' this is outta my league and if you're honest, outta yours too, Steve. Maybe we should as ordered let this one go?'

Steve sat back; his coffee was going cold, but he couldn't believe his ears. 'So, where's the guy I know? The one with a stubborn streak, like myself. The one who is, or was, a stickler for detail, truth and honesty. Where? Is that man now gone, Lieutenant, all because some ass in the Pentagon is involved? We're talking murder here, Lieutenant – multiple murders and don't think just because we may have a change of heart and stop any further investigation that it will go away. As I said, I'm a loose end. They have no alternative but to finish me. Listen, Lieutenant. They may or may not come after you; we don't know, but one thing is for sure, any doubt about anybody and they'll be taken out, no questions asked. Just a simple accident, as before.'

'What are you saying, Donaldson?' Chandler asked, fully aware of what was being said was true.

'I'm saying, Lieutenant, let's finish this but let it be us who does the finishing. Expose this rotten apple 'cause I believe it goes a lot further up the tree than Randall. The question is, how far?'

Lieutenant Chandler leaned back in his booth. This was insane. He mulled over everything Steve had said and most of it was true. These guys, no matter who they were, had to be exposed and stopped. The challenge was how, and it also depended on how far up the line all this went.

'So, if you're not meeting this Randall tomorrow, Steve … who is? I mean, I hope you don't think me or Johnston are going to act in this little charade of yours?' Chandler said.

Steve took his time; he swivelled his neck around his shoulders to ease the tension within, then just let go. 'I told Malone; I brought him in on this. That's how he knew about Rusty. That's how he could print his article. That's …'

'What!' Chandler exclaimed, jumping out of his seat. 'You told that motherfucker shitbag Malone? He's press, Donaldson. A goddamn reporter. I'm supposed to be your partner in this and yet you didn't consult me, and Malone, of all people. I mean, Donaldson, how's he going to meet whoever and play detective? It won't work Donaldson, and as of right now I'm out, Johnston too. You've gone too far this time. A squirmy little man posing as you. Does he know, Donaldson, who he's dealing with? Well, does he?' Chandler shouted, pressing his nose inches from Steve's.

Steve expected Chandler to be upset, but he'd underestimated the dislike Chandler obviously had for Jimmy Malone. 'Listen Lieutenant, you told me your cases were closed. Your hands tied. I … *we* … needed another player, someone with a hunger to flush out the info; someone with the balls to dig and dig and …'

'And some little shit who's a reporter,' Chandler interrupted.

'Let me explain further,' Steve said.

'Explain!' Chandler exploded, then resumed his seat. Other customers were glancing over at the two of them. 'This is all madness, I should have locked you up Donaldson when I had the chance; you're a liability. All this Jericho/Rubber Duck stuff, God, you must have had a good laugh to yourself and with that creature Malone. I mean, what do you call Johnston; Mickey Mouse?'

Steve couldn't hold himself back and started laughing.

'Okay wise guy. Tell me what's goin' down tomorrow and it better be good. Tell me that son of a bitch Malone doesn't play a major part. I can't, and won't, play with him on the team,' Chandler said, shifting uneasily in his seat.

Steve sat there, allowing the moment to pass. 'Malone's agreed to meet whoever Randall has arranged to meet me. He doesn't have to think too much; hopefully get paid and report back. If Randall does in fact show then I'll be able to identify him and so will Malone when we bring him to justice. If he doesn't show, Randall will still not know me on sight, as it's only Riker, Gennero and Rusty who met me, and as we both know, Lieutenant, they're all dead.'

Chandler just sat there. 'You do know I can't stand Malone?' he said.

'I got that, Lieutenant,' Steve replied.

'Ah don't care if something happens to him. I mean it, Donaldson. He's the lowest of the low.'

Steve realised he needed Chandler back on focus and so took the lead. 'Oh, you don't really mean that, Lieutenant. He does his job and, like us, he's good at it. Anyway, he's involved now, irrespective what goes down.'

'And what if this cocky son of a bitch fucks up? Where do you think that leaves us, to say nothing of my department, 'cause we ain't supposed to be involved?' Chandler started to shake. It was the first time in many a year since events and someone actually took over his being, and was making him unable to cope.

Steve witnessed Chandler's body behaviour. 'Listen, Lieutenant, Malone knows the risks. He's too long in the tooth to be careless, and …'

'Is he too long in the tooth to get himself killed, Donaldson?' Chandler said, then added 'there's always a bright side to everything.'

Steve smiled. 'Something smells here Lieutenant; something big enough to take out and cover up any trace or info that Claire Monroe knew about.'

'So, if it's in the Pentagon, the question is, how far up the line does it go?'

Steve and Lieutenant Chandler pondered, then discussed their plans for the next day.

Chapter 48

'Okay, I'm ready,' Malone said triumphantly.

Steve appraised the reporter up and down. 'It's not fancy dress. You're a bit OTT.'

Malone smiled again, then gave Steve a twirl. 'You think I'll stand out so they'll spot me?' Malone said, pleased with the outfit he'd chosen.

'Oh yeah! They'll spot you all right.' Once again, Steve eyed Jimmy Malone in his loud grey and black chequered jacket, pink shirt, and heavily patterned tie. His light lime green trousers with pink socks completed his look, along with his soft, small brimmed hat that he always wore and which had become part of his trademark.

'Didn't think you required to be so flamboyant, Jimmy? After all, they're expecting me; a PI impersonating Riker, not some clown that stands out like a sore thumb. You're supposed to just blend in, be Mr Average who no one will remember.'

'Ah just thought you'd need to be able to see me Donaldson, if...' Malone paused, 'if I needed your help,' he said.

Steve appraised Jimmy Malone. It would be unlikely if Randall or his men took a pop in such a public place, but Jimmy did have a point; people would remember him in his brightly coloured attire, should the inevitable happen.

Steve positioned himself in a vantage point as Malone sauntered around the Lake, watching kids and their parents queuing to hire boats. The South West-facing restaurant always attracted the more discerning diner, especially at this time of the year, and therefore the Boathouse was very busy.

Malone wandered slowly around the Lake, keeping close to the boathouse and occasionally glancing over at Steve sitting on a bench, feeling confident that whoever met him, he at least would be protected by Steve.

It was 1:30pm and as yet there had been no contact or approach made on him. Periodically he produced his handkerchief and blew his nose, which was the signal that was to be used to identify himself. Time was passing with nothing happening, and Malone was becoming bored. He had originally warmed to the decoy idea but now it seemed just another waste of time. It was pretty obvious now that this Randall character from the Pentagon was a no-show, and so he was about to call it a day and saunter slowly back to Steve, when he decided to purchase an ice cream; after all, he may as well get some treat for his afternoon's work.

'I can recommend the choc mint,' the ice cream vendor said. He was attired in a white uniform with a red apron and small white and red bordered hat with the logo "Mike's Creamy Ices Taste Better".'

Vanilla please,' Malone replied, giving his order as he scanned the area around him, not really observing Mike and his ice creams.

'Hey bud, as I said, the choc mint is the best and it'll match your outfit; all these pretty colours.'

Was the man taking the piss or what, but now he had Malone's full attention.

'That's a terrible cold you got,' the vendor said. 'You've been blowin' your nose all afternoon.'

Malone was now alert, staring at the man who kept his head down as he scooped two measures into a large twin wafer cone.

'There's a lot of it about,' he said as he pointed out another figure in a grey suit who was blowing his nose and staring at Malone.

The man in grey walked passed and Jimmy's eyes followed him.

'Hey bud, here's your change.'

'Keep the change,' Malone answered, not taking his gaze off the man in the grey suit, who once again blew his nose.

The man kept walking and Malone had to run gently to keep up with him and was unaware that he was being followed by the ice cream vendor, pushing his barrow.

The man in grey turned to face Malone who staggered to a halt. He felt strange. Had he been out in the sun too long? The grass turned into sky and back again. He remembered the ice cream vendor's barrow coming towards him as he slumped to the ground; his chocolate mint ice cream splattering the pathway.

Distant voices and screams were heard as passers-by shouted in shock. Malone was down but still conscious and the last thing he saw was the chubby cheeks of the ice cream vendor and the man in the grey suit kneeling beside him.

Steve had been distracted by a little girl who fell into the Lake just in front of him and without hesitation he'd rescued her. He was thanked by her grateful mother who panicked when her daughter fell.

Steve resumed his position, his eyes scanning the area and perimeter of the boathouse. Jimmy was gone. Contact had obviously been made.

'Shit,' Steve said quietly to himself, then reset his eyes where he'd last seen Malone. A crowd that had pooled were dispersing, and now Steve could see the ice cream vendor and another man in a grey suit helping a pedestrian back to his feet and dragging him away.

Shit, shit, shit. The body they were taking away was Malone. Steve recognised the brightly coloured trousers that Jimmy had worn. The three were headed along a pathway towards East Drive. The vendor's cart had been abandoned and Malone's famous hat lay on the ground beside it.

Chandler and Johnston had witnessed the abduction and Johnston was instructed to follow but at a discreet distance. Steve knew he had to catch up to Malone before his captors reached 79th Street Transverse where Steve assumed there would be a car waiting.

He quickened his pace, overtaking Johnston. He could see his quarry leaving the park area as the long, black Sedan slowly crept into view beside the Ramble. It only stopped a few seconds before heading off towards Central Park West. Malone had been taken.

Steve stood as he watched the car leave, its breaking tail lights ablaze as it hit the curve of the road. Steve was annoyed with himself. He should have been more vigilant. He had persuaded Malone to play an active role and even when Malone appeared in his outrageous outfit he felt some people would remember the brightly coloured clothes, but hey, this was New York, and anything goes.

Steve reclaimed Malone's hat from the pathway. He'd obviously been drugged and God knows what would happen to him now.

Lieutenant Chandler appeared at Steve's side. 'Well, that's another fine mess we're in,' he said flatly. 'Malone will spill the beans, especially when he knows I'm involved. I may as well go back to the precinct and clear out my desk.'

'Is that all you can say Lieutenant? You're not really bothered about Malone, are you?' Steve said.

Chandler stroked the side of his face and chin. 'Nope! Couldn't care less, Donaldson. He's been a thorn in my side for years; maybe this is payback time.'

Steve was astounded. He knew Chandler was a product of the old school. A good cop with a stickler for detail and justice, and who wanted very much to catch and expose criminals, no matter who they were or what influence they had. In fact, the bigger they were the more the Lieutenant liked to see them fall.

But here was Jimmy Malone, a New York Times reporter, and Chandler couldn't care less. Malone had put his neck on the line, albeit for a scoop, but also to expose dirty deals in the Pentagon and yet Chandler was just prepared to hang him out to dry without batting an eyelid.

Steve thought about Jimmy. A good reporter maybe, but he was not trained to take the punishment that would undoubtedly be administered. That was not in the game plan.

Detective Sergeant Johnston appeared. He'd followed the car as far as he could. He had its Virginia registration.

'So what do we do now?' Chandler asked. 'My job and career are on the line and that little shit Malone when pressed will sing.'

Steve fell silent. The last thing he had considered was Malone being abducted, but then on reflection it was obvious Randall, or whoever he sent, would not have negotiated in such a public place, especially as he knew Riker was dead.

Steve was angry with himself. He had not only jeopardised Jimmy Malone's safety but also any chance of solving Claire Monroe's murder. Somebody big in the Pentagon was involved, after all, the black Sedan used in the abduction had all the hallmarks of such an operation and Johnston had identified the Virginia registration plate.

Steve also realised that it wouldn't take long before whoever took Jimmy Malone knew Jimmy was not posing as Riker, and had not made the telephone call to Randall, but as Lieutenant Chandler pointed out, under physical pressure Jimmy would crack. He may be a hotshot reporter but under torture, well, that was a whole different ball game.

Steve wondered how much pain Malone would take under interrogation before he spilled his side of the story, but in any event, no matter how brave the little man was he would talk. After all, his only involvement was for the scoop to expose some bigwig in Washington.

The thought then occurred to Steve and he turned to Lieutenant Chandler. 'It'd be my guess Lieutenant that whoever took Jimmy could still be in the area. After all, they'll want whatever information he's supposed to know, then they'll wait for further instruction and finish him. Another loose end tidied up.'

'So, what are you saying Donaldson?' Chandler replied.

Steve thought for a moment. 'I'm thinking a disused warehouse. It's got to be close, somewhere where his captors can carry out their interrogation without disturbance; then, when they're sure about that, you'll probably be fishing another body out of the East River. Of course, the other alternative is that Jimmy might be braver than we give him credit for and after, shall we say some persuasive interrogation, he'll be released to expose ourselves and what each of us knows. Then Plan B will be put into operation and once Jimmy has fulfilled his needs and once we're all dealt with, well, he'll have written his last scoop. There are too many warehouses for us to check without help, and even then it would be like looking for a needle in a haystack.'

They fell silent, each thinking the worst.

'What about an airport?' Johnston volunteered. 'A private plane to take him out of the area. There would be no problem with security clearance; after all, it's Washington we're dealing with.

Steve glanced at Chandler. 'Johnston may just have offered another possibility,' he said.

'It'd still be too public. Whoever took Malone would, in my opinion, not risk another loose end,' Chandler replied.

Steve paused, deep in thought. 'What about another airfield?' he said.

'Where?' Chandler responded, his mind blank as he had no suggestion to offer.

Steve hesitated before replying. 'What about Teterboro, out past Ridgefield Park and Fort Lee? The car had headed towards Central Park West. It wouldn't take too long to hit the Henry Hudson Parkway, and then across the George Washington Bridge and onto the airport.'

Lieutenant Chandler started smiling, then, his eyes wide, began to laugh.

'What's so funny, Lieutenant?' Steve said frowning.

'Oh, I was just imagining that when these guys realise they have the wrong man and they're 20,000 feet up in the air; how they'll teach that little shit Malone to fly without a parachute and I'll never hear or see the son of a bitch again.'

Steve stared at Chandler. He had not appreciated just how much the Lieutenant disliked Malone.

Chandler now became serious. 'Okay Donaldson, it's over. Johnston and I are out, capeesh? Finished with this caper. We were prepared to give it a shot but hey, enough is enough.'

'Thought you wanted the same as me, Lieutenant? Thought you were a stickler for detail? Are you really telling me you are out?'

Lieutenant Chandler turned to leave and Steve grabbed his arm. Chandler eyeballed Steve, then finally removed Steve's hand from his arm. 'Goodbye, Donaldson. Johnston,' he said 'we're finished here.'

Steve watched the two detectives leave and gaped at the Ramble, where half an hour before poor Jimmy

Malone had been kidnapped. Jimmy only wanted his scoop and Steve had encouraged him to play an active role. It was an adventure for Jimmy, but Steve knew it would not be a game. Maybe if he contacted Randall he could save Jimmy's fate when they realised they had the wrong man?

It was a risk, but it was a risk worth taking.

Chapter 49

Glen Randall's direct telephone line rang out. It rang four times before he answered. 'Yeah!' Randall said.

There was silence on the line, then Steve spoke. 'Riker here, Randall. You got the wrong guy. I was there as agreed, waiting and watching your monkeys make assholes of themselves, picking off an innocent bystander, who knows nothing.' Steve was hoping that his call may save Jimmy Malone's life, assuming the reporter hadn't spilled the beans of his true involvement with unravelling the Claire Monroe case and his partnership with himself. Steve allowed for the fact that it would be a long shot if Malone hadn't talked, but at least he was giving it a go, especially as he was on his own again, as Chandler and Johnston had bailed. He was back to square one and not any closer to solving the murder of Claire Monroe.

'I still want paying Randall,' Steve let his statement penetrate the line.

Glen Randall sat bolt upright. He'd been told that the abduction was successful, but as yet no information surfaced as the target was still out of it with the drugs they had administered.

'Where are you … Riker, or whatever your real name is?' Randall paused. 'Riker is dead,' he stated flatly and with confidence 'so I don't know what game you're playing, but I ain't buying it. So, whoever and wherever you are, go fuck yourself.'

With that, Glen Randall terminated the call.

Chapter 50

Chandler paced his small office with its plain walls, old filing cabinet and simple desk, and stared at his office door with its glazed panel and his name and rank stencilled in large, black capital letters on the other side. He shook his head and threw an undrunk cup of coffee at his door; his frustration fighting with his conscience. He would need to meet Jericho. He had no choice.

Lieutenant Chandler stood under the awning of Rikki's Café on Mulberry Street. It was early morning and a damp, grey cloak hung over the city, enveloping it with clouds that would surely promise rain.

There were already drips from the awning from a previous downpour, their cascading bombs of water gathering weight as they crescendoed off the sidewalk before exploding into disintegration.

It had gone 7:00am and Chandler shivered in his blue lightweight raincoat. Once or twice he had turned towards the front door of the café expecting to see Rikki, or indeed Donaldson, but as yet there was no sign of movement from within.

Where was Rikki? Chandler thought, as he felt the dampness of the early morning penetrate his bones, and more to the point, where was that son of a bitch Jericho?

Chandler marched his feet up and down to keep his circulation going, and blew his hot breath into his cupped hands. There was still no movement from within. He did not see the other pair of eyes watching him and waiting patiently.

'Okay, Rubber Duck, let's go inside.' Chandler turned to face Jericho as Rikki opened the front door of the café, keeping the lights extinguished.

Chandler followed Steve to their usual booth as Rikki prepared their muffins and coffee. 'Where the hell have you been? I'm wet through, standing out there. What kept you Donaldson?'

Steve stared across the café, then fixed his gaze on his contact. 'I wasn't late Lieutenant. I just have to be sure you weren't being followed.'

'Hey, now you listen to me Donaldson. I'm here only because ...'

'Because! Because, Lieutenant, your conscience wouldn't let you walk away from all this and although you can't stand Malone you could never be party to him suffering his fate without some attempt to save him, and hopefully find out more of who's behind all this. I suspect, Lieutenant, you're as keen to find out who has the power to close murder cases and your department, just as I am keen to expose Claire Monroe's killers, and who also authorised my own demise.'

'Now you listen to me, Donaldson,' Chandler replied. 'I've had all this up to my neck,' he said, placing his right hand across his throat 'and you know what, I've changed my mind. I'm outta here. I'm sorry I came. All this cat and mouse crap. Jericho calling Rubber Duck, need to meet.' Chandler mimicked sarcastically. 'What do you take me for, Donaldson? This is not a game, and anyway, I'm too old for all this … got it? I've had enough.'

Chandler paused. He was angry, and so sat quietly, letting his anger go. 'Okay, you're correct, my conscience is bothering me but I'm not in any position to fight this and the fact that the Pentagon is involved rules me out. Understand? And if you're wise, Donaldson, you'll let it go too.'

'What about Malone, Lieutenant?' Steve asked.

'What about him?' Chandler echoed. 'He'd drop you and me if his butt was on the line. You got him involved, Donaldson, so you save the motherfucker.' Chandler's voice was rising in pitch, its decibels climbing.

Rikki produced their muffins and coffee.

'Take a weight off Rikki,' Steve said to his friend

Rikki pulled up a chair. 'You want me to listen Steve, okay! But I see and I hear but I don't get involved, all right? I run my café; that is my world … my life. Whatever you guys do you do, but I don't need to know.'

Steve smiled. He respected Rikki; after all he'd been there for Maria and for him when they both needed protection and a roof over their heads. 'Answer me this, Rik. Listen to what I have to say, then tell me in all honesty what you would do.'

'Hey, Steve, buddy, as I said, I don't get involved. You want a coffee, no problem. You want an Amaretto, no problem. I can fix it. You want my advice, whatever is going down, I … I … If it's as bad as I think it may be then walk away. Live for another day, you don't need whatever shit you're involved in.'

Lieutenant Chandler shrugged his shoulders. 'That's what I said, Rikki,' he said, now staring between Steve and the café owner.

'You agree with me?' Rikki blurted out.

'Yeah, I agree with you Rikki,' Chandler said smiling.

'You're a cop, Lieutenant. I hear a good one. Maybe you are. Maybe you ain't. But you're a cop.'

Chandler nodded. 'I hope a good one,' he said once again, allowing a smile to escape.

'Hey cop. Don't you smile at me. Ah got a business to run. So don't start to agree with me. Capeesh? Lieutenant, if Steve here needs your help it must be pretty big because he's good; ex-marine, Special Forces. Been on the Force too, so if he needs you Lieutenant, if it's for all the right reasons, then *help* him … okay?'

'I thought you'd just agreed – walk away. Live for another day,' Chandler said in surprise at Rikki's change of heart.

'Did I say that, Lieutenant? Forget what I said. Help Steve. That is my advice. There will be no charge for the coffee and muffins if you do. Steve is a good friend. He's helped my family many times and …'

'Hey, I wasn't payin' for the coffee and muffins anyway,' Chandler said.

'That's what you think, Lieutenant. We all pay somehow for decisions we make.'

Rikki returned to his counter, leaving Chandler and Steve alone once again.

'You're crazy Donaldson, you know that?'

'In or out, Chandler; just one last time,' Steve said.

Lieutenant Chandler narrowed his eyes, allowing his brows to break into a frown.

'For Malone, Lieutenant, if nothing else,' Steve said, hoping that Chandler would reconsider and stay on the case.

'I can't stand that little weasel, but I can't just walk away. Well, not yet, anyway.'

'Good,' Steve said.

Chandler shrugged his shoulders, then smiled. 'Where do we start?' he said. 'That little motherfucker better appreciate what I'm doing for him.'

Steve allowed himself a smile. 'Good decision, Lieutenant.'

Steve continued talking, just to bring Chandler up to date. 'I telephoned Randall at the Pentagon again; wanted to see if I could find out more about Malone's situation. Told him his clowns missed me and abducted an innocent bystander by mistake. He told me that Riker was dead and made it clear he wasn't buying my story. In fact, told me in no uncertain terms to fuck off. That in itself told me he's rattled, and it also meant that Jimmy Malone's position is not a good one.'

Chandler listened, then nodded. He extended his hand across the table. Steve returned the gesture as the two men shook hands.

'Let's do this thing,' Chandler said.

Lieutenant Chandler and Steve listed the facts in sequence as they knew them.

'Let's see what we got,' Chandler said.

'One. Claire Monroe murdered and made to look like a hit and run accident. There were no fingerprints taken. We knew her identity from her purse, and as it wasn't a crime – just an accident by some son of a bitch that didn't stop. No one came forward, therefore no investigation … case closed.

'Two. Nothing else in association with Claire's death until an attempt made on your life Steve, six months later. Had the hit and run been successful, it would never have been tied or associated to the Claire Monroe incident. And the fact that you were a PI would automatically rule out further investigation. No case to follow.

'Three. You get involved with Riker and Gennero. They've got your number. You find the car they used in Rusty's yard. They kidnap you, but you escape.

'Four. I pull them in for questioning on your hunch. They don't have credentials but they appear as if they're from the Department of Justice. Riker also threatened me to my face to close all enquiries. Very arrogant.

'Five. Fire at Rusty's junkyard made to look like an accident. Poor old Rusty dies. Probably set by Riker and Gennero.

'Six. Riker and Gennero become loose ends and end up fished out of the East River.

'Seven. The District Attorney's office instructs our department to close all cases from Monroe's to Rusty's and Riker and Gennero's. Their action is backed-up by my Captain.

'Eight. You break into Rusty's burnt out yard. You have a file with Riker's name on it; by the way, I assume you still have it?'

Steve nodded but let Chandler continue with his appraisal.

'Nine. Charlie O'Brien is also instructed to close the case on Riker and Gennero but gives me a number which he found in Riker's coat when bagging up his belongings.

'Ten. The same number appears in Riker's file that you have, but in reverse order.

'Eleven. The name Randall is disclosed on the file and when you ring it and follow it up you find your through to a Senior Military Liaison Officer at the Pentagon. In fact it's Colonel Randall.

'Twelve. You telephone this Randall again, arrange a meet at Loeb's Boathouse, Central Park, New York. You somehow involve that little squirt Malone of The Times; we watched and witnessed Malone's abduction. Randall's men assuming he's you.

'Is that about correct so far?' Chandler said.

Steve took several moments of reflecting the sequence of events. 'Yeah!' he replied, 'that's about right. I just hope I haven't done for Malone, that's all.'

Chandler leaned back in his booth. 'I'll not miss him Donaldson but that does not mean that I want him to end up dead somewhere wearing concrete boots, especially when he pretended to be you.'

Silence reigned between the two men as each contemplated Jimmy Malone's fate.

Chapter 51

'Okay! Wake up!' Jimmy's shoulder was shaken, then he was slapped on his cheek as the large spotlights focused on him. 'Come on, come on! Wake up!' the voice said, shadowing part of the spotlight ray.

Malone opened one eye. He tried to open both but the swelling from the blows he'd sustained kept his left eye closed. 'Ah don't know anything. You got the wrong guy,' Jimmy blurted out. 'I was just having an ice cream in the park. The last thing I remember is feeling dizzy, the sky upturned, then you guys were hitting me, so I don't know who you are or what you want, but I can't tell you anything.

The two interrogators under different circumstances may have released their prisoner; after all, his pleading, innocent expression of his face didn't fit with the profile they'd been given. Their remit was to obtain as much information as possible and then dispose of the poor son of a bitch.

'Okay schmuck. One more time. Who d'ya work for? You know Claire Monroe don't you?' the tall interrogator pressed.

'I told you, I'm a reporter for The Times. I don't know a Claire Monroe, in fact I know nothin'.' Malone said, struggling with his bonds and attempting to hold it together.

'So, what do you report? Eh! Eh?' his captor said, prodding him.

'Mainly crime, and anything that's of the public interest,' Jimmy answered as he felt and tasted the dried blood on his lips.

'Do you do impersonations of dead people?'

'What? What are you talkin' about? Ah don't understand.'

'Okay, we'll make it easy for you. Someone, maybe you, telephoned our boss, made a threat, then arranged a meet at Loeb's Boathouse in the park.'

'So? It wasn't me!' Jimmy exclaimed. 'Who's your boss?' he said.

'Oh! Wouldn't you like to know?'

'Well, who?' Jimmy asked again. 'Who am I supposed to have threatened?'

'None of your goddamn business,' his other captor said, as he then administered another slap on Jimmy's swollen eye which caused Malone's head to jerk sideways, jarring his neck.

'But you were there at the Boathouse, all dressed up like a clown and certainly not like a New York Times reporter. So, if you're not the guy we're after, who are you representing?'

'Ah told you already. I'm Jimmy Malone of The New York Times. Why would I make something like that up?' Malone replied, aware of his face stinging and the taste of dried blood being reactivated from the blow he'd just sustained.

'Ah need a drink … water please … Ah can't talk with these lights in my face.'

Jimmy Malone only heard the voice of the silhouetted figures and never saw his interrogators approach him out of the shadows. They set about him once more, hoping to force a confession, then one of his captors spoke.

'Get the punk some water,' he said to his associate. 'Maybe that will loosen his tongue.'

Water was received via a plastic cup and Malone gulped greedily. His gums stung on his tongue, but he was still dry.

'Now talk, Malone. If that is indeed your name.'

Jimmy hesitated. He had to get himself free. 'Okay, as I said, my name is Jimmy Malone of The New York Times. I'm a reporter. I was in the park following up a lead on a case I'd previously ran an article on.'

'Go on!' his captor's voice said.

'Had a tip-off that whoever killed a guy called Riker would be in the park at Loeb's Boathouse. I was informed that if I wanted the story then I was to be there.' Jimmy paused. 'That's all I have,' he said. 'I dressed like this so whoever called me would recognise me and who knows, make contact. I guess he never showed up because the last thing I remember is buying an ice cream and shadowy faces looking down on me. Then you guys beating me up and asking questions I don't have answers to.'

'So, who's your tip-off and what article were you writing about?'

'Oh, some dude and his partner washed up on the East River, but as far as my contact is concerned, it was just a phone call – a message; I never met him. He just mentioned Riker.'

'So, how did you know who to expect?'

'We'd agreed he would approach me but we'll never know now, will we, since you two clowns abducted me first.'

Malone didn't see the other blow coming, but he sure felt it. It was so hard that he fell over, still bound to his wooden chair which splintered into pieces, its back and seat still attached to his bonds.

'Don't get lippy with me,' the voice said. 'Now stand up.'

Jimmy Malone afforded himself a grin. 'You should be on the friggin' stage,' he said.

'Funny man, eh?' the voice answered, as his foot, encased in a high black polished leather shoe, connected with Jimmy's abdomen.

'Oh Christ! I think I'm gonna die,' Jimmy squealed.

The voice laughed. 'Maybe the next article you write will be your own obituary.' The voice then walked once again towards his partner, the bright spotlight shielding their identity.

'I need a piss,' Jimmy cried out. 'I mean I got to go now.'

His two captors ignored him and carried on whispering to each other.

'Ooh! I gotta go, please, please.'

The two men stared at one another. 'Okay, untie the little shit and take him downstairs to the latrines.'

The use of the word latrines told Jimmy that his captors were of military origin, although they certainly were not dressed that way.

'Okay, up you get.'

'Untie me, Jesus, I gotta go. Fuck, help.'

'Okay, okay. A switchblade knife was produced and the bonds that secured Jimmy to the remains of the broken wooden chair snapped, allowing the splintered wood to fall like spaghetti onto the concrete floor, their pieces forming points of a compass.

'This way, bud,' the younger voice said as he led Jimmy towards the stairwell. Malone was now aware of the derelict building he was being held in. The broken panes of glass housed in their steel frames depicted the age of unuse, together with the dark green painted brick with its off-white border at the top. Conduit piping was still intact in the ceiling in some places, although their distribution roses were without caps others were simply suspended vertically where their joints were broken with their wiring exposed. Peeling paintwork and worn steps told Malone there was very little chance of being discovered.

At the stairwell he noticed a large, red painted number 3; once again its paint old and faded. So, he was on floor 3 in a disused factory. Malone guessed maybe at the docks beside a pier. There were so many piers along the Hudson and he realised his escape would be a tall order.

Malone heard a plane go overhead. Wherever he was being held was on a flight path. He could hear the aeroplane engines cut back, so this location must be near an airfield. Malone racked his brains but the beatings he'd sustained were not allowing him to function properly.

His captor and he arrived on a long corridor and to the right, facing another set of stairs were signs in capital letters: "TOILET."

'Go relieve yourself, Malone. Don't try anything funny or I'll blow your brains out,' the voice said, tapping his jacket, indicating he was armed.

Malone entered the toilet area. The stink of unclean urine and excrement hit the back of his throat and even though his eyes were swollen and bruised they started to water. Cubicle doors hung loose, balancing on one hinge and covered with graffiti, signifying their abuse. Old paper was strewn everywhere and the slab urinal wore green and brown stains along its length where the sparge pipe was broken.

There was wire netting shielding the broken windows and the cords from the overhead fanlights being disconnected rendered their operation useless.

Malone relieved himself quickly. He was sore, his clothes a mess and his shoes stuck to the damp debris of the room, but he realised this would be his only chance of escape and he had to take it if he were to survive.

He glanced up at the old window panes, cracked, and in some cases, broken; all filthy with the film of dirt, birds' droppings and spiders' webs indicating that wherever his captors were holding him was certainly unused, and most likely derelict. Malone heard another aeroplane overhead, the drone of its engines, as once again the pilot cut the throttle. It was landing. Again, Malone thought he must be near an airport but where, and which one? He attempted to recall his last movements and moments but only remembered the pavement floating upwards towards him at breakneck speed. He did not remember anything else.

'Hurry the fuck up,' a voice shouted from outside, his captor impatient with how long it was taking for Malone to pee.

Shit!' Malone said. 'Wow!' he exclaimed. 'I've slipped, ouch! Help! Help me!' he shouted. 'I've done my back in, Fuck.'

'Hey, what's going on?'

'Help me please, I'm hurt,' Malone shouted, feigning injury.

'For fuck's sake, Malone, get your ass out here … now!'

'Ooh! God, I think I've broken somethin'! Can't move,' he shouted, with deep gasps and short breath outbursts.

'You son of a bitch, get out here.'

Jimmy fell silent now. He just stood there behind a division wall with the long 4ft rusty angle iron bar in his hands, held high, ready to swipe a clear shot.

'Malone,' the voice repeated.

Again. Silence.

Malone heard his captor sigh, then the shuffle of his feet over the debris as he walked into the male toilet area. The unsuspecting vicious blow that Malone inflicted as he swiped the angle iron bar with as much might as he could muster, using it like a baseball bat, connected first time, which was good because Jimmy didn't have the strength to repeat another.

He heard the bone crunch as the bar connected with his captor's head; blood spurted everywhere. His attack was successful as he witnessed the body slumped, helpless and unconscious on the dark, littered concrete floor.

'Take that, you fuck,' Malone said out loud to the body that lay motionless at his feet. Then, quickly sensing the passage of time, moved swiftly towards the stairwell. He saw the discoloured faded red number 3 on the slime-stained wall. The old plaster debris on the stairs was precarious, but Malone negotiated each step as quietly and as quickly as he could. He had reached the ground floor where the landing broadened to a much larger span space. He was taking his bearings when the shot ricocheted off the wall beside him. He didn't have to be careful now, just find a way out of the old ware-house.

Another shot pinged off another wall, but just like the first, missed him completely.

Malone ran, he could hear the voice yelling as its owner's feet scrambled down the stairwell, the sound coming closer and closer. Nowhere to hide, Malone real-ised he was better off outside, irrespective of what was out there.

He could see other buildings just like his own. All appeared disused, unoccupied. Where the hell was he?

There was a sudden quietness, except for the echo of his own footsteps and Malone stopped and turned. The man chasing him had disappeared.

Malone didn't take time to consider whether that was fortunate or not; all he knew was he had to escape. Jimmy Malone took risks to obtain a scoop but never before had his life been on the line like it was now. His adrenaline running high, he scrambled his way between the old discoloured peeling, concrete columns that separated the bays and obviously supported the upper floors of the old building towards the end where there was a large metal door; its sliding frame and guide rusted and deep-brown with lack of use. There was another smaller door handle within the frame of the broad door and Malone prayed that he'd be able to achieve his escape through it and away from his captor who obviously now had every intent to kill him.

Malone reached the door, frantically fumbling with its old lock and handle. The echo of his actions reverber-ated along the corridor he had travelled, but there was still no sign of his enemies.

'Fuck it. Oh shit! Open, you motherfucker,' he shouted at the door as he turned the handle and pulled with all his might.

Malone, although tired and perspiring, now gave it his all, then the door opened, making him fall backwards to the concrete floor. His hands were cut, his hair damp, his breathing heavy as he painfully rose to his feet. Gathering all his strength he stumbled outside, glad to be out in the open air. He crawled on his hands and knees. When he looked up, he froze.

Chapter 52

Randall's internal extension rang, its light flashing, signifying a call.

Glen picked up the handset. 'Randall,' he said.

'You got the package?' the voice asked, then, without waiting for an answer, continued. 'What does he know? You got all the information this time before you paid him?'

Glen Randall, recognised his superior's voice and slowly found the strength and courage to confirm his reply. 'Not exactly, we got a package, and some info but it's not correct, therefore payment has not been made.'

Silence filled the air, then Cleaver spoke. 'You'd better get over here and your story and reasons better be good.'

'Yessir,' Randall replied.

Cleaver spoke again. 'Has our situation been compromised?'

Again, there was silence on the line, indicating that there was a possible breach. Cleaver did not mince his words.

'Get over here now,' he snarled into the handset, 'and I mean now.' With that, Cleaver stood and ran his fingers over his head. He did not need any complications regarding Claire Monroe. Not now, not ever. He paced his office floor and took out the letter he'd received and re-read its contents:

MURDERER
RAPIST
CAYMAN
TRAITOR
I'LL GET YOU
YOUR TIME IS COMIN'

Chapter 53

On Grand Cayman, Rodriquez busied himself on final preparations to arrange transfer of the drug shipment from the incoming freighter. The Providence, which although registered in London, had been constructed in Mexico and was equipped with specially designed hidden panels to take such a cargo, and as a private commission these panels were unknown to regulatory authorities. The ship had passed its usual inspections and was insured through the proper channels with Lloyds of London.

The heroin was neatly packaged in two kilo plastic bags and protected by an outer layer of Visqueen and concealed in wooden crates with layers of straw.

The weather was fine at the moment, but there was a squall forecast which would mean the sea would be choppy. That could hinder and delay the transfer but on the positive side the cloud cover would protect any such movements from the Coast Guard. The transfer had to be completed prior to the usual custom check and certainly before The Providence docked on the mainland.

The risks were high and Rodriquez had competition from pirates operating out of both Jamaica and Haiti. So, as well as smuggling the merchandise and concealing it from the official authorities, he also had to contend with other operators who would gladly steal his contraband.

One consolation, however, was General Cleaver Harris made sure he was handsomely paid as well as providing enough funds to make sure Rodriquez organised the very best of protection to ensure each shipment arrived safely and on time.

The next few days therefore would be busy. Rodriquez had been reliably informed that the Authorities had been trailing The Providence for days. Spotter planes had been seen out in the Atlantic and although no other ship was in sight it was obvious that The Providence was under surveillance. There would therefore be a good chance of a full Customs search, and while this concerned Rodriquez he still felt confident that the cargo in the hidden panels would elude discovery. He had not informed Cleaver of the delay and undoubtedly pending search; that would only have brought more heat to the situation and besides, Cleaver paid him well to take responsibility of such matters.

Rodriquez radioed The Providence which was anchored out at sea, waiting on instruction. She was two days from port so the transfer had to be completed within the next eight hours.

Rodriquez looked at the sky as another aeroplane passed overhead. It was just a passenger jet, so he relaxed a little.

Rodriquez longed for the day when, after making enough money from his unlawful activities, he could retire. Live a simple and stress-free life; maybe even have a wife and children instead of having his manly needs catered for by the easy women who frequented the local bars.

He waited patiently for a response to his call as he patted his dog affectionately.

Captain Drummond spoke quietly. 'Thank you, amigo. Consignment is ready for despatch.' He then gave Rodriquez The Providence's location coordinates. 'Can you give me an ETA please?' Captain Drummond released his push button switch of his radio to allow the return message to be transmitted.

'Doctor arriving by water, approximately two hours. Be ready. Hope your patient okay till then.'

'Thank you,' Captain Drummond replied. 'We'll be ready,' he said, then signed off.

Chapter 54

Rodriquez Mahon was Cleaver's go-between from the shipping that brought the contraband into the US. His main role was to organise the shipment cargo onto a particular vessel manufactured to accommodate such a job. The captain's close officers were also involved and Rodriquez made sure they were handsomely remunerated for their involvement and also their silence.

He had links to the drug barons who were happy to negotiate business with him, just as long as supplies were regular and scheduled on time.

The money involved was unprecedented but Cleaver, with his own private administration and offshore accounts in the Caymans, made sure that there was more than enough to bankroll the operations. Cleaver's ambition was power and although he was powerful in the Pentagon, that was never enough to satisfy his driven ambitions. He therefore relied on Rodriquez Mahon and knew that as long as the money was being paid then Rodriquez and his business associates would be able to finance their operations and in turn make vast sums of profit.

Rodriquez was streetwise. He had to be, and although he resided on Grand Cayman near Seven Mile Beach, his operations did extend to Little Cayman and Cayman Brac as there were fewer occupancy numbers; Little Brac being almost uninhabited and apart from the abundancies of wildlife of sea turtles, lizards and crocodiles it was a great place to easily hide captured contraband for the next move in operating it along the chain.

The designated ship carrying the cargo would anchor at some given coordinates, then Rodriquez's interceptors – fast-moving speedboats – would take transfer of the goods and take them to one of the hidden caves on the Islands, just as the famous pirates and buccaneers had done many centuries before, when they used to capture Spanish vessels laden with gold and treasure returning to their homeland.

Rodriquez had a romantic notion that he was just like one of those buccaneers operating on the high seas in modern times, with stakes and profit much larger than his forbearers.

Cleaver worked with the man, in fact each had an understanding between them. As long as the money was right for Rodriquez then Cleaver through him could keep his ambitions alive and activate his specially trained and selected marines for his own benefits. Who really cared what the President thought, or the CIA and FBI for that matter? It was all about power and profit and Cleaver wanted it all.

Without exception, it didn't matter how it was achieved.

Chapter 55

Names were never used over the wire and certainly never any reference to the cargo being transferred. All manoeuvres were paid for and built on trust by the operators concerned. Any break in the chain could and would affect each other, so it was very important to keep that status quo; besides, many of the individuals involved were of influential positions and any exposure could topple governments as well as embarrassing exposure for those involved.

The Providence sat in the sea, the swirling waves cascading up and down her plumb line. Captain Drummond was anxious to move on. They too had observed the spotter planes overhead and knew that their stationary position would be reported.

The last radio call had been over three hours ago and contact was supposed to have occurred one hour before at the latest. Captain Drummond knew he would require to radio once more if no sign of uplift was forthcoming.

He scanned the horizon with his Navy binoculars. There was nothing. He swore out loud, cursing the delay as every minute without transfer increased the risk of a full-blown inspection by the Coast Guard.

Once again he lifted his binoculars to his eyes and was about to lower them when he saw it.

There was a small speck that hadn't been there before. In fact, there were three of them. Drummond concentrated on the fast-moving specks that sped towards The Providence, but they were still too far away to be identified.

It started to rain heavily; the dark, overcast sky shedding its tears, making the sea choppier. The Providence creaked and groaned, wanting to be free but was held fast by her anchorage.

Captain Drummond focused on the approaching vessels. Rodriquez was late; this could be his men now he thought, unless …

'Assemble all hands, Brown,' Drummond instructed his officer.

'Sir!' Brown replied, with a questionable tone.

'Just do it, man, and be quick about it. I fear we may have some unexpected visitors,' Drummond said, his eyes now glued through his binoculars at the fast-approaching boats.

Rodriquez and his men were never this late, and there had been no radio contact either, Drummond pondered.

The crew had assembled on the foredeck and Captain Drummond took his place to explain his fears. 'You will no doubt have observed the fast-moving approaching vessels on our starboard side. I can't identify them at this stage, and indeed there has been no radio contact from them. I therefore assume we are shortly to be attacked and boarded by pirates. Pirates who not only are interested in our cargo, but pirates who also want to seize this ship and you – her crew.'

Some eyes had drifted from their captain out towards sea as the remainder of his words were spoken. 'Brown, have the crew break out any weapons we have on board. Select your men. The remainder of the crew must hide. Go to the engine room, lock yourselves in, but hide and do not come out unless you hear my voice, or Mr Brown's, understand?'

The crew, for most part, did not understand but they were men who followed orders impeccably and so dispersed to carry out their instructions.

'What is it, Captain?' Brown asked, stepping closer to his superior and out of earshot of other crew members.

Drummond sighed. 'Our contact is late, Brown. There's been no signal either way. I fear we may be about to be taken over by pirates seeking to occupy our ship.

'Pirates?' Brown echoed.

Drummond nodded. He'd had previous experience of their activities when voyaging in Somalia, off the African coast many years before. 'Yes, Mister. They use fast small boats that can outrun a vessel of our size. They will be armed, probably with automatic weapons. It's not just our cargo they seek either. They'll want our ship, and more importantly, our crew.

Crew, Sir?' Brown questioned.

'Yes, Brown, our crew. They make good hostages for negotiation to acquire money and I fear some may die until their demands are met by either the owners of this ship or their relations. That's why I have ordered them below. I need you and your chosen men to stay up top and defend our ship and the impending attack.

Again, Captain Drummond trained his binoculars on the approaching craft. He could now see the wall of curtain spray that was being freed from the ocean from their speed. It would only be a short time before the inevitable occurred.

Captain Drummond had now forgotten about his hidden cargo. His first priority was to his crew and The Providence. There was no question he was about to surrender his ship; that just wasn't going to happen.

'Brown,' he shouted. 'Are the men safe in the engine room? Is the ship battened down? Are your men you've selected ready?'

'Yes Sir, yes Sir, yes Sir.' Brown replied.

'Okay Mister, let us prepare for this little fandangle.' Captain Drummond adjusted the focus on his high-powered binoculars once more and couldn't believe his eyes. 'Shit,' he said out loud, then added "we're about to be boarded. It's not pirates, Brown, it's Customs and the Coast Guard.' Drummond groaned as he spoke the words, fully aware that a thorough inspection of his ship was imminent.

'Keep to our story, Brown. We had engine trouble which is why we've been anchored. We then thought that we were about to be attacked by pirates and therefore took all precautions to defend our ship and secure our crew, should the worst have occurred. Is that clear, Brown?'

Officer Brown nodded. 'Yes Sir,' he muttered quietly.

'Is that clear, Brown? I didn't hear you.'

'Yes Sir,' Brown replied, more audibly this time.

'Okay,' Drummond replied. 'Let me do the talking.'

Chapter 56

The three interceptors were visible now. Captain Drummond could now see the armed men and the powerful searchlights from the Coast Guard's boats blinding the sky.

'You ready, Brown? We'll explain as I said, allow them to carry out a full inspection, then we'll be on our way.'

'What about our contact, Captain?'

'What about him?' Captain Drummond echoed. 'He wasn't here. We had no choice. Besides, these loons won't find anything and the fact that we've been cleared will protect us. Rodriquez will just have to wait until the return journey. In any event, that's his problem. It's hardly our fault he didn't pick up on time. Usual Caribbeans. Can't trust them.

'What's that approaching on our portside?' Brown said, observing the cloud of smoke on the horizon.

Captain Drummond swivelled his direction and raised his glasses. 'Oh God, no!' He allowed his binoculars to rest on his chest now, feeling their weight. 'It's the Navy,' he said quietly. All of a sudden his mind went blank. This was not happening. The Customs on one side, the Navy on the other. Obviously there had been a tip-off. That would explain the no-show or warning from Rodriquez.

This was no random inspection. Hell was about to be unleashed. God, he was too old for all this crap.

Drummond silently promised himself that once the inspection was over, and hopefully he could make alternative arrangements to dispose of his hidden cargo, that this would be his last assignment. He wanted out. Retire, buy a little cottage by the sea in England, or even better, a bar on the quayside in New Zealand. The image of New Zealand brought back fond memories and momentarily he was lost in those thoughts when he heard Brown's voice.

'They're here, Captain. Customs and Coast Guard.'

'I know, Brown, I know,' Drummond replied in a whisper.

Chapter 57

The large Navy cruiser moved closer on The Providence's portside. Captain Drummond could now see its crew on its deck. They were all at their posts; their guns manned and ready to fire.

On the Providence's starboard side a voice from a megaphone sounded, travelling across the air and penetrating above the noise of the wind and rain

'Prepare yourselves for inspection. Customs and Coast Guard here,' the voice shouted as the three Long Range Interceptors, or LRIs as they were known, docked on The Providence's starboard.

Captain Drummond completely ignored the Navy cruiser on The Providence's portside, and only waved in a friendly manner towards the Customs Captain.

'Better get the crew reassembled, Brown, we now know it's not pirates.'

'Yes Sir.'

'I have a call to make, Brown,' Drummond said, as he was about to make his way to the radio room.

'But Captain, they're docking now.'

'Then be quick with your orders, Mr Brown.'

Captain Drummond then entered the radio room. He switched the large transmitter over to another frequency and made the call. 'Lemon Drop to Mint Dulip. Lemon Drop to Mint Dulip. Come in. Lemon Drop to Mint Dulip. Being overrun. Do not pick up – do not pick up – over.'

Captain Drummond could now hear the heavy footsteps approaching down the white painted metal stairway and so quickly switched the radio transmitter back to its normal frequency. He stood up, swept back his hair with the palms of his hands, adorned his cap and moved forward in readiness to be interrogated.

The door opened and he was faced with his counterpart from the Customs team.

'Let me present myself, Captain. US Customs, Captain Wakefield is my name. We have orders to search your ship and trust you will comply fully with our wishes and cooperate on every level?'

Captain Drummond nodded. 'This isn't just any routine inspection then?' he said, appearing to be calm.

'Quite right,' Captain Wakefield replied and produced confirmation of his orders and handed them to Drummond.

Drummond was so engrossed in reading the orders that he didn't hear Captain Wakefield's question.

'What were you doing in the radio room? Who were you contacting?'

Drummond kept reading slowly. He needed to buy time to think how he could change his situation. He hoped Rodriquez had received his warning message and would stay away.

'Well, this appears to be in order,' he said, speaking as eloquently as he could and handed the orders back to Wakefield.

'I asked you a question, Captain,' Wakefield sneered. 'Who were you contacting from the radio room? Who were you warning?'

'Warning! I resent that remark,' Drummond said. 'We've been anchored here a few hours. A problem in the engine room. Sent a signal informing Authorities that we'd been delayed but could now proceed underway. Of course, now with your interruption, that situation has changed.'

'You betcha' life on it, Captain. Your delay has been extended,' Wakefield said. Drummond just stared into his counterpart's eyes, but said nothing. 'Come back to the Bridge with me while my men search this vessel. I trust your officer here will cooperate with my men and show them any area they wish to search?'

Drummond again stared at Wakefield. 'You have your orders, Captain, you don't really need my agreement.'

Wakefield smiled, then bent forward his lips close to Drummond's ear. 'We'll find it, you know. Your career is over. Maybe they'll go easier if you cooperate.'

Captain Wakefield stood back, his eyes glinting as he allowed his words to sink in as full realisation came that The Providence had been impounded.

Captain Drummond remained calm. Many years of service and experience taught him that; besides, he'd gone through heavy inspections before.

'You seem to be acting on information received,' Drummond said, attempting to find out more of how heavy the inspection had become. It was obvious to him that with the Navy involved this was no standard inspection, which explained the amount of times the overhead spotter planes had been seen. Drummond mulled everything over. Hell, even if they located the illegal cargo he was only involved in trafficking which was bad, but he'd still be able to talk that one through, given that the cargo was in specially built-in compartments which he knew nothing about.

He convinced himself therefore in any event he would be okay.

'Oh, yeah! We have information all right, and I know we'll find what we're searching for,' Wakefield said, then instructed his men to commence their job. 'You know what to do men; what we're looking for. Pull this ship apart,' he shouted.

Captain Wakefield then turned to Drummond. 'Oh, by the way, the Royal Navy's also here. They will be boarding The Providence and will be joining in the search. I can tell you, they have official orders too. So don't waste your time on that score. You'll not get away this time, Captain Drummond,' Wakefield stated satisfactorily. 'You're finished; your career, you! Everything you hold dear, Captain. All gone.'

Wakefield smiled as he delivered his last statement, fully expecting Captain Drummond to crumble.

'Well, good old Uncle Sam,' Drummond responded. Nothin' else to do but spend the taxpayers' money on one little old ship, which, incidentally, is not carrying anything illegal, and let me assure you Captain Wakefield, the Royal Navy's presence here in conjunction with Customs will not go unreported. In fact, this whole fiasco will be detailed in my report.'

Captain Wakefield stood back and stared at the master of The Providence. 'This is your last voyage, Drummond. We'll find the contraband. You're finished. So, let's return to the Bridge and allow our boys to do their job.'

Captain Drummond stood motionless to the spot as Wakefield covered his holstered SIG Sauer P229R .40 S&W pistol with his right hand, indicating that he would use it if provoked.

Drummond started up the metal stairway towards the bridge and witnessed first-hand both Customs crews and that of the Royal Navy scurrying about all around with automatic weapons.

'You expecting a war, Captain?' Drummond said sarcastically.

'Okay Drummond. I'll come straight to the point. We already know there is contraband aboard. We just have to find it. We also know this is not your first shipment, so you're already destined for jail. We know you're involved with organised crime and we're also aware that the funds derived from your involvement in smuggling this contraband is funding terrorism against the United States of America and her allies. We know these actions are unauthorised; unauthorised by some very influential personnel who are traitors to our Country. You, of course, Captain Drummond, may not be party to that side, but you are responsible for providing the necessary trafficking of goods in the first place. So Drummond, if you have any self-esteem you'd be wise to cooperate now. There will be a court martial; that cannot be avoided, but any cooperation by you at this stage can only go in your favour, or at least be noted. Maybe make a difference to your sentence, although you understand, Drummond, there are no guarantees.' Captain Wakefield waited patiently for The Providence's captain to respond.

'You're so full of bullshit, Wakefield,' Drummond replied. 'You couldn't wipe my ass. So go play your games, soldier boy.'

Captain Wakefield stood back, aghast. Whatever response he hoped or expected it certainly was not the insult that he'd just received. Wakefield composed himself. 'I can take it then, with those remarks Captain Drummond that you're not prepared to cooperate? Is that, Captain, what you want me to write on my report?' Wakefield paused, giving Drummond the opportunity to change his mind and retract his comments.

Drummond bent forward and whispered into Wakefield's ear. 'Go suck my dick, you Nancy solider boy.' Drummond now stood back smiling, his eyes watching Wakefield's response. He could see the humiliation on Wakefield's face; the anger welling up within him caused by those remarks, his face blushed, his temper being tested.

After a few minutes Wakefield spoke firmly but quietly, and with a stern authority in his voice. 'Fancy yourself, Drummond? Is that it, eh? Pity your colleagues in crime don't have your loyalty. They shopped you, Drummond. Hung you out to dry! I gave you a chance to help yourself today, but … you know what, Drummond? Fuck you. Yeah, fuck you. I'm now in command of this ship. Take Captain Drummond to his quarters. He will remain there until further notice. Post two armed men outside his cabin. He's not allowed any access to the ship.'

'Am I under arrest Captain?' Drummond asked. 'Just for the record,' he added.

Captain Wakefield breathed a sigh. 'If you wish to record it that way, then yes. You are under arrest. You can also include in your report that I, as Officer in Charge, placed you there because you would not cooperate with the US Customs or, in fact, the Royal Navy who are also present. That won't look good, or enhance your position, but please record your report.'

Captain Drummond knew he'd pushed his counterpart too far and now spoke. 'Listen Wakefield, I'm not guilty of anything. You've no evidence. No proof. Only a hunch and it's not my career that will be on the line, but yours, Wakefield. I can cooperate but I can also assure you, the Navy or Customs won't find a damn thing on board The Providence.'

Captain Wakefield smiled. 'That's not what our informant has told us. As I said Drummond, they've hung you out to dry.'

There was a pause, then Wakefield issued his instructions. 'Take him to his quarters.'

Chapter 58

Captain Wakefield, now happy that Drummond was secure in his quarters, signalled the Navy cruiser. He would have preferred to have taken all the credit for this inspection, especially when they discovered the illegal cargo, but the tip-off had come from the British which is how the Royal Navy became involved.

Commander Samuel Braddock of The Queen's Royal Navy now boarded The Providence and made his way to Wakefield on the Bridge.

He was a tall man, 6ft 5" with greying side-hair peeking from underneath his heavily braided cap. His long legs showed off the sharp crease of his uniformed trousers and his demure sent the impression that he was a man of integrity and discipline.

Both men saluted. 'Anything to report?' Commander Braddock asked.

'Afraid not, Sir. Have confined Captain Drummond to his quarters. He's not cooperating.'

Braddock paused before speaking. 'You do know, Captain, that our informant is an American, whose identity cannot be disclosed at this time; was employed at a very senior level and with government connections.'

Captain Wakefield shook his head negatively. 'I didn't realise. I thought it'd be someone with a grudge, just getting their own back. Maybe a fired crew member, or someone who had it in for Drummond.'

Commander Braddock smiled. 'I wish it were that simple. This situation is very sensitive. In fact, we, at this stage, don't know how or who's involved, but our understanding is, it goes all the way to the Pentagon. So you see, Captain, this is much more than a drug trafficking bust. This could unlock some very influential individuals and given it's the Pentagon, National Security could be compromised. I'll spell it out for you Captain Wakefield. If, as we suspect, that monies from these shipments are funding terrorists that are used against your Country and mine, then it's very important that we leave no stone unturned and find this contraband with the intention that when the goods fail to be delivered it may flush out the bigger fish in the chain. We, Captain, cannot fail in our endeavour to bring the culprit, or culprits, to justice. That is why our Countries are working very closely with each other.'

Captain Wakefield then offered 'Do you think there is a connection in the Cayman Islands? I mean, The Providence is anchored here within striking range, and ...'

Commander Braddock interrupted and nodded. 'It would be the obvious solution one would think, given all the circumstances and one that would seem to suit whoever is behind all this. I mean, we are aware of certain offshore accounts in the banking sector, and of course The Caymans are a British Colony, but even our Ambassador can't render any light on this matter.'

'Can't, or won't?' Captain Wakefield said.

Commander Braddock stared at the US Customs Officer.

'I hope you're not implying that our Ambassador has any implication in any of this?' he replied sternly.

Captain Wakefield paused. 'I didn't mean to accuse anybody, Sir, it's just that it seems to me that if this whole operation is as big as you say, then maybe your Governor, shall we say, would be able to shed some light on the matter?'

Commander Braddock still stared at Wakefield. Inside his mind he knew and felt that the Customs Officer had a point, but he was not going down that road. Not at this juncture, anyway.

Chapter 59

Captain Drummond was being interrogated once more by Captain Wakefield and Commander Samuel Braddock. Their crews had searched The Providence with a fine-tooth comb but as yet had discovered nothing. Nobody was talking, and if that situation remained then The Royal Navy and the US Coast Guard would have no option but to let the ship proceed to its destination. The Authorities would shadow her of course, after all, they'd been given a tip-off with times, coordinates and another name of a person involved.

'We know you're smuggling contraband, Drummond. We know its Class A substances. We know, you know. Save yourself Drummond. Your career is finished. Even if we let The Providence pass, you'll never be able to offload what's in her. Once her official cargo is removed and checked she'll be taken down to the breakers yard and eventually we'll find what we're looking for.'

Drummond smiled. 'Bit extreme, gentleman, I mean, the ship's clean, I'm clean, the crew's clean; everything is shipshape you might say and yet acting on a hunch, or information, you guys are prepared to suffer the embarrassment of a lawsuit, not only from the owners of The Providence but from me too and the crew, to say nothing of the embarrassing relations you will stir up between our two Countries.'

'A lawsuit from you, Drummond,' Wakefield said. 'On what grounds?'

'Deformation of character, Captain Wakefield. Deformation of character and false accusations, jeopardising the safety of my ship and fellow crew.' Drummond sat back, smiling now.

Captain Wakefield's eyes showed his displeasure. 'I'm only doing my job, Drummond.'

'Doing your fuckin' job?' Drummond shouted, interrupting Wakefield. 'You're a bit extreme, you bastard.'

'Now, you listen to me,' Wakefield uttered.

A seaman approached Drummond's cabin, knocked then entered. Commander Braddock, we have urgent news Sir, a communication from shore. Admiral Wilkinson requests you to make contact with him urgently.'

'Oops! Sounds ominous,' Drummond exclaimed, his eyes wide and laughing as Commander Braddock followed the able bodied seaman to the Bridge. 'Your ass is in a sling, Wakefield. Can't fault you for trying, but all said and done I reckon it's your career that will be over and not mine. What a pity,' Drummond added, sneeringly.

Commander Samuel Braddock listened carefully to his Admiral. 'You sure, Admiral? We have authorisation to hold the Providence and commence a search in the areas you have detailed ?'

Admiral Wilkinson confirmed his orders 'Proceed, Commander Braddock. You have all the backing of the Royal Navy and US Customs from the highest order.'

'Thank you, Sir. We'll report back as soon as we have anything.'

Chapter 60

Four hours had passed and both the US Customs and the Royal Navy had nothing to show for their inspection and impoundment of the ship.

Captain Wakefield reported to Commander Braddock of their unsuccessful search. He shrugged his shoulders. 'There's nothing, Sir. Just the cargo on the inventory. All appears to be in order.'

Commander Braddock was disappointed. His superiors had instructed him to take action on information received. Information from a very reliable source apparently, but information which now was incidental as nothing had been found.

Commander Braddock knew neither the US Customs, nor indeed the Royal Navy, could hold The Providence indefinitely even although he was reliably informed that the information was sound.

Had the illegal cargo already been picked up and transferred? Had the Authorities been too late?

Was that why The Providence's captain was so sure of himself?

'Captain Wakefield you have Captain Drummond in his quarters. I think some more questions need to be answered.'

Chapter 61

Glen Randall tidied his desk. He was not looking forward to his meeting with Cleaver.

He made his way from his bay along the corridor towards the ramp that would take him upwards to General Harris's office on Bay 3E225. Even with the many thousands of people employed in the Pentagon and the miles of corridors, one could easily make it between two random points using the radical hallways between the rings that connected them in several minutes.

It took Glen Randall just under 10 minutes to arrive at Cleaver's bay. He arrived and Barbara greeted him.

'Cleaver's expecting me. I'll just go straight in,' he said, as he knocked Cleaver's office door and walked straight in.

Barbara was taken aback. Normally she would clear that admission was convenient before allowing anyone to enter. She therefore followed Colonel Randall and began voicing her explanation to her boss.

Cleaver turned to face them. 'It's all right, Barbara. I'm expecting Colonel Randall. Can you bring us some coffee; oh, and Barbara, hold all calls meantime. Check my appointments, inform whoever I'm running late.'

Barbara vacated Cleaver's office, leaving the two men alone.

'Okay, Glen. Explain. What happened?'

'We … I mean … we got the wrong man. Got a call from this would-be Riker, informing me that we'd abducted an innocent bystander. Our men in New York abducted some clown dressed like an act from Coney Island. Thought it was our target being so flamboyantly dressed.'

'Obviously it's not when this imposter can inform me otherwise.'

'So, who do we have, Glen? Who have your men abducted?'

Chapter 62

Cleaver's direct line rang, its intrusion piercing between himself and Randall. He slowly picked up the receiver and listened.

Colonel Glen Randall sat and watched his General's expression change. Whoever was calling was not giving Cleaver good news.

'You mean delayed,' Harris said, quietly but confidently.

'No! I mean impounded. All aboard arrested, so there won't be any delivery for the foreseeable future.'

'You know that for sure?' Harris replied.

'I have said what I said,' Rodriquez replied, then hung up.'

Colonel Glen Randall searched his superior's face. It was showing signs of anger and concern.

Cleaver's brows furrowed, his eyes levelled at Randall staring at him. 'Remind me Glen how this all started? This New York thing.'

Glen Randall faced Cleaver. 'Where do I start?' he said sheepishly.

Cleaver searched Randall's face. 'At the beginning Glen. At the beginning.' Cleaver relaxed into his high-backed leather chair. 'Okay, Glen. Take me through it.'

Glen Randall paused a moment. 'Well! It all started as you know when Claire found out about our operations, the slush fund that had the offshore accounts, and of course she also found out about our friend in the Caymans.'

Cleaver sat quietly. He was aware of why Claire Monroe was put on the hit list. He was also aware of other factors that concerned Claire Monroe. Facts that Glen Randall was not aware of, and at this stage facts that Cleaver was not about to divulge.

'Well, when Claire relinquished her position here, approximately nine months ago, and then died in that automobile hit and run three months later, she had in that time put two and two together and was slowly busying herself into business that didn't concern her. She ...'

'Yeah, yeah! We know all that,' Cleaver interrupted. 'Speed up, Randall, we've not got all day. It's like War and Peace when you report anything.'

Glen Randall shifted uneasily in his chair, the leather cushion hissed air as he moved. 'Well, Claire had a meeting with a private investigator, a certain Steve Donaldson; small-time operator but he has a good record for succeeding. Ex-member of NYPD. Packed in the job after his marriage broke up. He was married to a Gill Browne; one daughter, Becky. No contact as far as I'm led to believe.'

'So?' Cleaver sounded impatient. Then thought could this be the schmuck who's sending the threatening letters to me?

Glen Randall continued with his report. 'Steve Donaldson just also happened to be a Marine in overseas Special Forces. Has a coded file, so he must have been involved at high level.'

Cleaver sighed. 'We don't need this,' he said.

Glen Randall then spoke again. 'Steve Donaldson was the last person to speak to Claire before Riker and Gennero took her out. We don't know what information she imparted but we decided to let it go, unless of course Donaldson himself took it any further. Six months lapsed, then Donaldson started making some enquiries. We discovered that he wanted the hit and run on Claire to have further investigation. There's a Lieutenant Chandler in Lower Manhattan, friend of Donaldson's I believe,' Randall said, as he held up his arms and fore-fingers, making an air quotation gesture, 'and I believe Riker even attempted to warn him off but, and it's only a but, Cleaver, we think Donaldson may have imparted what he knows to this Chandler.

'We realised Riker and Gennero messed up. They silenced Rusty who crushed the vehicles and therefore eliminating all evidence, but stupidly missed Donald-son.

'I let them have another go but as you know they failed. So they paid their price and we took action to close all investigations down relating to all activities.

'Now this son of a bitch threatens me by telephone. How he has my direct line is anybody's guess. Probably through Riker. After all, this Donaldson is resourceful and he's, I think, posing as Riker, requesting payment for the contract taken out on Claire Monroe.

'I know Riker and Gennero are dead. That's been confirmed so I decided to go along with the son of a bitch and arrangements were made to meet in Central

Park, New York, where we'd abduct him. Find out what he knows. The problem is, Cleaver, whoever we have isn't Donaldson. He telephoned me again and could inform me that our people took an innocent bystander by mistake. Our people can't confirm that, as whoever we're holding has not yet regained consciousness and therefore unable to speak.'

'Enough! Cleaver shouted. 'Ah don't do excuses. I charged you to take care of this Glen. This is your making. Your problem! Now you sit here asking me once again to solve it for you.'

'I … I… didn't mean to,' Glen Randall said, now standing. The last thing he wanted to incur was Cleaver's wrath; as he himself could manage most situations he was still no match for Cleaver Harris.

Randall now silently wished that the Riker incident had been solved. What had these clowns he employed done!? More importantly, not done. Heads would roll, he'd make sure of it.

'Sit down, Randall, I didn't say you could stand. I'm not finished with you yet.'

Randall remained motionless.

'Sit down,' Cleaver yelled. 'Sit down you overgrown oaf!'

Glen Randall started to shake. 'Cleaver, listen, I'll fix this, I … I …'

'Shut up,' Cleaver yelled again. 'You couldn't organise a raffle. Supposed to be a Colonel …Jesus,' Cleaver said, sighing.

Cleaver's telephone rang. It was Barbara.

'I have a call on line two for Colonel Randall, shall I connect you, or shall I take a message?'

Cleaver hesitated and glanced at his Colonel. 'No, put it through here,' he said as he handed the handset to Glen. 'Call for you,' Cleaver said. 'I'm now your bloody secretary,' he said sarcastically.

Glen Randall took the receiver and shrugged his shoulders. Why would a call for himself be transferred to General Cleaver's Office? Why had his secretary not just taken a message as usual?

Glen listened to the voice on the line. It was one of his men from New York.

'We got the wrong man. The package we have is a reporter for The New York Times, a certain Jimmy Malone. Says he was following up on a story. Says he was supposed to meet whoever in the park. What do you want us to do with him?' the voice said, expecting the usual answer to eliminate him.

Randall glanced at Cleaver and answered his caller. 'Let him go', he instructed, 'but keep tabs on him. Report all your findings.' Randall replaced the handset as Cleaver waited in anticipation.

Randall shook his head negatively, then stared at Cleaver before speaking. 'Apparently the package we have is a Jimmy Malone, a New York Times reporter. Apparently he was on a case, snooping for a story. Supposed to be meeting his contact who has obviously given him some information but only enough to keep him interested.'

'You think his contact is this Donaldson, Glen?' Cleaver interrupted.

Randall nodded. 'I think our friend Donaldson has fed this schmuck some titbits, got him all hot and bothered and to be a witness of our meeting at Loeb's Boathouse in the park. I also think that had Donaldson showed and we took him; it was insurance that he'd have a witness of any abduction and therefore enough ammunition to print a lead story which would undoubtedly get a follow-up, and who knows, maybe challenge our instructions to close all these cases.'

'So, let's assume this Donaldson was watching as your clowns apprehended the wrong target. He must have got a good laugh at that.' Cleaver's voice was angry now. 'How could they abduct the wrong guy in such a public place – how, Glen, how?'

Silence reigned between the two men, then Cleaver spoke again. 'This is your mess, Randall. You clear this up – now. Understand? Your head is on the line, Glen. Ah don't want to hear any more about this Donaldson and no more articles in The Times either. Claire Monroe is dead. She flipped, because she was a loose cannon; but she's out of it, so you do whatever it takes.'

Randall turned to leave when Cleaver spoke again.

'Glen, there's too much riding on this. We can't afford an enquiry, or any exposure at our door. We don't actually know what Monroe imparted to this Donaldson, or him to this reporter, but we are not going to allow any threat to undermine our business. You still have a contact in New York?'

Randall nodded affirmatively.

'Then deal with it properly. The reporter meets with an accident after he leads you to Donaldson. Get what info you can, then let your boys do their job.'

'But he's a reporter, Cleaver. That's like killin' a cop. They'll open the floodgates and the whole fuckin' issue will be at our door.'

Cleaver closed his eyes momentarily and sighed. 'Listen, Glen. This schmuck Malone ain't going to send you no valentine and you're not loved by Donaldson either. He can pin you to the murders of Rusty, Monroe, Riker and Gennero, so it's best all round. Get the bloody info, then finish it.'

'You inherited your commission, didn't you, Randall? Off the back of your family's tradition and military background, while I, Randall; I had to work my way up … up … up … You understand..? From nothin', Randall. Up to what I am now, a General, yeah, General Bob Cleaver Harris.

'You know why they call me Cleaver? Well, I'll tell you, Randall, it's cause I always get the job done, no matter what the cost, no matter what the odds. I have the ear of the President; you know, the President of the fuckin' United States of America. Yes me, General Bob Harris. I've worked my butt off for this country, and you, or some schmuck – ex-marine Donaldson, are not going to upset my plans, you understand?'

Cleaver swivelled his chair. He faced the stars and stripes flag that was there. His mind was racing; could it be this Donaldson was the one sending him the stencilled letters, threatening to expose him, and could he have got all his information from Claire Monroe in one short meeting? Cleaver mulled all the facts over.

Chapter 63

Cleaver adjusted his seating position. He made himself comfortable and let his mind rewind to his relationship with Claire. They worked together; they just clicked. It didn't matter what time of day or night, she never let him down.

Cleaver remembered too his first invitation for her to accompany him to the Cayman Islands. She had at that time refused. Made the excuse that she had to sort things out at home. She had parted from her ex-boy-friend, Mac, at Andrews Air Base on unpleasant terms and wanted to resolve that situation. It was her first vacation in a year and on reflection now her reasoning had been sound, but that was not how he remembered it. Cleaver recalled how displeased he was. He was not used to being turned down and in Claire's case it was the first time that she had not complied with his wishes. He had gone without her, full in the knowledge that had he ordered her to accompany him, then Claire would have done so.

Cleaver recalled too how Claire, after taking that long weekend at home, returned to her job in the Pentagon. She was different. She was so dependable in every way. They grew closer and closer and the next time he requested her to join him on one of his trips to the Islands she responded positively.

Cleaver smiled to himself as fond memories came flooding back.

Chapter 64

Cleaver looked out over the Potomac River and let his mind roll back to the first time Claire accompanied him to the Caymans. She had been working extra hard, day and night, on projects that he himself was orchestrating and he felt that a short vacation to the Islands would allow her some respite away from Washington, besides he wanted the opportunity to develop their friendship and hopefully take it to another level.

They boarded his private jet and Cleaver occupied his usual seat and motioned Claire to sit facing him. They smiled, and his long legs touched her knees, making their eyes lock together.

Claire was first to break the magnetism that held them both and for the first time since a teenager, actually blushed. She excused herself as she made her way to the small toilet to refresh her make-up.

The small talk between them was supposed to lighten the journey but Cleaver was not one for such conversation and so decided to impart his background and open up to his secretary. Claire had remained quiet for most of the journey, fascinated that the big, tough General everybody knew by reputation had in fact a heart, and one that was sensitive if one knew what buttons to press.

Touchdown arrived with a slight jolt and brief shudder as the jet's wheels met the tarmac. A car waited as the plane taxied to its designated parking slot and its engines whooshed as the turbines became stationary.

Claire was on her feet first, stretching for their hand luggage in the overhead locker. Cleaver also stood, anxious to stretch his legs. They were close to each other, almost touching; he could smell her perfume. God, his imagination could taste her very kissable lips with their red lipstick. He reached up to help and for an instance a special moment passed between them.

Cleaver wanted to hold her there and then, but it was the start of their vacation and he hoped that would come later.

Chapter 65

C leaver sat mesmerised as he remembered their first visit. He recalled how impressed Claire was by Governor Alexander Frederick Gordon and the opulence that exuded an ambassador's post in one of Britain's colonies. The evening had gone well; Claire learning and appreciating the more formal way of life and beginning to understand the whole meaning of protocol.

Cleaver remembered how attractive Claire had looked in her long black V-necked evening gown; so plain and yet on her so stunning and classy. Her only jewellery was a simple, silver locket which housed a picture of her mother and father on one side, and nothing on the other.

There had once been a picture of Mac and her, but that life had long gone and there had been no one in her life to date that could replace that love. That was until now. Claire had developed very strong feelings for her General and although she controlled them in her workplace at the Pentagon, her vacation with him to the Cayman Islands was quite another matter.

They had taken after-dinner refreshments on the terrace, both still dancing with each other's minds, both wanting to take the next step, but each holding back.

Cleaver had deliberately wanted to take it slow; after all, if he pushed his authority on her he would surely lose her affection, to say nothing of her worth to him as a secretary.

They talked easily with each other and then the time came for them to retire. They bade their goodnight to Governor Gordon and his wife and departed; Cleaver escorting Claire to her guest suite. He held her gaze then kissed her lightly on the cheek. He didn't want to take their relationship any further, and so acted like the perfect gentleman.

Claire had held him, reluctant to let her General go, but after a silence, when time stood still, they parted and Cleaver made his way to his own bedroom. He thought about Claire. Was she falling for him? Was he falling for her? That question he could answer.

He partook of another nightcap of brandy from a tray that Benjamin, Governor Gordon's butler had left, and planned how he would show Claire the sights and the Island the next day. Satisfied, Cleaver drifted into a deep sleep and did not hear the intruder tiptoe quietly towards his bed.

Claire dropped her silk nightdress, letting it shimmer to the floor, stepped out of it and slid her young, fit, tanned naked body under Cleaver's sheets. She gently caressed his manhood, pleased to find her General slept in the nude, her gentle touch stirring the man she wanted. Now she kissed his chest and then slowly, very slowly, worked her way down his body, her mouth now replacing what her hands had started.

Cleaver groaned with pleasure, his manhood at attention, and played with Claire's hair as she sensually worked on him. Cleaver came in her mouth and she savoured his sweet juices; very sweet, she thought, for such a big man. She then kissed him passionately on his lips, sharing his fluids with him. Cleaver responded by taking his turn to give pleasure as he worked gently and teasingly down her body, admiring and caressing her erect nipples. He could still smell her perfume even with the saltiness of the sex she had just given.

Cleaver was once again ready, and so entered her, thrusting long and hard, then slowing down before repeating the action, going much deeper; he felt her juices, her fingers fondling him and herself and as she came her body flexed repeatedly, enjoying the orgasm again and again.

Their bodies spent, they held each other under the white Egyptian cotton sheets, both completely satisfied. They kissed again, each savouring the moment of what had just occurred, Claire feeling secure for the first time in a long, long time; secure in her General's arms.

Cleaver too had felt the intimacy. He had planned to be the one to make the first move, but he couldn't complain, Claire had come to him and he was more than satisfied. He stroked her hair, then they kissed again, his tongue finding refuge as it intertwined with hers. Claire's body was rising again, and Cleaver did not disappoint as they partook of each other once again. Satisfied, Claire removed herself from the bed and clutching her rejected nightdress from the floor, made her way to the bathroom.

He admired her. She was gorgeous. He realised what he had seen in her long ago at the air show where they had first met. She had tenacity, and like himself, didn't need to abide by rules. She could adapt and change to any situation and Cleaver smiled as he saw himself in the woman who had just made love to him.

He stared over the Potomac River. He wanted to remember more.

***

Cleaver and Claire's relationship developed and any time he visited the Caymans Claire always accompanied him and soon they were regarded by Governor Gordon as a couple, albeit their relationship kept quiet and unofficial. Life was good between them and in their capacities suited each other, and when opportunity presented itself, pleasured each other. Claire soon discovered that Cleaver always needed time on his own at some point on their visits and although she had no choice or power over her man, was pleased when he'd rise early and take himself off for most of the day.

She only ever questioned him once and was told in no uncertain terms that it did not concern her, which upset her at first until Cleaver explained that he always at some point required to be on his own; away from the pressures of Washington, away from the protocol and even the hospitality of Governor Gordon, along with nature and time for himself to reflect and think.

Claire had accepted all that and Cleaver believed he'd sold the idea well. In reality Cleaver met his other business partner Rodriquez Mahon who resided close to Seven Mile Beach on the island.

A knock on his office door broke his concentration of his reminiscing. It was Barbara with papers that required his signature.

Cleaver admired his secretary. She was attractive and efficient and always immaculately dressed. He held his stare between them and something inside told him that she'd be willing to take up any invitation to join him in the Caymans, but she had refused when he had invited her, and so thought to himself he'd never know; besides, he had met Carla Roebuck and that experience was just too good to change.

Barbara turned to leave and Cleaver admired her silently again. She was good, he thought to himself, but she was no Claire.

Cleaver once again turned his chair and stared out over the Potomac and recalled the night when it all went wrong between Claire Monroe and himself.

Chapter 66

They were residing at Governor Gordon's residence in the Caymans and enjoying the usual warm hospitality that the Governor lavished, but Claire was tired as she had worked hard over the last few months non-stop and needed to rest.

She made her excuses after dinner and retired for the evening. Cleaver expected that this was a signal from Claire that she wanted some personal private time with him, and so he too retired. He followed Claire to her suite and did not expect her to decline or refuse his company. Cleaver remembered how upset he felt. After all, no one ever dared say no to him on any level. Claire had been adamant that night and Cleaver had no choice but to acknowledge her refusal for his company.

So, instead of retiring he headed for the beach, hoping the ambience of the night and the sea would cool his ardour and temper.

It was a dark night, the sea as black as a velvet cloak. There seemed to be no division between the sky and the ocean, except for the glow of the moon which cast a beacon across the water, detailing the ripple of a soft tide at the water's edge.

Cleaver's anger, for all the peacefulness of the night, was not receding and as he walked his anger was mounting. His words came out loud to himself, 'who the hell did she think she was, refusing me? Me …! General Cleaver Bob Harris. Nobody refuses me,' he murmured to himself. Why was she acting like this? He'd been good to her, and their relationship was solid. Or was it? Was there someone else? She had worked hard and long hours before and had never ever refused him. So what gave her the right to …?

'Not tonight, Cleaver,' he mimicked as he walked. Did she think she was a female Napoleon?

He continued to walk but his anger was not depleting. Then he heard the sound of a young woman. She was on the beach; she was moaning, or was she fighting off the young man on top of her.

Was he forcing himself upon her? Cleaver could see them both clearly now. The young woman had long dark curly hair, her firm breasts rising and falling as the young man on top was forcing himself.

'No! No! Not tonight,' he heard her cry. No! Not tonight had been enough for Cleaver to act. 'Another mother-fuckin' teasin' bitch,' he said to himself. He stepped up. He was over them. He yanked the young stud off the woman, rendered him unconscious with a single blow to the back of his head, then without further ado, unzipped his pants and took the young woman violently on the sand. He thrust and thrust and thrust into her, his full body weight taking control. The wide, frightened eyes of the woman stared back at him as she screamed, but she only screamed once because Cleaver hit her so hard that her neck snapped and she lay motionless.

Cleaver finished his business. He was perspiring heavily. He could taste her lipstick and the blood where she had bitten him.

He stood over her, dusted the sand off his clothes, zipped his pants back up, wiped his face and neck with a handkerchief and anxiously looked about him. There was no one. No one had witnessed what had taken place. He checked the young man. He was still unconscious but still alive. Good, he thought. He'll be the fall guy in all of this. Quietly, Cleaver departed the scene and returned along the beach to the Governor's mansion and the safety of his own suite. He drew a bath, lit a cigar and reflected on his evening, with no emotion entering his mind.

Cleaver had not seen the other pair of eyes on the beach that watched quietly and witnessed everything.

Chapter 67

Governor Gordon spoke to Claire over breakfast the next morning. 'Have you seen Cleaver this morning?' he said, as he sipped his freshly squeezed orange juice.

'No … not this morning … I think … he's gone fishing.'

Benjamin the butler interrupted. 'Was up early, usual Sunday. I saw him on the jetty.'

Governor Gordon acknowledged Benjamin's comment with a nod and then turned to Claire. 'Maybe you'd like to join us for croquet this morning Claire, that is, unless you have made other arrangements? I just thought with General Harris gone you'd be …' Gordon paused, 'somewhat lonely …' again, the Governor paused.

Claire, not expecting the invitation, hesitated before replying. 'Thank you Governor, but if it's all the same to you, I have preparations to make for our departure tomorrow, besides, I have a bit of a headache this morning.'

'Oh, oh I see. Benjamin, get something for Miss Monroe's headache immediately; we can't have you suffering unnecessarily, my dear.'

Claire raised her hand, looking at Benjamin. 'It's all right, Benjamin. I'll be okay. Just a bit too much red wine at dinner last evening. 'I'll take a walk along the beach; that should do the trick.'

Benjamin glanced at his boss.

'If you're sure, my dear,' Gordon said, watching Claire intently.

Claire smiled. It was the only time she would smile that day.

Time passed slowly and it seemed like an eternity before Cleaver returned from his trip.

'Hey you guys. See what I caught?' as he proudly held up his catch.

Governor Gordon and his guests were suitably impressed as Cleaver handed them to Benjamin to give to the cook.

Unknown to Gordon, or anyone else, Cleaver had not caught the fish, as Rodriquez had given the catch to him at their meeting on Seven Mile Beach, making sure that Cleaver had a suitable alibi.

Rodriquez and Cleaver had many meetings over the years and although friendly with each other when they met, they would never totally trust one another, and as far as Rodriquez was concerned, the relationship and partner routine worked as long as the money was right.

Cleaver sought Claire out. She was standing on the terrace, staring out over the ocean. She did not hear Cleaver approach and was surprised when he put his hands over her eyes as he stood behind her.

'Guess who?' he said, smiling.

Claire shrugged him off and instantly Cleaver felt her coldness towards him.

'Hey darlin' what's wrong now? Thought I'd go fishing, got quite a catch too. Gave it to Gordon's cook. You miss me, I didn't mean ...'

Claire didn't let Cleaver finish his sentence. 'Yes,' she whispered, I missed you. 'You've been gone all day and I ...'

Cleaver held her close. He did not see Claire's eyes crying but he could feel her anxiety from her body. Rather than question her, he consoled her now, holding her in front of him and wiping her tears with his handkerchief.

'You'll mess up that beautiful face if you keep crying,' he said, attempting to bring a jovial side to the situation. 'Surely I wasn't away that long?'

'No Cleaver, I suppose not. It's just, well, I ... I ... don't feel like talking right now. I would like to be on my own for a while. I'll see you at dinner, okay?'

Cleaver didn't understand. She had been off with him the previous evening and now for the second time he was being dismissed. 'Anything wrong, Claire,' he ventured. 'You had bad news? Have I done anything wrong?' he said anxiously.

Claire didn't answer immediately, then mustered enough courage. 'I want to return to Washington. As soon as possible – today, or first thing in the morning. Can you organise that, Cleaver?' she said coldly.

She then walked off into the Mansion House, leaving Cleaver astounded and alone on the terrace.

Chapter 68

The flight back to the States was quiet to say the least. The atmosphere between them electric. He had attempted conversation but the lack of response was dragging him down and he was not a man to be trifled with.

'Look Claire, don't know what the hell is going on between us. If I've offended you then tell me; what it is I've done? If, on the other hand, it's something you women go through then I'll try to understand, although I'm a man and I can't pretend that I'm going to get it.'

Claire remained silent and for the first time in his life Cleaver was lost for words. Touchdown in Washington was still frosty between them and once their baggage had cleared Claire bade Cleaver goodnight.

'See you in the morning, Sir,' she said as she made her way out through the terminal.

'Hell, you stop right there, what's all this "Sir" business? 'See you in the morning, Sir,' Cleaver mimicked. Now, stop right now and tell me what's wrong. You've been hell on heels for the last 24 hours and all of a sudden I'm "Sir", just like I don't matter. Don't we have a relationship together?' Cleaver said, hoping to appeal to her and the good times they had shared.

'Okay, Cleaver, I've changed. I don't want to work for you, or anywhere else in the Pentagon, for that matter.'

'What?' exclaimed Cleaver. 'Now, what is this all about, Claire? You owe me an explanation.'

Cleaver then softened, his mind working overtime to unlock the solution between them. 'Claire, you're tired. Go home, get some rest. You'll feel better tomorrow. We'll discuss it then. I shouldn't have gone fishing, I'm sorry. I know that now. Leaving you all day with Gordon and his cronies. I apologise. Please let me make it up to you.'

Claire's eyes had been closed as she listened to Cleaver's words. Now she opened them, allowing her tears to run as she spoke her final words.

'Cleaver, it's over … It's all over. You … me … the job … everything. Now, if you'll excuse me, I want to go home. I need to be alone, so don't call and don't come round. Tomorrow I'll pack up my desk, then I'm gone.'

'Claire, you can't be serious. What the hell – *who* the hell do you think you are? I gave you everything. It was me – I brought you to Washington. I taught you. I loved you … love you. What's changed Claire – what?'

'I've said all I'm going to say, Cleaver.'

Chapter 69

Cleaver sat at home, bewildered. They hadn't fallen out, so there was no obvious reason why she would react in this way. He had become very close to her, maybe too close. But why all the extremes?

Cleaver could not understand. Everything seemed fine at the Governor's house in the Caymans until they came to retire. True, she knocked him back with some lame excuse, but surely that wouldn't have resulted in her packing in her job; putting her whole career on the line and surely not because he'd gone fishing. No! There had to be something else. Something she was not telling.

Cleaver reminded himself of his actions on the beach on Saturday night, but was sure no one had seen him. The young girl had died in a tragic accident of actions by an overzealous boyfriend. A lover's tiff that went too far.

It was even reported in the local newspaper as such and no further investigation was made by the Authorities, but something had changed. Had her hotshot pilot re-entered her life without his knowing? He then dismissed the idea, besides, he had ordered other plans for Mac.

Maybe the workload of the last few months had taken more than he anticipated? He had thought that time away with him in the Caymans would have been an adequate solution, after all, it had never been a problem before.

Maybe it was extreme mental exhaustion and maybe time in the Caymans had not been such a good idea after all. Maybe full-time leave was what was required. He could always bring a temp in, or use Glen Randall's secretary temporarily, and as far as the relationship was concerned he'd need to take a backseat. Take it slow; let Claire come out of whatever she was in. Let her choose to come back to him.

Cleaver relaxed now, full in the knowledge that he had at least formulated a plan. A means to an end and a solution to his problem.

Next morning Cleaver was at his desk early. He wanted to make sure he would be there before Claire arrived, but it was Cleaver who got the surprise. Claire had already been in and cleared out her desk.

She had appeared during the night. Security knowing her let her pass, assuming she was on official business and so did not question her movements, or reasons for being there.

Cleaver, once again astonished, couldn't fathom it out. He tried ringing but her telephone just rang out. He went round to her apartment but there was no response and it looked deserted. What was all this about, he thought, as he returned to his office in the Pentagon.

For a whole week he'd attempted to contact her but nothing. He'd even involved Colonel Glen Randall and his network to trace her, but each enquiry drew a blank.

Claire Monroe was gone. Disappeared off the face of the Earth.

Cleaver broke away from his meditation and memory of Claire Monroe. He had other complications on his mind. The call from Rodriquez, although brief, was not good. The ship, The Providence, was currently impounded by both Customs and The Royal Navy, even although there was nothing untoward to sanction their actions. Rodriquez had also informed Cleaver that The Providence's Captain Drummond had been arrested.

Someone had obviously tipped-off the Authorities. The ship, the cargo, the time and position. There was certainly a mole in his organisation. Cleaver knew he had to find that mole and when he did, he would squash it like a fly.

Chapter 70

Jimmy Malone was on his hands and knees, his neck creaked as his eyes fell onto the six highly polished black shoes at the bottom of sharp pressed grey trousers. Jimmy prepared himself for the onslaught and the beating that was sure to come, and therefore tensed himself, coiling like a spring. If he was going down, he was going down fighting, after all, he was supposed to be Steve Donaldson, Private Investigator.

'Okay, whoever you are – get up!'

'What for? You big tough guys gonna give me a goin' over again; all three of you?'

'Get up I said,' the gruff voice repeated.

Jimmy struggled to his feet, he wanted to look into his captor's eyes but then things went hazy and everything began to spin as he felt the muzzle over his mouth and nostrils. He inhaled the chloroform, the sky above him, hit the ground and in turn the ground became the sky. In seconds he fell deeply into unconsciousness.

The three men in grey suits carried him to the waiting limo, secured his body in the trunk and sped off in the direction of New York City. The two grey suits who travelled with Malone never spoke as they carried out their latest instructions. Their other partner was back at the old warehouse, making sure there was no evidence left of any abduction and dismantled all equipment they had used.

Fort Lee was still a tourist attraction, as films had been once made there. The old warehouse, of course, was hidden away in a backlot, and free from public scrutiny. However, Randall's soldiers required to be thorough and every effort was made to leave no trace of their visit.

The black Lincoln limo sped ever onwards over the George Washington Bridge and the Henry Hudson Parkway, along Central Park West onto 79th Transverse Road and the Ramble.

One hour had lapsed before Jimmy woke and found himself seated and propped up on a park bench. His head pounded. He felt nausea and tried to remember the chain of events and his ordeal and interrogation at the old disused warehouse.

Was it a dream he thought,? then he remembered the bright lights, distant voices and felt the bruises on his face. It was no dream, and he could now hear the sound of traffic from the busy streets as commuters commenced their day.

A young woman, headband on, wearing bright red shorts, white top and running shoes jogged towards him. Jimmy tried calling out but his mind was still half asleep, and anyway, he doubted she would have stopped as she probably thought him just another down and out who slept in the park at night. Jimmy felt rough – looked rough, which did not match his brightly coloured attire he'd been wearing when abducted. His memory was returning slowly.

He'd been working on a case, impersonating Steve Donaldson, Private Investigator. He looked hazily across the Lake in front of him, the image of the ice cream vendor entered his mind. It had been a beautiful day, he was to make contact with whoever and Donaldson would be watching.

He remembered falling, the path coming towards him and the faces – hazy faces – all staring at him. He remembered being helped to his feet by two gentlemen. He now looked down at his shoes, their toe caps all scuffed where he'd been dragged. He now remembered the disused warehouse, obviously an industrial site. He remembered running, he remembered hitting his captor with an iron bar; it was all flooding back now, the shots that rang out against the concrete pillars as he ran. He remembered his panic at the metal door, his temperature and adrenalin rising as he fought to escape. He then remembered the three pairs of polished black shoes and their sharp, grey trousers that belonged to the legs of … Jimmy paused. He never saw their faces. He remembered the sky turned with the ground, yes, it was all coming back, but he couldn't remember how he got to the bench in the park.

In the park where it all had begun.

Jimmy staggered to the nearest phone booth and dialled.

'Donaldson's Private Investigators,' Steve answered, using the plural to give the impression that his organisation was much bigger than himself.

'It's me …' Malone sighed. 'I need you, man. I'm totally fucked.'

Steve stared at the handset and wondered if Malone's captors were using him as bait to entrap him. Steve decided he would need to take that chance. Maybe his telephone call to Randall had saved Jimmy after all, and with that in mind he replied.

'Where are you? Are you alone, Jimmy?'

'Yeah! Am in the park next to Loeb's. Whoever they were dumped me back here; left me on a bench. Can you collect me? Am a bit of a mess.'

Steve considered Jimmy's request. It could be a trap.

'I'll arrange pick-up Malone. Just sit tight, okay?'

'Hey man, whatever the story is, it's too way over my head,' Malone said, then hung up.

Steve reflected on Malone's call, pressed the two black buttons on his telephone making sure the line was clear, then dialled.

Chapter 71

'My name is Jericho. Is Detective Sergeant John-ston available?' Steve said.

The line extension was connected and Johnston answered.

'You have a pick up at Loeb's Boathouse, do it yourself, understand?'

'But, what is it? When … How will I know …?' Johnston said.

'Just do it, Sergeant, and do it now. When you see it, you'll understand. By the way, tell Rubber Duck to meet me, usual time and place tomorrow morning. Tell him Jericho needs to meet. It involves Malone. I know there's no love lost between them but I don't believe your boss would just hang him out to dry.'

There was a click as Steve terminated the call.

Sergeant Johnston knocked Chandler's door. 'Got a minute, Lieutenant? Just had Jericho on the wire.'

Lieutenant Chandler kept his head down on the papers in front of him, but let his eyes roll to the top as he stared as his sergeant.

'He apparently wants to meet, usual time and place. Says he needs you. Oh, and also, there's a package to be collected at Loeb's Boathouse.'

'What! Who the hell does he think he is? Who's runnin' this goddamn department? This ain't no game, Johnston,' Chandler shouted, then quietly murmured 'Jericho and Rubber Duck. What a friggin' mess.'

Chandler closed his eyes momentarily. 'Any news from Charlie O'Brien on that homicide that was brought in yesterday?'

Johnston shook his head negatively. 'I'll get right on it,' he said, then departed to contact and chase up the Coroner's report.

Chandler was angry. He understood why he kept himself in the loop. Steve Donaldson had stumbled onto something big. Something rotten at the top which, by all accounts, involved the Pentagon. That was way out of his jurisdiction and way above his head but if he didn't act, who would? Chandler was frustrated. He could not allow Donaldson to call the shots in the precinct, as there would be no stopping the private investigator in the future.

It was obvious that anyone connected to Claire Monroe paid their price, and Donaldson would have as well, had Jimmy Malone not agreed to be his decoy.

Chandler thought about Malone. Thought about Donaldson. 'Shit, shit, shit!'

Chapter 72

Chandler couldn't concentrate on other cases and certainly couldn't contain himself any longer. He burst his door open and stood beside his sergeant.

'You said there was a package to be collected!'

Johnston eyed his superior. 'Yes, and it sounded urgent. In fact, told me to do it myself. Said when I saw it I would understand.'

Detective Chandler furrowed his brows. 'At Loeb's Boathouse, you said?'

Johnston nodded.

'Well! Let's go, Sergeant. No point sitting here when Mr Steve Donaldson has given us an order. Let's just drop everything for the son of a bitch,' he said sarcastically.

The two detectives arrived on East Drive and walked slowly through part of the Ramble; then they saw him.

Jimmy Malone was sitting on a bench by the Lake, his hair dishevelled; his brightly coloured clothes that he'd worn on the day he was abducted creased and dirty. He was unshaven and Chandler observed the remnants of the bruises that had been inflicted upon the reporter.

'What you doin' here, Malone? Bird watching, or waiting to hire a boat?' Chandler said mockingly. He didn't like the little man but even Malone was entitled as a taxpayer to be protected from violent crime.

'Had a rough time, Jimmy, by the looks of things,' Chandler said. 'I assume you're the package we've to collect?' he added.

'Hey, who sent you guys? Had enough interrogation to last me a lifetime, so if it's all the same to you, Chandler, fuck off.'

Lieutenant Chandler ignored Malone's outburst, then answered. 'Your partner in crime, Malone, phoned us to pick you up, make sure you're all right and take you home.'

'Who phoned you? What you talkin' …? Don't need no cops to get home,' he said, now thinking that contacting Steve Donaldson had been a mistake.

'Well, you know, Malone. Your friend and mine. Steve Donaldson, of course.' Chandler then added, 'I need to know what happened, Malone, I know all about your involvement but first, let us get you cleaned up, then you can fill us in.'

'I ain' sayin' nothin' till I talk to Donaldson. After all…'

'Hey, now you listen to me, you little shit,' Chandler growled, as he grabbed Jimmy by the collar. I'm the law around here – well, as far as you're concerned anyway, and if I want information about you, or anything else for that matter, then I expect to get it. Is that loud and clear, Malone?'

Jimmy struggled, Chandler's grip was strong and he couldn't speak, so reluctantly nodded his head.

'That's better, Malone,' Chandler said, then loosened his grip and wiped his hands with his handkerchief.

Jimmy Malone just stood there, watching Chandler and Johnston. They were taking him home, so he said nothing more.

Chandler then turned towards him. 'Suppose you still want to be a player in this caper?' he said.

'Jimmy nodded, 'and I don't mind tellin' everything that happened, but I do want Donaldson present, after all, he's the one that's to blame for all of this.'

Lieutenant Chandler afforded a smile. 'Okay, Malone, be outside Police Headquarters, 6:00am sharp, then we'll go and meet Donaldson. Don't be late 'cause we won't wait.'

'Where we meetin' him?' Malone asked.

'Just be at HQ, 6:00am. Now, let's get you home.'

Chapter 73

Six am and Malone met Lieutenant Chandler and Detective Sergeant Johnston outside the Police Headquarters. They then, under Chandler's instruction, made their way to Rikki's Café on Mulberry Street.

It was now 7:00am and the three men were cold. They had been standing under the awning of Rikki's Café for some time now, and Donaldson's no-show, together with the sharp rain falling, chilled their bones, which was beginning to agitate them.

Chandler cupped his hands over his face as he held them against the glass entrance. There was no sign of life inside but he'd been here before with Steve and knew he probably was already in there, and so started to bang on the glass doorway, hoping for a response.

Jimmy Malone stamped his feet, his arms wrapped around himself as he laboured to keep warm.

'Okay, enough is enough!' he shouted. 'Do you realise what I've been through lately, I've been …'

'Shut up you schmuck,' Chandler shouted. 'You don't know anything. You feed off other people's misery, so for once Malone, SHUT THE FUCK UP. Oh, and if you really want to go, then go. You'll be doin' us all a favour,' Chandler said.

'Hey, no way Lieutenant, I'm in this for the long haul. I'm in all the way, same as you. So get used to me, Lieutenant, 'cause I'm here to the end.'

Chandler stared at Malone. His dislike of the reporter was evident and the heavy air that hung like a cloud filled the atmosphere between them.

Johnston broke the deadlock. 'I think there's movement inside,' he said.

Chandler immediately turned towards the café entrance door.

Rikki opened up. He eyed Malone suspiciously. 'Steve's in the back; usual table. I assume it's coffee all round?'

Rikki waited for confirmation but Chandler was the only one to respond. 'That'll be great, Rik,' as he pushed past, leading the way for his two accomplices to follow.

All seated, Steve looked at Jimmy. 'Okay Malone, tell us what happened. Oh, you've probably told the Lieutenant here but hey, repeat it for my benefit. What! What you say?'

'Ah told them nothin'… nothin'! Okay? I wouldn't talk to this snake in the grass,' he said, eyeballing Chandler, 'and as for the goons that abducted me, ah told them nothin' either, except that I was a Times reporter working on a story. A tip-off who wanted to meet in the park. They obviously thought I was you, though somethin' 'bout you phoning and threatening their boss.'

Did they say who their boss was?' Steve asked.

'No … no … ah took a bit of punishment, as you can see,' Malone said, fingering the bruises on his cheeks and around his eyes.

Steve nodded sympathetically. 'Did you see or hear anything that might give us a clue to where you were being held?'

Again, Jimmy shook his head negatively. 'But I was held in an old, disused warehouse, crap everywhere; broken windows, peeling paint and it wasn't on the waterfront. There were other similar buildings nearby and they all looked much the same. Obviously been an old industrial area and on a main flightpath. I could hear the planes overhead cut their engines as they came into land, but which airport, I couldn't guess.'

Steve pursed his lips, then Jimmy spoke again. 'Oh, one other thing, I do remember the tyres of the limo I was in lapping over joints in the road; not big ones, 'cause they seemed very repetitive and every few seconds.'

'You mean like a bridge?'

'Yeah,' Malone replied, 'yeah, like a bridge. You know, b-dump, b-dump, b-dump,' Malone said, smiling.

'Hey, quite a detective, Donaldson.'

Chandler rolled his eyes. He did not like Jimmy Malone of The New York Times.

Steve thought for a moment. 'The men that abducted you sped their limo headed from the Ramble, 79th Street, Transverse towards Central Park West. Now they could have gone in any direction, but let's assume they took you to a holding unit, a disused warehouse where they wouldn't be disturbed, and let's assume we're dealing with Washington, 'cause the limo had Virginia plates.' Steve glanced at Johnston. 'Correct, Sergeant. So the location wouldn't be far from an airport. The big gun can fly in, unobserved, or, indeed, you can be taken out.'

Malone remembered when he did escape and for a brief moment was outside. 'The only other thing I thought strange, although I didn't get much opportunity to observe anything, was that although the other buildings were disused they seemed so perfect in character, just like a scene from a movie, know what I mean?'

Steve then spoke. 'You mean, like a backdrop, Jimmy?'

Malone nodded.

Steve searched his memory. 'I bet you were in Fort Lee. It still attracts visitors to the old film sets when they used to make movies there. Bet you ten to one that's where they held you. The tyre lap you heard was when they crossed the George Washington Bridge and onward to Fort Lee, a stone's throw to Teterboro Airport.

Steve sat back, in his mind satisfied that now they knew where Jimmy Malone had been held. He also appreciated that his captors had let Jimmy go. There had to be a reason for that. Firstly, his phone call to Randall informing him of his soldiers' mistake and also they had released Malone, probably to still flush himself out. If that was the case, then Randall would still have a tail on Jimmy because the only persons that knew Steve on sight were dead.

'Did anyone follow you guys here?' Steve said, glancing at Chandler. No one spoke.

'Okay, Steve, you may be right, but that still doesn't get us any closer with who we're really dealin' with,' Chandler said.'

'I know, but it's background, albeit supposition and in my experience sometimes it's not so much what you know, it's very much about what they think you know. Malone's abduction, or rather mine, supposedly was to ascertain what information Claire Monroe had passed on to me. Claire's dead; Riker, Gennero and Rusty too. Once I unloaded it was my turn, but they made a mistake in grabbing Malone here and I've got to hand it to you, Jimmy, you didn't give our relationship away – thank you for that, and as for the hell you've been through, I owe you a beer. Anyway, as I was saying, me telephoning Randall in Washington made them realise they did abduct the wrong man, so rather than take you out, which would guarantee finality, they didn't want any more threats from me; better to hear what I actually knew, they doped Malone again and returned him to where it all began at Loeb's Boathouse. He wakes up, can't remember too much, in the same location, been mugged; after all, it's Central Park.'

Just then Rik appeared. 'Thought you guys would like some bagels and doughnuts along with your coffee,' he said, as he placed a large plate in the centre of the table.

Malone had his hand on the chocolate doughnut on the platter. 'Anybody mind if I go first?' he said, not waiting for a reply as he stuffed a large bit into his mouth.

Everybody smiled at the reporter.

Chapter 74

Back in his office Steve checked the time – it was 11:45am – then dialled Randall's line. It rang out, its tone going unanswered. Nearly Noon, the Pentagon was always like a circus at this time of day. Randall would be busy but Steve hoped not too busy to answer his direct line.

The line went live and as usual Randall didn't speak.

'Want another meeting?' Steve said flatly. 'Prepared to meet you on your turf in DC … make it more convenient for you. Will contact you tomorrow for time and place'.

Steve hung up, not allowing Randall to offer any response. He wanted time to discuss this meeting with whoever was the real power behind the Claire Monroe story.

Steve opened his mail. There was a long, white envelope amongst his usual bills. He opened it casually, then sat bolt upright as he read the stencilled words:

MURDERER
RAPIST
CAYMANS
TRAITOR

It was obviously a copy as the envelope was marked Pentagon. Someone had mailed it by hand to be included in his mailbox.

Steve now moved to the side of the window, hoping to catch a glimpse of the watcher who'd be interested in his reaction. There was no one – well, no one that he could see.

Steve sat back down at his desk and re-read the threatening letter.

He smiled as he realised someone else also knew what was behind Claire Monroe's death, and more importantly, he figured they knew who!

Steve wondered if Randall knew about the letter. Better not mention it on the telephone when he called next. Better to wait and expose this information at their meeting, especially if the boss of the whole operation would be present.

Better hold at least one surprise up his sleeve.

Steve considered informing Stuart Chandler to keep him in the loop, but decided against it. He would hold back the information meantime. He therefore photocopied the letter, sealed it in an envelope marked "Lieutenant Chandler" and filed it in his desk drawer, should something happen to him. At least Stuart Chandler would have something to go on. Something to connect all the relevant details pertaining to Claire Monroe. And who knows, maybe the person who wrote the letter?

Chapter 75

Next day arrived. Steve read the time on his office wall clock. It was two minutes to the hour. He sat and stared at the black numbers on their stark white background and waited patiently as the second hand made its sweep, allowing the minute hand to move closer to the hour. He watched as both clicked together at noon. It was time to contact Randall. Randall's direct line ran out. Brr! Brr! Brr! Brr! Brr! Brr! Brr! It then connected and the line went live. Nobody spoke in that instance, then Steve asked,' you decided where to meet me, Randall?'

There was still no reply, or confirmation. Steve listened for a click, signifying that someone else may be listening, but there was none. A secure direct line should have been exactly that, but now that Randall's number was out there Steve wouldn't have been surprised if that line had been compromised.

The silence seemed endless, so Steve spoke again. 'Meet me at Arlington Cemetery, 1:00pm Friday. The price is $5 million Randall, cash of course, and no funny business. Just you, the money and of course, Mr Big, who's pulling the strings.'

'How will I recognise you,' Randall replied cautiously, his mind racing as he could imagine Cleaver's response to his caller's demands.

'You won't have to Randall, I'll recognise you. Put the cash in an attaché case. That shouldn't look out of place, but be warned, Colonel, I won't be as easy to apprehend, like your goons made their mistake in Central Park.'

'You got it all figured out, eh?' Randall said into the handset. 'What guarantees do I have that after paying you a bundle of money and allowing you to just walk off into the sunset, that whatever info you have dies; what guarantee do I have that you won't want more?'

Steve let Randall's questions hang in the air, then with a chuckle, replied, 'you don't … you schmuck. All I can say, Randall, if it's a no-show, or I ain't paid, or in the unlikely event of something happening to me, then there's a letter detailing all the evidence against you and your organisation, which will keep the Authorities busy; to say nothing of the press coverage which will blow your cover. I can see the headlines now: "Corruption and Murder in the Pentagon".'

Steve let his comments sit over the line. In reality he knew nothing, but Randall didn't know that, otherwise there would have been no attempt on his life and he certainly would not be having this telephone conversation.

'You're pretty sure of yourself,' Randall replied.

'Sure enough,' Steve said.

There was a pause, then Randall spoke. 'Okay, Friday, 1:00pm, Arlington. Don't be late.'

Steve studied a map detailing all routes in and around Arlington Cemetery and could now understand how and why the Pentagon had been constructed on its present site of the old, disused Hoover Airport. Had it been built on its original site at Arlington Farms then there was a strong possibility that the view to Washington, DC would have been obstructed.

The Pentagon's shape was deliberate to suit the shape of its original location and being practical in design, never changed when relocated to its present site. The design afforded the building to be lower than normal while allowing the capacity of tens of thousands of military and admin staff to operate from its premises.

Its layout and shape meant it sprawled over a large area but its design ensured that its main circular corridors all converged with concrete ramps to each floor, making accessibility to each area efficient and quick.

The roads between Arlington, Virginia and Washington, DC were used daily by thousands of commuters, so Steve was content that he, and hopefully Chandler, could blend in and disappear after the meeting with Randall without too much trouble. Steve's main concern was what Randall and his buddies had in store for him. They were not about to hand over $5 million without a guarantee, and the only guarantee these people understood was permanent ones. They had already proved how they dealt with loose ends with Claire, Riker, Gennero and Rusty. He did not want any of his own colleagues done for either. Jimmy Malone had come within inches of his life and Steve had to make sure that a repeat performance was not on the cards.

Steve's formative years in Special Forces gave him the ability to think out every possibility and he recalled his time on missions overseas, both official and unofficial. Some of those missions were classified, and even unknown to The Chief of Staff, which made Steve think that maybe whatever Claire Monroe knew it was not in the best interests of the Country, but probably still all paid for by good old Uncle Sam. There had to be a driving force behind it all. Steve knew it wasn't Randall; after all, his number was in Riker's coat pocket, to say nothing of the fact that it was also in a file in a junkyard.

So, Randall, a Colonel, was the go-between. Who could influence such a person in such a high position?

Chapter 76

Steve mulled the case over in his mind. Who would give an order for Claire Munroe to be executed? How far up the tree did Claire's knowledge go? Very far, obviously.

Steve recalled the copy letter he'd received. It had mentioned murderer and traitor. Someone who was still alive knew more about this caper but were still staying in the shadows. Steve racked his brains; was it someone else that Claire knew? Had she spoken to somebody else before approaching himself? Could there be another link in the chain that he'd missed, or hadn't considered?

Steve shook his head. He rotated his head, releasing the tension in his neck and as he did so it came to him. General! Of course. It was always Generals who instructed or commanded missions. It was always a General who gave the ultimate orders.

Steve closed his eyes and allowed the thought to sit with him. Had Claire Monroe worked for a General at the Pentagon? Was that the connection?

Nobody had actually checked who Claire had worked for. Nobody had really thought about it. What was Claire's real background and story?

He was to meet Stuart Chandler the next day at Rikki's. They now had a new angle to go on, but first he would return to his apartment and rest.

Stuart Chandler did much the same. He took time out by himself. He wandered through the park, observing young mothers with their children laughing and playing and the dog walkers, all enjoying the fresh air and the park's amenities. None of these people, of course, would have ventured into the park at night, for fear of mugging, or worse, rape and murder.

Chandler thought as he watched these people of how his days and nights were spent. His job was to clean up the city of its ugly garbage who transcended the law. Day or night his task was endless and sometimes pointless, as on many occasions the sharp lawyers in good suits either managed to reduce the sentence for their clients and sometimes got them acquitted totally. For them, it was just a game.

'A game,' Chandler repeated out loud to himself. He shook his head sadly. It was clear in his mind. Claire Monroe's story – whatever it was – certainly was no game. He was totally committed now Donaldson had made sure of that. He would work hard to expose the rotten apple in the Pentagon. He only had one regret. He had agreed that Jimmy Malone of The Times was also on the team.

Chandler thought some more and muttered Malone's name under his breath.

How he hated that little man.

Chapter 77

Steve Donaldson searched the faces of his partners: Lieutenant Stuart Chandler, Detective Sergeant Johnston and New York hotshot reporter Jimmy Malone.

'The meeting with Randall is at 1:00pm, Arlington Cemetery, Virginia, this Friday. Now, I don't really expect Randall to show, but like before,' Steve said, glancing his eyes in Malone's direction, 'somebody will. They know you now Jimmy, so you can't take my place this time.'

'Hey, who said I was gonna? I won't be a schmuck a second time.'

Steve laughed and smiled with his eyes. 'No, I bet you won't Malone, but I'm willing to also bet that if there's a story in all of this you'll be there.' Steve held the reporter's eyes with his own.

Malone just waved at him, smiled, then helped himself to another doughnut.

Lieutenant Chandler now spoke. 'I don't really know what you expect of Johnston and myself Steve. I mean, we can't just go waltzing down to Virginia. We have jobs and superiors to answer to. Besides, we've no jurisdiction and may I remind you, nothing officially to investigate. The Claire Monroe case, along with Riker, Rusty and Gennero's murders are closed. No further action to be taken and that instruction came from way above. There's a rotten apple here Steve, and it's got a link between Claire Monroe and the Pentagon, but I don't see how Johnston and myself can just swan off to Washington without a by-your-leave. You're playing cat and mouse, Steve, with this Randall. You can't beat the odds this time. He's already shown his power and authority, to say nothing of how easy it proved to abduct Malone here, who really, when all considered, was supposed to be you.

'We're meeting this guy on Friday at Arlington. He's on his own turf and bound to have more power to repeat the same thing, only this time Johnston and myself – to say nothing of Malone here will be included. That can't happen Steve, and you know it.' Chandler sipped his coffee and silence reigned.

Steve appraised Chandler for a few moments and then replied, keeping his eyes on his coffee cup. 'I'm disappointed, Lieutenant. Thought you were in the whole way. Thought you'd want to expose this son of a bitch. I mean, what if Claire Monroe was your daughter and information came to light that someone, because of what she knew, had her killed? What would your response be then, Lieutenant?

'What if I told you that I think there's a high-ranking General involved? What if I told you National Security could be threatened? What if ...'

'Hold it,' Chandler interrupted. 'What's all this National Security stuff, Steve? We can't just proceed on "what-ifs" regarding this. We'll get one crack at this motherfucker and if we miss there will be no threat 'cause we'll be gone. We, at this point, are acting unofficially so it won't go any further.'

Steve sighed. 'That's why I left the department. Too much red tape. Too much bending to please powerful people and allowing bad guys to walk, no matter how good or tight the evidence was. I need you, Lieutenant, and Johnston too. Jimmy here is already on board. He'll get his scoop. The scoop of the century, but I believe it'll take the four of us to pull it off.'

Jimmy Malone smiled. He was overwhelmed by Steve's inclusion of himself.

'There's one other thing I should tell you.'

Chandler pursed his lips. 'What golden words of wisdom are you gonna tell us now?' he said.

Steve's hand located the envelope inside his jacket pocket. 'This was in my mail. You will note there is no postmark but it is marked Pentagon. Whoever put it in my mailbox did so personally. Read it, gentlemen. There's obviously another player in this game. A player that's goin' all the way.'

Steve let Chandler open the envelope and allowed him, Johnston and Malone to read its threatening contents.

Steve eyed his other three accomplices. 'Now, who's comin' to Arlington with me on Friday?'

Chapter 78

General Bob Cleaver Harris sat quietly in his office. He looked out his window across the Potomac River and the Washington Monument in the background, his mind once again working hard and digesting everything Glen Randall had told him.

Barbara his secretary knocked and deposited his mail on his desk, then departed.

Cleaver casually turned then saw the long, white envelope marked "PERSONAL!" He held it in his hands, then slowly opened it, and read its contents:

GOT YOU NOW
NO SHIPMENT DELIVERY OOPS!
YOUR TIME IS RUNNING OUT
MURDERER –
TRAITOR

Cleaver searched his mind. Who could be doing this? Was it this PI Donaldson; an ex-marine with a coded file and who was the last person to speak to Claire Monroe before she died? If so, what did he know? If so, what did he want?

Cleaver thought hard. He allowed his memory to travel back to the days when he first met Claire Monroe at an air show. How she had impressed him when she stepped into an unknown situation, when a co-pilot had failed to show. Cleaver was impressed. He'd brought her to Washington, and as his secretary she proved her worth. Claire put her job way above everything else and even above her hotshot boyfriend at Andrews Air Base. She had become Cleaver's right arm. Her grit and mental attitude to get things done always excelling, especially where it concerned him. Cleaver thought fondly of Claire and allowed himself a small smile. She was like him – get the job done, worry about the consequences later. He thought about that seriously now. He had seen himself in her and at the time he liked what he saw.

Chapter 79

Cleaver re-read the most recent warning letter he'd received:

GOT YOU NOW
NO SHIPMENT DELIVERY OOPS!
YOUR TIME IS RUNNING OUT
MURDERER –
TRAITOR

Cleaver read the words once more, all the time his mind racing. He then compared it to the first notice he had received:

MURDERER
RAPIST
TRAITOR
CAYMANS
I'LL GET YOU
YOUR TIME IS COMING

No one had seen him in the Caymans with the local girl on the beach. Her boyfriend wouldn't even remember how he became unconscious, but somebody obviously had information on him. It couldn't be Claire; she was dead. Randall and his crew had carried that operation out successfully but the questions remained. If Claire knew anything, what did she know? And more importantly, who did she tell? Did she tell anybody? Or did these letters come from another source? Maybe through Randall?

Then, of course, there was this person, Donaldson. A PI with a distinguished background in Special Forces, designed to operate overseas and survive under the most horrendous and difficult conditions. Randall was meeting him at Arlington on Friday. Maybe he should remain here in Virginia, meet this Donaldson character along with Randall. Find out what he really knows, then formalise a solution. A permanent one.

Cleaver considered his options, but in the end decided to keep his appointment in the Caymans. He had to speak to Rodriquez. Find out what had gone wrong. Maybe he would have more information on the Customs search and who supplied the information.

Then, of course, there was also Carla Roebuck. She was an incentive all by herself. Cleaver sat back, more relaxed now. He had made his decision. He looked forward to rekindling his friendship with Carla. He would, he knew, enjoy himself.

Chapter 80

Friday morning arrived and Cleaver made final preparations with his secretary Barbara. He had given her the necessary instructions to carry out her duties for the remainder of the day. He also had a private meeting with Colonel Glen Randall.

'Don't mess this up this time, Randall. I don't care how you do it, but I want this monkey Donaldson off our backs. Find out what he really knows and if he has a partner, or if there's anybody else involved and once you've completed that then shut it down, you know, containment. No further issues, understand?' Cleaver said, his voice severely abrupt and in a no nonsense tone.

'Cleaver, I can only try …'

General Bob Harris raised his hand. 'Stop right there Glen. No... "Try" will not do. CONTAINMENT GLEN, NOTHING ELSE, CONTAINMENT, FOLLOWED BY TERMINATION AND CONCLUSION. AN END!!!'

Cleaver paused. 'Nothing in-between, Glen. Nothing short – got it? Are you clear Randall?'

Colonel Randall nodded, then replied, 'Yes, General, full containment and termination.'

'Good,' Cleaver said. 'Because I have to sort out the business in the Caymans. Find out who's been upsetting the applecart. You understand?'

Again, Randall nodded.

Once again, Cleaver repeated himself, his eyes narrowing as he uttered the words. 'Containment and termination to all who betray us and to all who have breached our security.'

'Yes, Sir,' Randall replied, not sure of what else to say. He knew enough that this time there had to be no mistakes. There would be a finality to the whole Claire Monroe issue.

Neither Glen Randall nor Cleaver Harris ever knew why Claire Monroe resigned all those months ago; never knew why she broke up with Cleaver, and never understood how, with all their power and network of people, ever found her. It was only three months after the day she resigned that a sighting of her came to General Bob Cleaver Harris's attention, and only after an incident which involved unauthorised entry into his private files that unlocked a path to trace her. Randall's network had worked hard when they found her in New York and whilst under surveillance for a few days it was decided that rather than bring her in and confront her to find out what she knew, the word had come down to eliminate her; take her out so that whatever information she knew would die with her.

General Bob Cleaver Harris had given that order via Randall. 'Find her, make like it's an accident; no witnesses, just a simple accident but make sure no trace can come back to ourselves, and if you find any other persons involved then the same thing for them, but there can be no link between the deaths, understand? Take time between these operations if you can, unless otherwise, but we have to tie this loose end up completely, with all guarantees in place.'

Chapter 81

Cleaver arrived in Grand Cayman and was greeted by Governor Gordon's chauffeur, and after the usual pleasantries was whisked away in the long black Lincoln to Government House in Georgetown.

Cleaver always admired the mansion, with its pure white stucco walls, its colonial elegance and opulence, with palm trees in its gardens beside the concrete drive-way, the balustrade balconies of the building; while giving privacy to the upper residencies, allowed its oceanic, privileged views over the Caribbean Sea.

Grand Cayman was changing; progress and expansion on the way. Its population was increasing, and although sound as a British Colony, was related to Jamaica by the Treaty of Madrid. There were rumblings that Jamaica wanted independence. Grand Cayman and her other two islands being smaller, never felt the need for this forthcoming independence and Govenor Gordon certainly wanted to remain with the status quo and be related to Jamaica in the Caribbean but remain a Colony of the British Crown, especially now that the new airfield which had opened six years previously, and replaced the small seaplane service that previously existed and with the new hotels and first Commercial

Bank now open, and the fact that women now, for the first time, had the right to vote and with the dependency to Jamaica gone, but still a Colony of the British Crown, Grand Cayman was flourishing.

Alexander Frederick Gordon greeted General Bob Cleaver Harris personally. 'Good flight I trust, Cleaver?' he said, extending his hand.

'Yes thank you, Governor. It's always a pleasure to return. I do love these islands and, of course, your generous hospitality,' Cleaver replied.

'Dinner at the usual time, General, usual guests this time; no one you don't know ...' Gordon hesitated, 'and, of course, Carla Roebuck will also be attending ...' Gordon winked as he nudged Cleaver's arm. 'Hey, what?' he added.

Cleaver smiled. 'Thank you for accommodating me, Governor. I'm very pleased Carla could make it.'

'Not at all, old boy. In fact, when I told her you were attending and asked after her, well, quite frankly she couldn't wait to meet you again. Must have made an impression, old boy, what, eh?! Wink, wink.'

Gordon was now boring Cleaver. 'Mind if I freshen up, Governor? It's been a busy week.'

'Of course, Cleaver, of course. Benjamin has taken your luggage up already. We'll meet for cocktails prior to dinner. Usual time, what!' Gordon said in his pompous English colonial accent.

'Thank you, Governor. I look forward to that,' Cleaver replied, thinking how was he going to sustain this bullshit all weekend without company that he could relate to? Thank God Carla Roebuck was at least here tonight, and hopefully she'd still be in attendance tomorrow, Saturday; then Sunday he'd speak to Rodriquez – find out exactly what had gone wrong and who betrayed them by tipping-off the Customs.

'See you at cocktails, Governor,' Cleaver said, then made his way up the wide marble covered staircase, with its portraits of past Governors. A new portrait of the new, young Queen Elizabeth, although commissioned had not yet arrived, but there was a space on the wall already reserved for the painting.

Cleaver met Benjamin. 'I've unpacked for you, General. Everything as usual. Anything I can do for you?'

'No, Benjamin, everything's fine. Just need to rest, then freshen up and I'll be fine.'

'I've taken the liberty of providing a tray with your favourite bourbon, I hope that my anticipation has been correct?'

Cleaver smiled genuinely for the first time that day. 'Benjamin, that's just what I need right now. I've said it before but I wish I could take you home with me, you just always get it right.'

Again, Cleaver smiled and Benjamin was pleased his duties as butler were appreciated.

Cleaver poured himself a large measure of the Tennessean liquor Benjamin had left on a tray. He savoured its taste as it travelled down his digestive track. He had brought his dress uniform which Benjamin had hung pristinely, ready for its owner to wear later that evening.

Cleaver showered and paraded about in his room, just wrapped in his large white cotton towel. He was so looking forward to seeing Carla again and hopefully another night to remember.

Chapter 82

Arlington Cemetery could be seen from the White House across the Potomac River. There were always many visitors so Steve was not conspicuous, as he looked as if he was attending the passing of a family member killed in action.

Jimmy Malone and Detective Sergeant Johnston grouped themselves together in another row behind, where they could monitor anybody approaching Steve.

Lieutenant Chandler's role was to keep a safe distance and watch for, hopefully, anybody approaching Steve, and as his back-up, if necessary intervene, using his shield as identification; although he didn't have any jurisdiction or authority, it still signified that Steve was under some form of protection.

One o'clock had come and gone. Steve was uneasy as nobody had showed. He felt sure he was being watched, but maybe only to really identify him and the rest would follow later.

He stood there, pretending to read a headstone, but all the time remembering Claire Monroe's visit to his office, all the time remembering how he refused her; all the time remembering how it put his own life in danger and that of Jimmy Malone's who attempted to help him solve the mystery. What had Claire known that could invite such heat? He himself knew nothing, but that was not the point. The big guns were taking no chances; take him out anyway. A specialist sharpshooter could take him out right now, even from a mile away. It'd be over in a second. A shot to his head and brain. No witnesses, no kidnapping. Sure, there'd be an almighty backlash from media and even the White House, especially such a crime being committed on such sacred ground.

What if the White House is implicated? What if? 'Oh hell, let that go,' Steve said to himself. If he had lived his life on a "what if" basis, he'd never have achieved anything.

It was now 1:20pm. A Colonel in service uniform moved slowly among the headstones and eventually stood four stones up from him.

Steve glanced at the man who never lifted his head or eyes from the headstone in front of him.

He was tall; Steve guessed 6ft 1". His highly polished shoes pristine, creased trousers and jacket with the officers' ribbons above the breast pocket. He held his cap in his hand. His complexion was pale but his mouth was sharp, as was his eyes which peeped out like two coals in the snow. His haircut was typical regulation, and his clean-shaven face wore the scars that merited the braiding above his breast pocket.

Steve averted his eyes for a moment, scanning the rest of the headstones in his vicinity.

'So, what d'ya know, and how much do you want?' the voice from the Colonel said.

Steve hesitated, then kept staring at the headstone before him. 'Well, I want paying … Randall. I assume you are Randall?' Steve continued, not waiting for confirmation, 'and I want assurances that there will be no more attempts on my life.'

'What puts you in a bargaining position, Mister? You're not Riker. Riker's dead. So I can only assume you're Donaldson. A private eye, trying to make a fast buck on a hunch … otherwise …'

'Otherwise, Colonel, you think I'd have gone further up the tree? The DEA, for example?'

Colonel Randall shrugged his shoulders but still never made eye contact.

'Claire Monroe was killed, Colonel. Killed, by your people. You made a mistake in attempting the same thing with me, then abducting an innocent person at Loeb's Boathouse in Central Park. You clowns don't get it. All the organisation and you still bungle it. Wouldn't want your kind on a mission with me,' Steve said.

'Oh, that's right, Donaldson. Forgot you have a military background. Overseas Special Forces, I understand. Coded file and all. You must be a handful, Donaldson, and yet you've exposed yourself here, this afternoon. Who would question a tragic automobile accident, especially after visiting a fellow comrade here in Arlington? You're finished, Donaldson. Name your price; also tell me what you know, and if you promise to move elsewhere that'll be an end to it. We can all forget about Claire Monroe.'

Steve smiled, then let out a small snigger. 'All very neat, cut and dried, Colonel, but as you said, I was in Special Forces and we wouldn't leave a loose end like me walking about, irrespective of what I know.'

'You don't trust me?' Randall replied.

'No, Colonel, I don't. You're full of bullshit and you know it.'

Colonel Randall's eyes scanned the vicinity. 'You alone, Donaldson? That was big of you.'

Steve didn't reply.

Randall then touched his right ear with his right hand, raised and prodded his middle finger into his lobe, then removing it, changed his statement. 'Oh, sorry, you've brought some "friends" with you. They're behind us; one's the guy we abducted in Central Park by mistake. Who's the other one?'

'Supervised by radio,' Steve said, 'I knew you wouldn't dare come alone, you sorry son of a bitch.'

Randall smiled. 'As I said Donaldson, name your price, but first tell me what you know. We'll call it a day and your friends can go free too.'

'If I believed that, Colonel, then I'd be a dead man. No, first I want to know why Claire was taken out. The information I have wouldn't warrant that action. Also, Riker and Gennero were taken down and the whole case undermined and closed down. Why Colonel? Why?'

'It's a matter of National Security, Donaldson. You know I can't fill in the blanks for you, but I can authorise your safe passage and a payment that will keep you in a lovely lifestyle for the rest of your life.'

'And how long would I live, Colonel? A week, a month, six months?' Steve said.

'Hey, we all gotta die sometime,' Randall replied.

Steve thought for a moment. Maybe he should try a bluff, see how much Randall would go to. See how much was at stake. 'Okay Randall. There's four of us involved who know about Claire Monroe's secret. Three are as you said, here, but there's one that's watching; watching to see whether we're successful today or not.'

'And if not, Donaldson?'

'If not, Colonel, he knows what to do, and more importantly, who to go to, and Randall? It's way above the Pentagon.'

'So, what's your deal?' Randall said.

'Well, as I said, there are four of us. Let's say a million apiece; plus one for luck – that's five million bucks,' Steve said, then added, 'cheap at the price, I would have thought.'

Colonel Randall now stood beside Steve.

'Now, you listen to me, motherfucker. Extortion does not become you, or your little band of playmates. You have no idea who, or what, you're dealing with,' Randall retorted.

Steve eyeballed him. 'Listen Randall, we ain't a bunch of cowboys, if that's what you think. This is not the OK Corral and your guys ain't any Wyatt Earp, so go and fuck yourself. You've heard my terms. Five million bucks; we'll go quietly, if not, Randall, the stink we'll cause in Washington will be so bad that'll make your head spin. Oh, and Randall, the first head we're talking about is yours. Now, you get a meeting arranged with Mr Big. He can't hide forever, besides, he's aware of his threats, even although he thinks it's just some crank. We'll tell him I also know who's blackmailing him.'

'What? What are you talking about?' Randall said.

'Just arrange a meeting. He's got to be present, with you too! Get the money certified, Randall – that's the least of it – before you're all held accountable for treason and murder, to say nothing of what upset you'll cause your Colombian partners.'

Steve now stood back. He turned to leave, then faced Randall. 'You can add rape to that list too, Colonel. I'll call you tomorrow Randall. You better have good news for me.'

With that, Steve glanced over at Detective Johnston and Jimmy Malone, then walked away.

Malone and Johnston followed, keeping their distance.

Colonel Randall spoke into his cuff. 'Stand down. I have the info I required; I repeat, stand down.'

Randall walked slowly towards the entrance/exit on the Southeast side of the cemetery. What the hell did Donaldson mean, threats? Threats against who? He referred to Mr Big. Did Cleaver know something he didn't? What the hell was he doing in the goddamn Caymans this weekend? Then he remembered their connection with Rodriquez Mahon. What a mess, all because Cleaver couldn't keep his dick in his fuckin' pants.

Chapter 83

Lieutenant Chandler, Sergeant Johnston and newspaper reporter Jimmy Malone listened as Steve repeated his conversation with Colonel Randall.

'You asked for five million bucks?' Malone echoed. 'Gee! You got balls, Donaldson, I'll give you that.'

'Never mind all that,' Chandler interrupted. 'I ... *we're* not interested in the money. It's unlocking the solution to the various crimes that have been committed, to say nothing of the exposure of some very high-ranking individuals.'

'Not interested in the money, Lieutenant? Have you forgotten I was the one who was drugged, kidnapped, tortured, beat-up and had to run for my life, all because you guys messed up,' Malone said, as he touched his face which was still tender from the blows he'd sustained.

'Listen, you little shit. You're lucky we haven't booked you for interfering in police business, so shut the fuck up, you little parasite. If it wasn't for Donaldson here you'd have no involvement in any of this.'

'Okay, okay you two,' Steve said, attempting to appease the situation. 'We're all on the same side. Let's all read from the same hymn sheet. I threw down the gauntlet at Randall. Told him about the threatening letters to see his reaction. Guess what? He didn't know what I was talking about. He didn't say as much, but I could tell he was surprised.'

'So, what's your take on this, Donaldson?' Chandler asked. 'What do we do now?'

'We wait, Lieutenant. Then I'll contact Randall. Arrange another meet with him and hopefully Mr Big, but this time it will be in New York at a venue we choose. I have to phone him tomorrow.'

'And don't forget about the money,' Malone said, in a gushing tone.

Chandler just eyeballed the reporter and was about to speak when Steve held his arm. Chandler said nothing, but his expression showed he was not pleased.

'It's this reference to the Caymans ah don't get,' Malone said. 'What's the connection there? They're a British colony, or something,' he said.

Steve smiled. 'Yes, that's right, Jimmy. They are part of the British Commonwealth, so whatever their connection, could start an international incident and ...'

'Oh for God's sake Donaldson, now you're in la-la land. You've been watchin' too many movies?' Chandler said.

Steve just stared at his other three accomplices. 'Listen, there's a lot of stuff done that involves the Caymans. Offshore accounts for one, and drug handling too. You'd be surprised the kinda figures we're talking about, to say nothing of the people involved controlling it all.'

Next day Steve telephoned to arrange the meeting with Randall.

'I told him that Tuesday was the deadline and if he and whoever didn't show then our information would be released to the nation via the news and media.

Whoever is leading this operation uses Randall efficiently and wisely but keeps him in the dark sometimes, but still expects him to operate to his or her satisfaction.'

'Who sent you the copy letter, Steve?' Lieutenant Chandler asked.

'Told you – don't know, but it's someone with a vindictive streak and somebody who wants revenge big time and is prepared, I think, to expose their identity to take whoever is responsible down.'

Lieutenant Chandler asked, 'Can I see the letter again, Steve?'

'Sure,' Steve replied, as he took it from his inside pocket.

Lieutenant Chandler read the letter out loud, the black capitals raised on a white background signifying its contents.

'MURDERER

RAPIST

TRAITOR

CAYMANS

I'LL GET YOU

YOUR TIME IS COMING

'And you've no idea, Steve, who sent this?'

Steve shook his head negatively. 'No, Lieutenant. It would unlock so much if I did.'

Steve telephoned Randall once more and confirmed their meeting.

'Okay guys, it all goes down Tuesday. We meet Randall and Mr Big at the Loeb Boathouse, Central Park as before but this time there'll be no abductions. This time we'll meet the person behind Claire Monroe's killing and answerable to all the other poor souls involved like Rusty and Riker and Gennero, and how many others that we don't know about. So, any suggestions guys, because right now I could do with all the help I can get.'

'Do you really think the big fish will show himself Donaldson?' Malone said. "Cause bud, let me tell you, I ain't buying any more friggin' ice cream. You got that?'

Steve allowed himself a smile. 'Hey Jimmy, according to you, you showed them what was what. I don't think they'll mess with you twice.'

Lieutenant Stuart Chandler smiled. 'And if they attempted to abduct you a second time Malone, I would just spring into action and save your butt.' Chandler was now laughing.

'Very funny Lieutenant. You wouldn't help me if hell was freezin' over.'

It was Johnston's turn to laugh.

***

Steve headed for his office to catch up with his mail he'd taken from his mailbox.

He was sorting through the usual bumf as he walked, then realised his office door was ajar. Putting his mail on the corridor floor, he pressed himself against the wall and withdrew his .38. Stealthily he edged himself towards his office. There were no lights on and he strained his ears for any sound of movement. There was nothing.

Steve squatted as he held his gun in both outstretched arms. He kicked the door open and rolled in and over and into the room, then balanced himself on one knee, his gun pointing all around.

Steve's eyes fell on the intruder in the corner. He stared, his mind fighting with his eyes at the person that stood before him.

Chapter 84

Cleaver checked himself in his long, freestanding mirror where he could see his full self, and reflect that he did really look good. Okay, he wasn't the young buck of his youth, but yes, he had a mature charm and murmured to himself, 'Yeah, very good, Cleaver. You'll do very nicely.'

He again thought of Carla Roebuck. He hoped the evening would go well with her. At least she had some spunk – a fiery personality, but he liked that, apart from the fact that she was so damn sexy and God, so attractive.

There was a soft knock at his door. It was Benjamin. 'Excuse me, General, but Governor Gordon has sent me to inform you that Miss Roebuck has arrived and is already having cocktails downstairs.'

'Thank you, Benjamin. Tell the Governor I'll be down directly.'

Cleaver checked himself in the mirror one last time, adjusted his tie, then let his eyes sweep around his room. It was tidy, as was his normal fashion. He opened his door, turning the round, heavy brass handle and made his way downstairs.

Cleaver was last to arrive and Benjamin met him with an offered tray of dry champagne which Cleaver accepted graciously.

'Ah, Cleaver,' Governor Gordon said out loud, signifying his welcome and making all other guests turn and stare at Cleaver. 'Oh, my, you do look splendid,' Gordon said, admiring the sharpness of Cleaver's attire in his pristine evening dress uniform, with his scarlet waistcoat and miniature campaign medals.

'Thank you, Governor,' Cleaver replied, as his eyes rotated around the room, recognising the usual acquaintances who frequented Gordon's hospitality, like Peter Morgan of Barclays Bank, the first commercial bank on Grand Cayman, which had operated since 1953. There was the Chairman of the Chamber of Commerce, William Eden, and two other gentlemen: Stanley Church and Sandy Foster, both hoteliers. Their businesses had sprung up on the back of the new airfield as the tourist numbers increased visiting the islands. Cleaver nodded at each of them in turn, his eyes still rotating until they came to rest on Carla Roebuck. She was in busy conversation with Neville Lowther, Chairman of the Caymans National Festival who organised The Pirates Week, amongst other events during the year.

Carla's head turned. She was smitten as she gazed across the room at Cleaver. She could not help herself but admire the tall, powerful man in his dress uniform and smiled teasingly as she remembered fondly of their last encounter.

Cleaver was still staring at Carla as each of the wives present came forward to greet him. First up was Mrs Elizabeth Eden. She smiled as she approached.

'You look very distinguished tonight, General.'

'Why, thank you, Ma'am.' Cleaver replied and returned her compliment with a charming smile. He received much the same comments from the other ladies present, each speaking to him one by one and Cleaver behaved admirably, but his mind was still on Carla Roebuck who was on the other side of the room.

Slowly, Carla made her way towards Cleaver, mingling as she drew nearer. Cleaver had also moved in her direction, stopping and chatting to Governor Gordon and hoteliers Stanley Church and Sandy Foster before discussing pleasantries with Peter Morgan of Barclays Bank, then the two met.

Carla stared at her General, and he back at her. 'Long time,' she said, 'and I must say, you do look wonderful in that uniform.'

'Thank you,' Cleaver replied. 'You look pretty good too, in fact, I feel like a kid in a sweet shop; all this candy, but don't touch.'

'Oh! I don't know, General. Who knows what the rest of the evening may bring?'

They were playing cat and mouse with each other, their eyes and smiles locked together, oblivious to the other guests.

'Ladies and Gentlemen,' shouted Benjamin. 'Dinner is served!'

The announcement found guests matching their part- ners, and filing into the large dining room, Governor Gordon and his wife Mary leading the entourage.

Cleaver downed the remainder of his champagne. 'Shall we?' he said, as he allowed Carla to take his arm.

Carla and Cleaver never really had the time for all this protocol, but hey, they were together once again, and if that meant following some stuck-up formalities then who were they to rock the boat?

Dinner went well, the ladies present very much in the limelight as the Caymans had just received its first written confirmation ceasing it to be a dependent of Jamaica, and also granting the vote to women.

It was late and Cleaver had had a long day. He had his usual Romeo and Juliet and brandy with the other gentlemen present, talking about the new business the Islands were attracting and, of course, the politics of the day, while the ladies kept themselves separate, talking about their opportunity and the change that was affecting them in the Caymans.

Cleaver approached Carla. She was on the terrace, looking out over the lush gardens, all clouded in the black night. The ripple of the Caribbean could be heard faintly as its waves gently fell to zero on the beach.

'Mind if I join you?' Cleaver said, another champagne flute in his hand.

Carla turned and smiled. 'Why General, thought you'd never come. You men, talk, talk, talk, putting the world to rights, but nothing ever gets done,' she said, then added, 'well, not really. It's all just a game, isn't it, General?'

Cleaver considered Carla's statement, his dark brown eyes searching her beautiful green ones, her soft skin complementing her long, dark hair, her full breasts, small waist and proportioned hips giving her the perfect hourglass figure.

He watched Carla's full lips as they talked, but his mind was focusing on their last encounter at Governor Gordon's mansion and Cleaver felt instantly aroused.

They played the teasing game, each enjoying the challenge of each other's intellect and the promise of what the rest of the night may bring.

Re-joining other guests for a short time, they each bade their host goodnight and headed for their bedrooms. Carla, once inside Cleaver's bedroom, hesitated. She had changed her mind.

She kissed Cleaver, then whispered into his ear, 'I don't think we'll go any further tonight, Cleaver, after all, I'm sure you're still on the rebound after that secretary of yours – what was her name? Claire … She made such an impression on you. What happened, Cleaver, did she not like it rough? Rough, like you can give?' Carla laughed in his face.

Cleaver was taken aback, but angry now, especially since he'd been looking forward to Carla's company all evening. 'Rough?' he echoed. 'Rough? I'll show you rough, Carla,' he said, as he spun her around so that she was facing away from him. He held her over the bed, face down, his strong hand and arm locking her down in a vice-like grip, then lifted her black sequined dress, exposing her buttocks; took one look, then spanked her; spanked her hard, four, five, six times, then he unzipped himself and forced his large, erect manhood into her, thrusting harder and harder, still holding her face down. He didn't stop until she cried out.

'You're hurting me, you're hurting me.'

'You want it rough, Carla, well, here it is.' Again, he thrust himself hard into her, then abruptly withdrew. He still held her, but pulled her back up towards himself.

She was still facing away from him. He was satisfied with his action.

His grip on Carla softened, and he expected a retaliation, an attack, but Carla, still not facing him, just arched her body close to his, her cheek now resting against his with her head thrown back. She gazed into Cleaver's eyes, and smiled.

'I love you, Cleaver,' she said, her green eyes dancing the words she spoke.

Carla then turned full-on to Cleaver and kissed him passionately. They broke free and again she repeated her words. 'I love you, Cleaver.'

Cleaver eyed the beauty before him. 'I know you do,' he said, then ordered her to leave.

Chapter 85

Next morning Cleaver went to Seven Mile Beach.

'Okay, Rodriquez, what the hell happened? Do you think Drummond is playing against us, to furnish his own ends?'

'No, General, I don't. I think somebody tipped them off about The Providence, they pulled the Royal Navy in as well as the Coastguard and, of course, Drummond and his crew didn't stand a chance. Someone, somewhere, General, is feeding them information about our shipments and I can assure you General it's not from my end, although our compadres in Colombia don't care whose fault it is; they just want the merchandise. Too many people depend on us, we are a key link in the chain, and if we break then it affects everybody down the line. There's a lot of money at stake here General, but I'm sure you know that and I'm sure ...' Rodriquez paused, 'you'll fix it. Square this deal; keep our Colombian friends happy and off my back.'

'What was their take, Rodriquez, had the shipment been made?' Cleaver asked, now thinking on his feet and with good reason. It was costing him a fortune too. Cleaver thought maybe Randall will come to the rescue;

eliminate this Donaldson. Hopefully he's the one behind all this trouble.

'So, what am I in for, Rodriquez?' Cleaver repeated.

'Oh, Señor, at a guess, \$50-60 million, maybe more.'

'That much?' Cleaver said, pursing his lips.

Rodriquez shrugged his shoulders. 'Can you fix it General?'

Cleaver thought for a moment. 'Maybe Rodriquez, but not here in the Caymans. I'll require to return to Washington.'

'Okay, Señor, but whatever you think you can do, do it quickly. These people; they don't play games and patience is, how you say, not their strong point.'

Cleaver nodded. He had already decided to return earlier than planned, his discussion with Rodriquez just confirmed the situation.

Cleaver hoped Randall would have at least solved one part of the puzzle. Together they would sort out the challenge of the shipment and appease their Colombian counterparts.

***

The telephone rang in Governor Alex Frederick Gordon's mansion. Benjamin answered the call. It was Colonel Glen Randall from Washington, DC on the line for General Harris.

'I'm sure the General's about, Sir. Please hold while I locate him and bring him to the telephone.'

Benjamin knocked gently but firmly on General Harris's door. 'Yeah! Come in, I'm decent,' General Harris replied.

Benjamin entered, his white gloved hands still on the door handle. 'There's a telephone call for you General, a Colonel Randall from Washington, sounds urgent,' Benjamin added.

'Can it be transferred through here to my room Benjamin?'

'No Sir. These instruments are purely internal lines Sir, in case you or any guest requires assistance. I'm afraid the only direct line out is downstairs in the lobby, apart from the one in the Governor's study.'

'Can I call him back?'

'Suppose so Sir, but he's hanging on for you at the moment.'

'Okay, go ahead, tell Colonel Randall I'm on my way to speak to him.'

Benjamin raced ahead and delivered Cleaver's message, keeping Randall hanging on the line until the General appeared.

Cleaver took the receiver off Benjamin and mouthed a thank you for him to depart. 'Randall, Cleaver here. What's so urgent? Then, not waiting for a reply, carried on speaking, 'you got that thing sorted out?'

Randall's voice was quiet. 'If you mean Donaldson – not exactly, but he knows something else too.'

'I'm listening,' Cleaver said.

'He says you've been receiving threatening letters, says you're involved with some other stuff. He said you'd know what I was talking about Cleaver, what the hell is going on? Cleaver … Cleaver … you still there?'

General Bob Cleaver Harris was still there all right, as Randall's comments hit him and he thought about the two anonymous letters he'd received.

'Well, Cleaver, what does he mean? What is he referring to?'

Cleaver didn't answer for a moment, then said coldly into the black Bakelite handset, 'I'm returning to Washington, Glen. Be there as soon as I can; arrange for my usual transfer from Bolling field.'

'Cleaver … Cleaver!' Randall yelled, but the line was dead.

Cleaver ordered a cab.

'Benjamin, say goodbye to Governor Gordon for me, something's come up and I have to return to Washington immediately.'

Benjamin nodded. 'Will there be anything else, Sir?'

Cleaver hesitated, smiled; his memory returning to his time with Carla Roebuck. 'No Benjamin, I took the liberty of ordering a cab earlier, so there's nothing except to thank you once again for looking after me. You never disappoint, Benjamin. The Governor's very lucky and fortunate to have someone as reliable and trustworthy as you.' Cleaver's mind was triggered by his last word; how he would love to know who was betraying him in his organisation.

Cleaver shook Benjamin's hand. 'Take care of yourself,' he said.

General Bob Cleaver Harris settled down in his cab and set off for the airport.

Carla Roebuck just watched from her window as the cab sped down the long driveway.

'He didn't even say goodbye,' Carla said out loud to herself, then turned away.

'Come back to bed darlin'. He ain't worth the trouble.'

Carla shot a glance towards Peter Morgan of Barclays Bank.

'Get out!' She shouted. 'Get out!'

Chapter 86

General Bob Cleaver Harris arrived back in Virginia. He was in Randall's office.

'How, Randall? How did this schmuck find out about the letters?' Cleaver needed Randall all the way on this one and had let him read the threatening information he'd received.

'Cleaver, what the hell are you involved in? Besides, our deal with Rodriquez. What's this about murder and rape?'

'Glen, this is neither the time nor the place. We have to find out if this Donaldson sent these letters which I assume he did, since he mentioned them to you, but how, or what, he knows must be extracted from him before his demise. There can be no stone unturned Glen, you do understand that, don't you?' Cleaver said, his eyes wide and staring. 'Glen! Glen! Colonel Randall, answer me!' Cleaver shouted. He was pushing Randall, who was still trying to figure out what it was that he didn't know, and what the information was that he had to extract from Donaldson. The very thought of what he may find frightened even him.

'Where are you meeting Donaldson on Tuesday?' Cleaver asked.

'Me? Listen Cleaver, unless you're there he won't meet anyone. That's the point; he wants his five million bucks in cash, but he wants you there to give it to him.'

'Oh! Fuck's sake Glen, I won't be there. He's an amateur PI, playing way out of his league. Meet him at the boathouse, Central Park, but string him along and whoever's with him, give them a story, then put them through the routine and take them out. Job done. Play will resume as soon as things quieten down.'

Colonel Glen Randall sat in his chair. For the first time, he felt Cleaver was wrong.

'I think you, or *we're* underestimating this Donaldson. He plays his cards close to his chest. He knew about Claire Monroe, he figured out the attempted hit on himself, exposed Riker and Gennero and involved a police lieutenant from Manhattan. We – I – had to shut all enquiries into all those cases down. Even the one that involved Rusty the junkyard man who died in an accidental fire, but Donaldson found out otherwise, and I believe that's where he got my name and number. Don't ask me how, but I think it's where he made the connection to this office. So don't think, Cleaver, we're dealing with some schmuck who is chancing his arm. After all, he's also an ex-Special Forces marine, like yourself.'

'Oh yeah! I'd forgot about that,' Cleaver replied, then fell silent.

Glen Randall didn't speak either, so the two men sat, each trying to figure a solution to their problem.

Cleaver was first to speak. 'What about The Providence?' he asked. 'Has she been released from Customs yet?'

Colonel Randall wiped his brow with the back of his hand. He closed his eyes for a couple of seconds, then opened them and shook his head negatively. 'I'm assured to date the Authorities have not found anything on her, but as far as I know they won't release the ship. They have their captain, Drummond, under guard. Seem to be acting on information received. Information that was very specific of where they would be and what they were carrying. It's all very pat but right now I can't unlock any doors. I believe the Royal Navy's involved too, so it's not just the US Coastguard we're dealing with.'

Cleaver thought for a moment. 'Who's the man in charge of this operation? The man at the top, overseeing both US Customs and Her Majesty's Royal Navy?'

'You won't get to him,' Cleaver.

Randall checked his notes. 'It's an Admiral Wilkinson, according to his records on file. Very untouchable.'

'Glen, we need that shipment to be released. Our Colombian friends rely on us and although I can't divulge any more information to you, let me say that it's crucial The Providence is set on her way!'

Colonel Glen Randall just shrugged his shoulders, then added, 'Maybe we should just sit this one out a bit longer,' then asked, 'Cleaver, what rape is Donaldson referring to in those letters?'

'Christ's sake Randall, I don't fuckin' well know, I've never raped anyone in my life,' Cleaver replied as he quickly remembered his sex with Carla Roebuck at Governor Gordon's mansion in the Caymans. 'So, I don't know what he's talking about.' Cleaver's voice was rising now; its tone and decibels showing signs of frustration and anger.

Glen Randall took his time with his question, then spoke quietly to his superior. 'Did you ever rape Claire Monroe, Cleaver?' he asked, his eyes staring at Harris's face, searching for an expressive response or clue that would signify the truth.

'No … no, I never raped Claire. True, we were in a relationship and I thought it was great. Then the bitch just got up and quit – quit on me, quit her job; after everything I'd done for her.'

'You sure, Cleaver? We never did find out why she left the service.'

'Now you listen to me, Randall, Claire Monroe and I were good together, but I never forced myself on her sexually. There's no reason for any allegations from her to say otherwise. Anyway, she's dead, and one thing I've learned Randall; people can't speak from the grave.'

'We took her out; she knew too much. She was too close to me. I didn't like giving you that order but it was safer and tidier to be absolutely sure. Anyway, our other friends would probably have done the job anyway, 'cause they don't like loose ends either, but as God is my judge I never ever raped her.'

Colonel Randall sat back. 'Well, she must have told this guy Donaldson something that night because it's been hell ever since.'

Cleaver Harris rotated his head and neck; he could feel the tension in his muscles. 'You say we meet this Donaldson, Tuesday, Central Park?'

Randall nodded. 'Well, I'll be there. Just as this Mr PI requested. Organise the money. We'll play his game but if this motherfucker thinks he's going to collect $5 million and just walk off into the sunset, he's got another think coming.'

'We'll play his game Randall, then take him down.'

'Get the money, usual fund. I'll sign the authorisation.'

General Bob Cleaver Harris stared at Colonel Randall. Both men remained silent for a while, each in anticipation of what was going to happen on Tuesday in New York.

Randall's direct line burst into life. The two men, taken unaware, just stared at the instrument as its constant tone pierced the silence.

Glen picked up the receiver and held it to his ear. 'Randall,' he replied.

'It's me …' Steve said, then, not waiting for any acknowledgement, said, 'slight change of plans, Randall. It's still Tuesday, and it's still at the Loeb Boathouse, but not outside …' Steve paused. 'I'll be inside at the restaurant – not the café – the actual restaurant. We can talk easier there. I have a table reserved.' Steve paused again. 'Oh, and Randall, bring Mr Big and, of course, the money. One without the other and there's no deal.'

Chapter 87

Tuesday morning arrived. Jimmy Malone had been sent ahead with Detective Sergeant Johnston to check out the surrounding vicinity of Loeb's Boathouse. If there were any of Randall's foot soldiers about then hopefully Malone would recognise them from his previous ordeal.

It was still early although the park was busy with its usual daily joggers and dog walkers. There was certainly no ice cream man and no sign of any other suspicious characters. The usual beat police had also passed clearing the park of the bums that used it during the night, so all seemed normal.

'You think this son of a bitch will show?' Malone asked Johnston.

'I don't know Jimmy, but there's a good chance Donaldson will pull this off,' Johnston replied, as his eyes kept scanning the pathways, benches and trees around him.

'I don't really get it, Sergeant,' Malone said, extending the conversation and hoping Johnston would enlighten him with more information on the case.

'You're fishing Malone? You know what I know, check out the guy in the suit other side of the Lake, he's talkin' to another guy; they're shakin' hands, dressed in suits.

Can you see them? Do you recognise them?' Johnston asked, keeping a direct stare at the two figures in the distance.

Jimmy Malone shielded his eyes, placing his right hand across his forehead from the morning sun as he stared eastwards across the lake, past the boathouse.

'Can't really tell from this distance. Could be, but not sure.'

Sergeant Johnston watched the two men who were still in deep conversation as he once again scanned the surrounding area.

'They're on the move,' Malone said quietly.

Johnston's eyes focused more directly now. The two men, whoever they were, walked away casually; they seemed okay. They were laughing as they made their way towards the park exit.

Detective Johnston checked his watch. It now read 11:00am. 'Let's take another walk around, Malone. You take this side, I'll wander over past the boathouse, check out the others; let's say we meet back here in half an hour, okay? Then we'll check out the Ramble together.'

'Suits me,' Malone said, as he started to walk on his second reconnoitre of that morning.

'Oh, Malone, don't stray too far, I need to keep you in sight, just in case anything … you know/'

Malone smiled. 'Hey Johnston, I can handle myself,' he said cockily, 'and besides, I'm not the one they're after. They, whoever *they* are want Donaldson, so I don't think they'll jeopardise their mission taking me; I mean, they do know I'm just a reporter, so if they're watching they won't make their move until after the drop has been made at lunchtime.'

Detective Johnston eyed Malone. 'We'll make a detective out of you yet, Jimmy. Maybe you should consider joining up; leave that trashy industry you work in.'

'What, and miss all the gossip, miss all the scoops? Hell, Johnston, that's what keeps me going and besides, I'm good at it. Good at my job, Johnston. I ain't cut out to be no Rubber Duck – or Jericho, for that matter.'

The two men laughed, then parted, each taking their route; each wondering what the afternoon would bring.

Steve sat with Lieutenant Chandler. They were having coffee and muffins at Rikki's Café. Chandler was overindulging himself this morning as he bit into his chocolate doughnut.

'Do you really think "Mr Big" will show?' he mumbled, his mouth full of doughnut. 'Do you really believe he and Randall are just gonna hear what you have to say and hand over five million bucks and let you walk? They'll take you out, Steve. You do know that, don't you?'

Steve nodded. 'I expect them to try Lieutenant, but I have other plans. Besides, I have a surprise up my sleeve which will rock the fuckin' boat so much that it'll bring tears to their eyes.'

'A surprise, Steve? You mean the threatening letter; what's that going to achieve? Anybody can send a threat, it's quite another thing carrying it out, and for all intents and purposes, they think it's you who's sent them and you want paid-off; trading your information for the cash. That doesn't mean you're going to collect, Steve,' Chandler said, wiping his mouth with his hand.

Steve paused. 'You, and I suspect Randall too, have overlooked one small detail.'

'Oh, what's that?' asked Chandler.

Steve allowed himself a smile. 'It's not the money Lieutenant, the five million bucks is incidental. That's not the issue. It goes much deeper than that, in fact, a whole lot deeper. I can't divulge that, not even to you Lieutenant, but you'll understand when the meeting takes place and all the parties connected are present. It will all be made clear once Randall and his superiors are locked in and exposed.'

You're keeping me out of the loop, Donaldson, what else have you got? Tell me, you son of a bitch, tell me what it is I don't know.'

Steve sat back. He checked his wristwatch. It's almost noon. Time to go, Lieutenant.'

Donaldson, tell me – what is it that I don't know?'

Steve eyeballed Lieutenant Chandler. 'You'll know in one hour Lieutenant; one hour and I guarantee if you play your cards right they'll be offering you The Captaincy of your precinct.'

Steve rose to leave. Chandler grabbed him, he could feel the power and muscle of Steve's arm. He obviously kept himself fit. Very fit. After all, he had been a US marine, but that was a long time ago.

Steve glanced down at Chandler's arm, then stared into his face. 'You with me on this Lieutenant? Do you trust me?' Steve let his words ring with a tone that saw Chandler release his grip of Steve's arm.

Steve nodded. 'Good, then let's go. We have a tiger to snare.'

Chapter 88

Steve checked in with the Maître'D at the Loeb Boathouse restaurant. It was almost 1:00pm when he and Lieutenant Chandler sat down. He'd already explained to the restaurant manager that they'd be joined by the rest of their party sometime soon.

The reservation had been made for six people, but at Steve's instruction an extra seat had been added, albeit without a place setting. They were not dining, even although they were in the formal dining room, as Steve had arranged for coffee and biscuits to be provided and also adjacent tables either side to be cleared as he had informed the manager that the meeting was of a sensitive nature. Steve had also promised that any loss of business incurred would be met by his party, so the restaurant need not miss out.

Lieutenant Chandler's badge secured the accommodation and Steve felt somewhat relaxed as he sat there waiting.

One o'clock came and went. Chandler checked his watch. He shifted uneasily in his seat. 'Where are they? They do know we're inside the boathouse and not outside?' he said, then added, 'I'll go check.'

Steve grabbed the Lieutenant's arm. 'Sit down, they know where we are. They'll be here.

'What makes you so sure?' Chandler said, staring at Steve, then shooting a glance at his sergeant and Malone.

'Eh? What are you not telling us Donaldson? Come on, what?'

Steve just stared at the Lieutenant. 'Sit down, please. You're a stickler for the truth, you always tell me that, remember? Well, be patient a little longer and all will be revealed.'

Lieutenant Chandler sighed, then retook his seat. He was not happy; Donaldson was holding something back, something he should know and as the Senior Investigation Officer on this case and the only one there with any real jurisdiction.

Steve glanced across the restaurant. The adjacent tables were not in use as he requested. The nearest table in operation was occupied by a lone diner, dressed in black with a tilted fedora hat that covered the eyes. The diner was enjoying hors d'oeuvres, and all consumed with their newspaper in front of them. The only other table in close proximity was a group of old-timers; obviously they'd been sailing their rowing crafts on the Lake and enjoying each other's company over lunch.

There was a shuffle at the reception desk. Two military personnel appeared in their standard issue uniforms. Their presence in their attire caused people to turn and stare but the larger of the two, and the most senior ranking, was not phased as he followed the Maître'D to Donaldson's table. Colonel Randall followed, carrying two attaché cases.

Steve stood, extending his hand. 'Good afternoon General,' he said.

He did not receive an acknowledgement, nor a reaction of his gesture.

'Let's get on with this,' the General said, and sat down opposite Steve.

Colonel Randall fell in line, sitting beside Cleaver and across from Lieutenant Stuart Chandler. He put the two cases on the floor beside him.

Steve sat back. He appraised the powerful man before him. He checked out his decorations sewn into his uniform jacket above the breast pocket.

'You've been on many missions, General. Successful ones too, judging by your decorations on your jacket. I bet you can tell us all a few stories, General, Eh?'

Steve was about to continue when General Harris held his hand up, signifying him to stop and shut up.

'We're here for a purpose, Donaldson. I've made myself available. We've got your money, however, can't think what you know that's worth all that and then what are you gonna do, Donaldson? You and your friends just give us some bullshit of a story and disappear into the sunset? Well, this is not the movies Donaldson; John Wayne don't just ride off without a hell of a good story or reason, or more importantly, proof. I say proof, Donaldson, because I assume you're the one who's been sending me the threats? At first I didn't take them seriously, but now I want to know what exactly you do have?

'So, Mr Private Eye, what information do you have on me, or Randall for that matter, that's worth $5 million? You see Donaldson, I think you're full of bullshit; you're an ex-marine all washed up, no real career, no wife, lost your kid. You're attempting to make amends for mistakes you've made and you've bluffed it so far. Am I right, Donaldson, or am I right?'

Steve paused – he glanced at Lieutenant Stuart Chandler and made the introduction. 'This is Lieutenant Stuart Chandler of the New York Police Department, General. You, via Randall, have shut down his cases. Your men, Riker and Gennero tried their usual bullying tactics on him and me, but when that didn't work authorisation went higher, General – I suspect from you to shut every case down that could be traced back to Claire Monroe. Riker, Gennero and Rusty; just pawns on the large scale of your game, were disappointing and so were taken out.

'They all knew Claire Monroe as they'd delivered the hit. It was reported as a hit and run. No big deal on the face of it. No real investigation into a traffic accident; just another statistic, but for one small thing. Claire Monroe had come to see me before she was fatally wounded that night. She had hidden from you and your organisation, then she reappeared. Randall here organised surveillance, then Riker and Gennero did the business. You're a military man, General, you don't like loose ends.

'You had me watched but took no action, therefore not alerting anybody, especially the Lieutenant here, as he may have put two and two together since I was the one who forced him to reopen the Claire Monroe case.

'The fact that Riker and Gennero attempted the same procedure on me testifies that Claire Monroe knew more than she should. She left your employ on a spur of the moment. Left you personally in the Cayman Islands when you expected her to be her more than accommodating self. She paid dearly for her action, General. She disappeared but when she resurfaced she, as far as you were concerned, was a loose cannon; a loose end. You gave Randall the order and he instructed Riker and Gennero to carry it out.

'You see, General, you're in all the way up in this shit; all the way up to your neck and it doesn't get any easier for you, after all, what went down in the Caymans; all your visits there, Claire Monroe with you, but she was not privy to everything, was she General? You made sure she knew some of your activities; after all, you and she were so close but she found out about the real you, General, and that's why she got herself out.'

Steve stopped talking as he sipped his coffee, his eyes fixed staringly on General Harris who sat across from him.

'Okay, Claire Monroe and I were an item for a while. It happens; boss and secretary. That does not implicate or prove I had anything to do with her death. A tragic accident Donaldson, nothing more. You have no proof. There's no one to back-up your story.'

'No one except Colonel Randall,' Steve interrupted.

General Harris laughed out loud. 'Oh! I see, and Colonel Randall here is gonna come all over and nice and put me and himself in the frame and pay you $5 million to boot. I don't think so, Mr Steve Donaldson. As far as I'm concerned, this meeting is over. Glen, we're leaving, bring the money. This cowboy schmuck has nothin'. Nothin' that we can't handle.'

'Is that a threat, General, in front of witnesses?' Steve said.

General Harris smiled as he examined the faces he was up against: Chandler, Johnston, Malone, and, of course, Steve's.

'You've got nothin' Donaldson. Now, I'm leavin', I have a plane to catch.'

General Harris stood and screwed his eyes up. 'I'm dealin' with amateurs; knew I was. Just came to see what you had Donaldson, and I must say, I'm slightly disappointed, you being an ex-US marine and decorated too for services in Special Forces, really disappointed.' He turned to Colonel Randall. 'Glen, we're leaving.'

Colonel Randall now stood, his two attaché cases in hand.

'Cleaver,' Steve now said, referring to the General by his nickname. 'I'm sorry you feel that way. I mean, does the name Drummond – Captain Drummond – of the ship The Providence mean anything to you?'

'You know my nickname, Donaldson. Well, bully for you, then you'll know I'm not a man to be trifled with, and Drummond – a Captain, you say? Never heard of him. Another shot in the dark Mr Private Investigator? A line that goes nowhere.'

'That's not what Rodriquez Mahon says. He's with Admiral Wilkinson as we speak.'

It was Cleaver's turn to feel awkward. 'A name, that's all Donaldson, a name.'

'Well. What will your Colombian friends say, Cleaver, eh? I don't think they'll be so accommodating, as we are being right now. So, you leave General, and deal with them on your own, or sit down and listen to a very interesting story I have to tell you.'

Chapter 89

General Bob Cleaver Harris glanced at Glen Randall.

'What have you got to lose, Cleaver?' Randall said, shrugging his shoulders. 'We're here now anyway; anything this schmuck has to say we may just as well hear it. Won't change anything, but let's humour him.'

Cleaver searched Steve's face, but couldn't read it. He then glanced at Randall but still did not resume his seat.

'Do you remember a girl called Marietta de Palos?' Steve said.

'Can't say that I do,' Cleaver replied. 'Should I know her? Next you'll be tellin' me she's a pole dancer in a strip joint Donaldson, so if that's your story you've got the wrong man and I'm outta here.'

'Paco Montero, then. Do you remember him?' Steve pressed.

'No, don't know any of these names. Should I?' Cleaver asked.

'You tell me, General. Do you need to know a woman's name before raping her, then killing her, or is that something you would do just for the hell of it?'

Cleaver stared across the table. He didn't reply.

'Well, is it, General bloody Cleaver Harris?'

'I don't know what you're talking about Donaldson, and I've never heard of the people you refer to. I haven't killed or raped anyone, for that matter.' Silently, Carla Roebuck's image jumped into his mind. Could she be behind all this? Then he thought, but Carla couldn't – wouldn't have any cause to … seek out Steve Donaldson. His strong mind then returned to the present situation.

'Is that your story, Donaldson? Is that all you've got? Some cock and bull made up story to threaten me; me, General Bob Harris? You do disappoint me Donaldson. You bring threats that are unfounded; you can't back them up. I don't know who you're talking about and I believe you don't either.'

Steve leaned back in his chair. 'Maybe that's correct General, but let's take you on another adventure; one that I think will amaze you.'

'What are you up to Donaldson? What dirty tricks are you fabricating this time?'

'No dirty tricks General. I think what I'm about to divulge will absolutely blow your mind.'

Chapter 90

'Okay, General Bob Harris. You're better known as Cleaver Harris. That's your nickname which you were given in the Marines, and as I understand, because no matter what the assignment, no matter what the difficulties, or the odds, Bob Harris always got it done. Chop – just like a cleaver. Get the job done at all costs. You moved up the career ladder quickly, because you could be relied upon and General, your nickname Cleaver stuck. Promotion after promotion, Cleaver Harris always got the job done.

'That's all great General, and you had immense influence and power but all that wasn't enough Cleaver – may I call you Cleaver? Because you wanted more wealth, more power; you wanted everything your way. With your present rank you found you could access virtually anything you desired. You developed your private army of mercenaries, handpicked men, each with individual and special skills; men that could survive in the most abnormal of conditions. Men who could carry out your instructions without question, and men who were loyal to your cause. Men for hire General, men who operated outwith the sanction of normal military missions. In fact, I bet some of the missions they were involved in were probably against their fellow Americans. That didn't matter, or concern you, of course, just as long as the mission was completed and completed to your every direct order and satisfaction.'

'This is all bullshit Donaldson, and you know it. You're trying to impress your friends here with all this shit. This is absolute crap Donaldson, and it doesn't wash. You've been in Special Forces as a US marine. You know first-hand what goes down. It's not always a bed of roses, but there's nothing that's not official. This is not Hollywood Donaldson, so if that's all you've got, that and two people that I've never heard of, or met, then I suggest *you* need help, not me.'

'So, you are denying the night flights that leave from a Mississippi base, and unscheduled missions that take men overseas, then back again with nothing logged? You deny the assault of Paco Montero and the rape and killing of his girlfriend, Marietta de Palos on the beach in Grand Cayman? You deny that when your own fuckin' ego was dented when Claire Monroe gave you a knockback that evening when she didn't want to have sex with you, that you were so angry; your temper rising and rising, someone saying no to General Bob Cleaver fuckin' Harris, that you couldn't bear it? Especially since it was Claire Monroe; your secretary and lover. You couldn't have anyone saying no to the famous General Cleaver Harris and certainly no one so close to you. You stormed out General, and you found yourself on the beach. You heard a young couple making out on the sand, enjoying their pleasures with each other; pleasures that you'd been denied by Claire Monroe that very evening. After all, General, isn't that one of the reasons Claire accompanied you on these trips to the Cayman Islands? You couldn't stand the fact that here was a young couple in full process of making love, the very thing you'd been denied. You, General Cleaver Harris.

'You made sure you were not going to be denied, so you hauled Paco Montero off his girlfriend, rendered him unconscious with a blow to his head, then proceeded to rape Marietta de Palos; she fought General, didn't she, but her neck broke when her head snapped back. You finished your business, and thought no one witnessed you, General. But you were careless; someone saw you. Saw the whole incident. You left a crime scene, knowing full well that when the couple would be found it would be regarded as a rape gone wrong and both parties – one dead and the other injured – would be recorded that very way, nothing to do with General Cleaver Harris who was supposed to be in his guest suite at Governor Gordon's mansion all evening.'

Steve's voice was rising as he spoke his words, full in the knowledge that he knew the man across from him knew the story so well, and would remember that night now that it was being recalled to him.

General Cleaver Harris shook his head. 'God, you're an imaginative son of a bitch. Why do you dislike me so much that you want to frame me for every crime under the sun? Hey, I wasn't there; don't know the people. It's all pie in the sky,' Harris said, in a confident composure.

'We have a witness who saw you,' Steve said dryly.

'Oh, a witness, now, humph, let me see, some coloured being paid a few bucks to say whatever you tell him to.' Harris laughed. 'As I said Donaldson, you ain't got no witness and you can't tie me to a crime when I wasn't there. And even if you did, you couldn't prove anything, not really. It would be my word against a coloured.' General Harris looked around the table and again laughed sarcastically.

'Our witness, General, is not a coloured. You made a mistake. Through anger you inflicted your control over a poor, defenceless young woman and you're gonna pay for that.'

Again, General Cleaver Harris laughed.

'So that's murder and rape we have on you General. Then there's the recruitment and abuse of the specially trained corps carrying out specialist unauthorised missions overseas, and yet all paid for by generous Uncle Sam.'

'You should write a book Donaldson. Again, your imagination is running riot. You have no records, no statements, no witnesses; no proof, Donaldson. You ain't going far on that set of charges either, so if it's all the same to you, I'll leave now with the $5 million in these cases; you do what you think you have to do, but be sure of this Donaldson, come against me again and I'll swat you like the lowlife fly you are. Your ass will be mine, Donaldson – understand?'

'Are you threatening me, General?'

Cleaver smiled. 'I don't make threats …! Understand?'

Cleaver and Randall rose once again to leave.

'Oh, I wouldn't leave just yet General, I, or, we, haven't finished yet. I've saved the best till last.'

'You may not have finished Donaldson, but I'm through listening. You do what the hell you like, am outta here.'

'You organised the hit on myself, General. Instructed Randall here to get his boys, Riker and Gennero, on the case. A pair of amateurs; messed up. Got themselves killed, didn't they, by your instruction. I guess then, of course, it all started when Claire Monroe left you and her work. You knew she had information on most of your activities and because of your personal involvement with her you confided in her on certain aspects.

'You authorised the hit, General, but she disappeared. Disappeared off the face of the Earth, and even you, with your power and people working for you couldn't find her whereabouts until, of course, she came to me. She wanted my services to put you away General, as she realised the real monster you are and the power-mad maniac who'd stop at nothing to ensure you achieved your goals and had more power.'

General Harris stared at Donaldson. He shook his head. 'Claire Monroe was very special to me. We had a good working relationship and it blossomed into that of a personal nature, that I do admit, but I don't think I'll be the first boss to fall for his secretary, and I certainly would wish her no harm.'

Cleaver spoke quietly, his eyes welled up, crocodile tears blurring his vision. 'I really loved that woman. You know what's so galling? I took her away from her navigation at Andrews Air Base, working on mundane map coordination and, of course, her hotshot flyer of a boyfriend Mac ... God, I can never remember that son of a bitch's name. Is that who's putting all this together for you Donaldson? A vengeful old flame of Claire Monroe?'

'Not quite, General. Not quite.'

'You heard of Lomax, Goldman and Corbett, General?'

Harris searched his memory. 'Sounds like lawyers,' he answered, smiling, 'but I can't say I know them.' Harris turned to Randall and asked the question with his eyes, 'you know them, Glen?' he said.

Colonel Randall shook his head negatively. 'What have they got to do with anything?'

'Oh! First, let me explain. Their main interests are personal injury but they have a very strong department that deals with criminal law. They prosecute the bad guys, and even when the DA refuses a case they seem to win. Lomax and Goldman started the company many years ago. They were fortunate enough to have in their employ a young man by the name of Peter Corbett. He was a bright star in the making. He seemed to win all his cases. He was ambitious and his young bride Barbara wanted a family. They found, rather unfortunately, after being pregnant with their first child, which she lost, that it would be impossible for her to ever conceive again. Corbett had been made a partner in the firm. He had excelled in all areas pertaining to his work, but all they ever wanted as a couple was a daughter.

'An unplanned opportunity arose after a couple were killed in a terrible road traffic accident. The woman was pregnant, and although the doctors managed to save the babies, only one could be taken by the mother's family. Reluctantly, the second child was put up for adoption.

'Peter and Barbara Corbett came on the scene and it wasn't long before papers and documents were completed and they had a daughter, who they named Christine. They lived in San Francisco where Lomax, Goldman were based and she grew up loved and well cared for. She had a good education. She did well in high school; went from there to college and onto becoming a legal secretary. You can understand there was no shortage of money, so Christine had the best. She was attractive, intelligent, and, in fact, moved her career up to become a lawyer. She won many of her cases, just like her father; in fact, she earned quite a reputation and was a force to be reckoned within any courtroom.

'Years passed and the two girls, never knowing each other, forged out their own individual careers. That was, until one day, while reading a newspaper in San Francisco, a certain young woman read an article about this female lawyer. There was also a photograph. The rest is a fantastic story of two sisters being reunited after so many years. The Corbetts were delighted. They had discovered a new daughter and they welcomed her with open arms. The whole situation could not have been better as the other sister's relatives that had taken her in had died and she really had no family. Her career too (while she had been successful) had gone belly-up, which is why she found herself in San Francisco in the first place.'

'Is this a sequel you're running here, Donaldson?' Cleaver said, smiling. 'Should I come back tomorrow for part two? Do they all die, or do they live happily ever after?' Cleaver said, now laughing out loud. He started coughing with the hilarity of it all.

'I ain't finished yet,' Steve broke in, now raising his voice.

'Hell you have Donaldson, you're all washed up; we ain't listening to any more of your ramblings.'

Cleaver scrutinised Lieutenant Chandler, Detective Sergeant Johnston and New York Times Reporter

Jimmy Malone. 'I feel sorry for you guys, dragged into all this mumbo jumbo. All in for the cash; nothing ever changes,' Cleaver added, as he once again drew a broad smile.

'If there's nothing in all this, General, then, 1. Why did you consent to come today, and 2. Why did you organise and bring $5 million in cash with you, which is the amount I requested for the pay-off; not just to keep us all quiet but for the information I'm giving you today?'

General Cleaver Harris again beamed a smile across the table at Steve. 'But you have nothin' Donaldson; a whole lot of circumstantial claptrap and a story that belongs on Heart to Heart radio show. You've no proof Donaldson … no proof that I'm involved in anything, or Colonel Glen Randall here, so you know what you can do with your accusations and threats, you can …' Cleaver was about to tell Steve where to shove all his evidence, when he was now fully aware of another person standing beside him. It was the lone diner who was dressed in a black trouser suit and black fedora hat pulled down low across the eyes.

'Hello, Cleaver, long time, remember me?' The young attractive woman said, as she removed her hat completely.

Cleaver turned, followed by Randall in total disbelief, as they stared into the eyes and face of a women they both knew.

Chapter 91

'Cla... ire... You... You're alive? My God... how are you?' Cleaver said, now standing and attempting to hug her.

Claire immediately took a step backward, avoiding contact. Colonel Glen Randall was also standing, so Steve, Lieutenant Chandler, Sergeant Johnston and Jimmy Malone followed suit.

'Where have you been?' Cleaver asked. 'I tried to find you … after you, eh … left your job at the Pentagon. How …? Where have you been …? How are you …?'

Cleaver again took a pace towards her and again Claire took a step back.

'Don't come near me. I've been very busy since you ordered the hit on me through your bulldog Randall here, but I'm here. Here to expose you Cleaver, and your organisation. You're going down, Cleaver. Hear me? Going down.'

Cleaver was aghast; really taken aback. 'Claire, what are you saying? I've not done anything … Claire … listen …'

'No, Cleaver, you listen. I'm the one who sent the letters to you. You know, with the statements of what you really are. You are a murderer Cleaver. I saw you.

Yes Cleaver, I … I saw you. I was on the beach that night in Grand Cayman. Remember when I didn't want you to come to my bedroom? You didn't like being refused; nobody ever says no to the Great General Bob Cleaver Harris. No … nobody dare, otherwise they'll be for the chop. But I said no Cleaver, and you stomped off.

'I watched from my window as you walked towards the beach. I had a change of heart I suppose, so I followed you; I kept a discreet distance, still unsure if I had totally changed my mind. I saw the young couple; I saw you, jealous and conscious of them making love. I watched, Cleaver, as you approached them. They were laughing with each other. I watched as you hit him, rendering Paco unconscious. I then watched in horror as you unzipped your pants and raped the poor defenceless girl Marietta; she attempted to fight you off. Then you hit her, and her neck snapped. That didn't stop you finishing your business you monster, then you wiped your neck and forehead, discarding your perspiration from your body after your attack. I saw you search around, making sure no one witnessed the incident, then you left, leaving a young girl dead and raped, the boyfriend unconscious to make it look like a lover's fight. Him forcing himself or her, but I saw Cleaver. I saw you and saw what you did and what really happened. So, you are guilty of murder and rape Cleaver, and it all took place in Grand Cayman where you were a guest of Governor Gordon at his house.

'That's not all that happened in the Caymans though, is it?'

'Okay Claire, enlighten us all with more of this rubbish you're making up. A woman scorned, is that what has happened to you?' Cleaver said. What else do you want to tell?'

'That's right Cleaver, I started making my own enquiries. Finding the source and the information wasn't easy, so I needed help. I had read and heard about Steve Donaldson, Private Investigator; how he solved a big case involving The Rosenbergs and thought he may be the man for me. I didn't have all the information to give him but I'd heard that he would, or had, proceeded in other cases on a need to know basis. So I thought that by working with him bit by bit we together would be able to prove how guilty and treacherous you really are, and how dangerous an enemy of our Country you are.

'Remember Cleaver, when I worked for you as your private secretary I was privy to much more than just liaison work. The fact that we were lovers Cleaver allowed certain – shall we say – secrets to be shared. I could handle everything Cleaver, until that night on the beach when you raped and murdered that poor girl; a girl you didn't even know, not that it mattered. She was there and your need was great, so much so that you carried out her execution without the blink of an eye. I realised Cleaver, that if you could behave like that with a stranger; be so cold and brutal, then what would you be like with someone close and personal to you? I was close to you Cleaver, but I had denied you your pleasure. I also realised I knew a lot of information on your other activities, to say nothing of the rape and murder I witnessed. I therefore realised you would find a way to kill me. To use your famous words Cleaver, "I'll squash her like a fly. No loose ends". Well, I wasn't going to wait around till you decided how, or where, so I got out. I ran

Cleaver, and kept running anywhere, but as long as I was away from you.'

'Claire, I must say, you have a fertile imagination. Now, sit down, you're embarrassing yourself and these gentlemen here,' Cleaver said, as he majestically waved his arm, sweeping it in front of Steve and Chandler.

'No Cleaver, I won't sit down. You see, I ran. I ended up in San Francisco. It was me who read the article in The Post; saw the picture of Christine Corbett. She looked exactly like me. That was when I found out I had an identical twin. You, nor anybody else for that matter, could not tell us apart, except for two small freckles she had below her left eye and you'd need to be looking for them to spot them.

'I learned she was a successful lawyer; we shared out past upbringings and cried when we thought of our real parents dying so tragically in an accident, just as Mr Donaldson told you. We then agreed that she would help me to bring you to justice, along with anybody else involved with you. Our aim was to free our Country from the evil that was, and is, emerging from the very top.

'You're a traitor, Cleaver. All those secret clandestine missions with your own specially trained troops, often to the highest bidder, even if it meant killing some of our own guys. You, Cleaver – a traitor as well as a murderer, rapist, and illegal smuggler.'

'Ho! Ho! A smuggler now?' Cleaver shouted, 'quick, hoist the main sail, I've got a scorned woman on my trail. Who the fuck do you think you're talking to, Claire Monroe? I'm not Blackbeard; operating out of the Cayman Islands on some trumped-up charge.'

'No, Cleaver, Blackbeard was an angel compared to you.'

'You can't prove anything, Claire. You're all wind and no knickers.'

Claire Monroe shouted at her former boss. 'You never used to complain, Cleaver, when I didn't wear any knickers.'

Jimmy Malone sniggered, 'I'd like to have been a fly on that wall' he added.

'Shut up you little shit of a parasite,' Cleaver responded, his decibels rising. He was in a corner and he didn't like it. His only experience to defend himself was to go on with the offensive. 'So, come on Claire Monroe, what other little gems do you want to air, 'cause this is the last time you'll insult or discredit me. When I think of all the things I did for you; your career, your promotions, my trust, my love, my all.'

'No, Cleaver, not your all. It's always been General Cleaver Harris. The man who gets things done. The all-powerful General, who never fails and must always win, but I said in my letters that I'd get you, and today is the day, Cleaver. You're going down. And for a long, long time.'

Cleaver showed bravado and laughed. It wasn't the first time he laughed in the face of his enemies and as far as he was concerned, it wouldn't be the last.

'As I said, Cleaver, I needed the help of Private Investigator Steve Donaldson. He would proceed on a need to know basis and Christine, my new found sister and identical twin, offered to help.

'We exchanged places in New York. She pretended to be me. I gave her my purse with my driving licence, library card; all identification to prove that she was me should Mr Donaldson request proof of identity. I gave her so much information, but not everything. Anyway, I had more to find out at the time and relied on Mr Donaldson's services to help me, or should I say, Christine.

'Unfortunately, Mr Donaldson did not take the case, and Christine departed without having given any information that we held on you and Colonel Randall here, but your guys didn't know that. Christine was crossing the street to meet me and bring me up-to-date of her meeting with Steve Donaldson. We all know she didn't make it, Cleaver. We all know she was murdered by Randall's rookie so-called Justice Department agents, all directed by your authorisation, Cleaver. I mean, Colonel Randall couldn't tie his shoelace first without asking your permission. Christine had all my identification. It looked like a hit and run. There were no fingerprints taken and the case was logged accordingly. You managed to close down all investigation into Christine's murder; a murder that you thought was mine.

'You also organised or instructed Randall to take out Riker and Gennero. I knew I was getting close when that happened. No loose ends, eh, Cleaver?

'Steve Donaldson didn't know about my identical twin sister, or indeed our story, and how we were separated, but he did have enough savvy to realise that whoever killed me would come after him and sure enough, they did. As Christine had all my details; driving licence etc, then I was presumed dead, Cleaver. Did you miss me Cleaver?' Claire smiled. 'Don't answer that. As I was dead, I could move freely as no one was looking for me.

The rest of the evidence is clear and once they examine the body, her dental records will confirm her true identity. You see, Cleaver, you authorised the killing of an innocent young woman, and you'll be held accountable for that.'

Tears welled up in Claire's eyes as she thought of her sister. 'With regards to your smuggling activities which helps you fund your own private army of specially trained handpicked men for your clandestine operations, that is done by bringing and distributing drugs to Colombian cartel friends. They get their cut, you get yours. That, in itself, brings you more power, Cleaver.

'So General; Mr High and Mighty; you're going down. Down, down, down; not just for the murder of my sister, but for all the families involved over the years because of your personal ambition and greed.'

'You can't prove any of this Claire. Now, why don't we go somewhere and discuss all this? We used to be ...'

'Cleaver, I don't think you've grasped the situation you're in. Rodriquez Mahon is in custody with Admiral Wilkinson of The Royal Navy and he's singing like a canary. He's been offered witness protection, and he ain't holding anything back. The Providence is gone. Its cargo exposed and confiscated. Captain Drummond jailed. You're next Cleaver and all because Steve Donaldson here wouldn't take the case until I was supposedly killed. On a need to know basis, Cleaver. That's what betrayed you. Donaldson started investigations after that. Lomax, Goldman and Corbett will be the prosecutors on this one. You're finished, Cleaver.'

Four Military Police appeared to take General Harris and Colonel Randall into custody.

Lieutenant Chandler turned to Steve. 'You played that pretty close to your chest, Donaldson. Why didn't you tell me?'

Steve sat quiet for a moment, then nodded. 'On a need to know basis, Lieutenant. On a need to know basis.'

Now read an exclusive extract of the next
Steve Donaldson thriller

THE ANNIVERSARY

BY CRAIG SIMPSON

Chapter 1

It was the small hours when I left Winn in her apartment. We had a thing going and it was good. Good because we were both relaxed with each other and the fact that none of us felt pressured made our relationship work.

Winn wanted me to stay. In fact, I had planned to do just that, and then that same old feeling reared its ugly head and I remembered what day it was. It crept up on me like a snake in the grass. One minute it wasn't there, the next it was.

Two years had passed since Maria had died, gunned down by Karen Rosenberg as she stepped in to save me. Maria's father, Gabrielle, died that day too, in fact, many people met their maker in that incident, not least Michele Salvadori and some of his soldiers, and although Lieutenant Stuart Chandler of the NYPD applauded the demise of the Mafia Don he also appreciated the price I'd paid.

Winn and I therefore were taking it slow. We had met professionally on many occasions, and although attracted physically, neither of us ever crossed the line. Me a PI, and Winn, a highly successful and respected lawyer. Times change; people and situations too and Winn and I finally crossed that line and became an item.

A takeout, a bottle of wine, quiet music, dim lights and close conversations till late, before making out in her bedroom seemed perfect.

We both lay there feeling good. Me feeling no pain while Winn took another drag on her Marlboro. I didn't like her smoking; it wasn't just that it was bad for her health, it wasn't too pleasant to kiss her on the mouth after she'd had a drag. She wasn't a heavy smoker though, she just enjoyed one at certain times, especially after meals and certainly after sex.

I kissed Winn's forehead. 'Gotta go,' I said, as I stood up and started dressing.

'Don't go, stay here. Please, Steve' she said, as she stubbed her cigarette out.

I tried to explain but the words wouldn't come. My inner self still wanted to be alone at this time; the anniversary of Maria's death.

Winn was understanding. She maybe didn't agree with me that we could have a relationship, and yet at certain times I held back and transported myself back to the same old memories and the same old love that had now departed.

Winn had always said take time to remember Maria fondly and gently, very gently, move on. Her words used to sting my mind. She was right, of course, but each time that date came around I found myself back to square one and wanting to be on my own. I patted her house cat Sophie, who was asleep on the couch, and headed for home.

This is why I found myself sitting at traffic lights at 2:30am, my eyes watering, feeling bad that I'd left Winn, but also knew how I'd react when I returned to my apartment to grieve alone as if that made everything within me all right. I knew I'd have a few JDs before crashing out in my easy chair, but hey, its me and that's what I did.

I was distracted by the sound of sirens and the flashing lights of the emergency vehicles as they crossed the junction. It was not an unusual sound for a city that never sleeps, but it was enough for my mind to go blank and without further hesitation I changed direction and joined the wagon train.

Chapter 2

We were on 42nd Street, passing Bryant Park, the not so lovely part of the city, where the pros and the pimps conveyed their business. Tenth Avenue was soon on us, it being easy when tailgaiting emergency vehicles with their lights flashing.

My mind travelled back once again to Maria as we rolled passed 44th Street and I looked towards Eleventh Avenue and knew The Blue Parrot where I'd first met her was in the vicinity.

The Birdland district was next with all the famous jazz clubs, and where some of the most famous artists had played and in many cases, like Count Basie who, made this their New York headquarters.

The convoy ahead of me ground to a halt. Vehicles became stationary as the cordon blocked the road at the front of the Paradise Club. Police cruisers were already in abundance and the area was in the process of being taped off.

I parked and alighted from my car, only to duck down for protection as an explosion went off, shattering windows of adjacent properties and allowing the audible screams from inside the club to expand into the street.

Curiosity aroused, I peered through the dust and recognised the figure of my old friend, Lieutenant Stuart Chandler. He was entering the club, his usual sidekick Detective Sergeant Johnston at his side.

This was my ticket to gain entry and find out what was going down.

Chapter 3

I flashed my wallet and announced that I was NPYD which gained me entry. So much for security.

On entering the main area of the club, everything was in disarray. People and glass everywhere. The glitter ball was shattered on the floor, no more revolving and shedding its neon coloured lights.

Scantily clad hostesses were attempting to cover themselves as the shock and reality set in. Clients sat in the red velvet booths unable to move, frightened to ask for assistance in case they should be recognised.

Lieutenant Chandler was speaking to an attending officer and I saw his eyes stare up the stairs where there was obviously another part of the club. Chandler moved towards the upper level and I joined him at his side.

'Hey, Donaldson, what you doin' here?' his eyes staring into mine.

I shook my head without uttering a word.

Chandler kept his eyes focused. 'Get out! You're not wanted here.' His command was direct and to the point and I felt it was my turn to speak.

'Ah was just passing. Thought you could use my help, but if … you don't need me Lieutenant, I'll go.' With that, I retraced my steps towards the exit.

'Okay, stop. Stop right there, Donaldson,' Chandler's voice shouted.

I smiled inwardly. I knew he wouldn't just let me walk out of the club without interrogating me first. 'What d'ya say?' I said, as I turned to face him.

Chandler stared again, his severe expression burning my eyes. 'Come with me,' he said, and we both climbed the stairs to the club's more intimate and private rooms.

An officer was standing outside an open red door, and beckoned the Lieutenant.

'In here, Lieutenant,' he yelled, as a shocked, whimpering hostess was being helped along the corridor, unable to control herself.

'Bit of a mess,' the officer said. Chandler glanced at him and thumbed his arm in my direction.

'He's with me,' he said as he entered the room. I just nodded as I followed Stuart Chandler into The Scarlet Room – well, that was the name on the door.

The scene inside matched perfectly, but on this occasion, not in a good way.

Chapter 4

The bodies were still in their dead positions as the medics and forensics had not yet examined them.

'Phew, it's Tony Cafarelli,' Chandler exclaimed. 'I've been trying to put this dude away for years.' Chandler bent closer to the dead body; he'd been shot twice through the head and a large piece of mirrored glass stood upright, embedded in his broad, hairy chest. Chandler's eyes moved upwards of what was once a mirrored ceiling for playmates to watch themselves and their hostesses perform on a large round divan bed.

'Well, goodbye TC,' Chandler said out loud as he turned to face me. 'You know this guy, Donaldson?'

Again, I shook my head negatively. 'No,' I replied. 'Heard of him. Big player in the Mob, I understand.'

Chandler nodded. 'He controlled hookers; both in clubs and on the streets. Narcotics too – big time. Grand theft auto was another of his interests. In fact, you name it, Cafarelli was involved somehow. He was backed heavily by the Mob, and he used and abused that privilege to excess. You could say that Tony Cafarelli knew no boundaries. He forgot nothing and never left anything to chance.'

'Well, he's miscalculated big time. 'Cause someone knew he was here and when and what he'd be doin'. Would the Mob put out a hit on their man?' I said, thinking out the possibility.

'Yeah, if he crossed the line, but he wasn't a snitch, Donaldson, if that's what you're intimating.'

I frowned, 'If he was into all you say, how come you guys never nailed him and sent him down for a long time?'

Chandler didn't like my question and his resentment showed. 'Well, it's not easy dealin' with these people. They have their own connections in the system and, of course, it doesn't help when there are lawyers like your girlfriend going about defending them.'

'Hey, Chandler, don't you start with Winn, she's with the Prosecution Department now, and ...'

'And nothin' Donaldson. She was a defence lawyer, and on more than one occasion got our friend here off. He was as guilty as hell, but he walked, thanks to Winnifred Atkinson.'

'I don't like what you're implying,' I replied.

'Who cares?' Chandler said, as he now walked around to the body of the young hooker who was slumped against the wall.

Her long dark hair cascaded over her face and shoulders. Her red silk dress was folded down below her pert breasts. She wore no panties, but still adorned her gold sandals.

Chandler resisted any action to check her over. He knew he would need to wait for the Coroner to do his preliminary examination. Blood ran down the girl's face. You did not need to be a Coroner to see she too had been shot in the forehead, and also her heart.

'What d'ya make of this, Donaldson?'

I surveyed the scarlet room. It was obvious it was for discerning customers only, and anything imagined would be fulfilled. There was a drinks cabinet, full of every drink I'd heard of, and some that I hadn't. The remnants of a coke line was on a table adjacent to the bed, together with a large bucket of ice.

The mirrored ceiling had been blown apart; probably by gun shots. There was blood everywhere – on the walls, the silk sheets and even on the shattered glasses at the side of the bed.

My eyes took it all in, and without stating the obvious, replied, 'I guess someone didn't like TC.'

Chapter 5

Detective Sergeant Johnston appeared, guiding the Coroner Charlie O'Brien.

'Okay, let me in,' he said, as he cautiously shuffled passed the uniformed officer at the door. Johnston stopped in his tracks as his eyes surveyed the room and the dead bodies. 'Is that who I think it is?' he said, staring at the lifeless body of Tony Cafarelli.

'Yep!' Chandler replied. 'Every cloud and all that,' he said.

Johnston stared at me with questionable eyes but made no comment.

'Jee … sus! Bloody hell! What went down here?' O'Brien said, as he etched his way towards the deceased. 'Professional hit, Lieutenant, eh?'

'Is that your diagnosis, Charlie?' Chandler said.

I remained quiet, watching and waiting in the background. There was no need for me to remind everybody of my presence; after all, I shouldn't have been here at a crime scene and now wished I'd stayed home with Winn. It would certainly have been more comforting than witnessing this shit.

O'Brien was examining the girl now. 'Yeah, I guess she was against the wall when she was shot in the heart.

She'd die instantly. The other bullet to the head was after she slumped to the floor. It's been fired at close range 'cause the bullet has come out the other side. You can see the mess on the wall. Looks like a professional hit Lieutenant, given Cafarelli's background. The girl was just in the wrong place at the wrong time. She'd be so shocked she wouldn't know what hit her.' O'Brien paused. 'It would be over in seconds. Cafarelli, on the other hand, would see his attacker but he'll never be able to identify him, or …' again, O'Brien paused, '… or her,' he added.

'Hey,' Chandler echoed. 'Do you think a woman has done this, or possibly been involved?'

Charlie O'Brien smiled. 'I didn't say it was a woman. I just meant that whoever killed TC here could be either gender. I mean, both the girl and Cafarelli had been executed like a professional hit. It's like a signature, except on this occasion we don't know whose.'

Charlie continued his examination. 'It looks like a 9mm and it's had a suppressor used. I'll know more after the autopsy.'

'What else?' Chandler pressed.

'Oh I don't know, Lieutenant. The hostess with the mostess was definitely playing and TC was probably in heaven; you can see the faint trail of semen on the bed and again down the girl's legs. Well, as I said, I'll know more after I examine them downtown.'

'Anything else, Charlie?'

O'Brien stared at Chandler. 'You're the bloody detective, you figure it out; but look at the ceiling, its shot to hell. Observe, Lieutenant, the large piece of broken mirrored glass embedded in the deceased's chest. That didn't kill him Lieutenant, but it would be painful, given the speed and the height it would fall onto our friend here. No, whoever carried out this hit probably wanted Cafarelli to know the reason why he was going down, and would possibly take some satisfaction in telling him.'

'Who's the detective now, O'Brien?'

'Oh no, just a simple observation. As I said, I'll know more once I examine them properly.'

'When?' Chandler started to ask.

'Hey! It won't be today Lieutenant, so don't even ask.'

Chandler stared at O'Brien. Charlie caught his stare.

'Okay, tomorrow then, since it's you.'

'Thanks Charlie,' Chandler replied.

The disturbance and noise from the other parts of the club distracted everyone's attention.

'Better go and see what all the commotion is about Johnston,' Chandler said. Then he turned to me.

'Want to hang about for a while Donaldson?'

I stared at my ex-lieutenant. 'You want me to?' I asked.

Chandler nodded. I smiled.